It's Never Too Late to Look HOT

By Heather Estay

IT'S NEVER TOO LATE TO LOOK HOT
IT'S NEVER TOO LATE TO BE A BRIDESMAID
IT'S NEVER TOO LATE TO GET A LIFE

It's Never Too Late to Look HOT

Heather Estay

AVON
TRADE

An Imprint of HarperCollins*Publishers*

IT'S NEVER TOO LATE TO LOOK HOT. Copyright © 2006 by Heather Estay. All rights reserved. Printed in the United States of America. No part of this book may be used or reproduced in any manner whatsoever without written permission except in the case of brief quotations embodied in critical articles and reviews. For information address HarperCollins Publishers Inc., 10 East 53rd Street, New York, NY 10022.

HarperCollins books may be purchased for educational, business, or sales promotional use. For information please write: Special Markets Department, HarperCollins Publishers Inc., 10 East 53rd Street, New York, NY 10022.

FIRST EDITION

Interior text designed by Elizabeth M. Glover

Library of Congress Cataloging-in-Publication Data

Estay, Heather.
  It's never too late to look hot / by Heather Estay.—1st ed.
    p. cm.
ISBN-13: 978-0-06-083691-7
ISBN-10: 0-06-083691-1
1. Middle-aged women—Fiction. 2. Female friendship—Fiction. 3. Divorced mothers—Fiction. 4. Domestic fiction. I. Title.

PS3605.S73I77 2006
813'.6—dc22   2006007475

06 07 08 09 10 JTC/RRD 10 9 8 7 6 5 4 3 2 1

For dear Alli:
Spud and I will never forget you,
your playfulness, and your gentle loving nature.
We miss you, sweet pup!
(P.S. However, Spud is thrilled to be exonerated
of all trash can raids from years past)

Prologue

"Oh, look! She's getting ready to throw the bou-quet!" Gwen pulled me to my feet.

"Who knows, Angie?" Marie's eyes twinkled as she pushed me from behind. "You might be next."

The heat was becoming extreme. I felt my face flush and the sweat pour down my front.

"Is it just me or is it becoming uncomfortably hot in here?"

"Later, Angie!" Jessica's face lit up with excitement as she yanked me into the crush of panting single females. "Get ready for the catch!"

Jenna, my beautiful daughter, waved her bridal bouquet like a matador's red cape, taunting the herd of half-crazed bulls (uh, make that cows). She turned her back to us as the crowd shouted the countdown:

"One! Two! Three!"

Jenna lofted the bouquet high over her shoulder. Up, up, up it went and landed with a soft plop in Jessica's hands.

"Eeek!" Jess squeaked in panic, swatting wildly at the flowers like they were Venus flytraps out for her blood. The bouquet flew with adamant trajectory into Gwen's open arms.

"Ugh!" Frantically, Gwen launched the hapless spray of roses into the air. It flew gracefully over the ceiling fan, pausing dramatically before it reentered the stratosphere and headed straight for me.

"Yaaa!" I pitched it back to Gwen instantly, a well-trained first baseman setting up a double play in the last game of the World Series.

For the next thirty seconds, the three of us batted that bouquet back and forth desperately, a good imitation of the US Olympic volleyball team in a life-and-death game of Hot Potato. Suddenly, a huge purple rhino charged into the fracas with a ferocious body block. The force was great enough to send all three of us spiraling into Marie, who (though innocent of any bouquet batting) is one of our very best friends and therefore certainly would be thrilled to join us in the resulting pileup.

"I got it! I got it!" the rhino, Clarisse, yelled triumphantly. She held her trophy, the sadly battered bridal bouquet, high above her head.

Jessica, Gwen, Marie, and I lay panting, arms and legs entwined, a tangled purple heap of middle-aged bridesmaids.

"What on earth was that all about?" Marie demanded, her head mashed under Jessica's left hip. She did not sound at all thrilled to have joined us in the pileup.

"Angie! For God's sake, say something so I know you're alive!" Tim exclaimed anxiously. He, along with Jack, Whatsis Name, and Wayne, nervously sorted through the jumble of their significant others' legs and arms, searching for a familiar limb to pull out of the purple wreckage.

"Angie! I'm coming!" Bob bellowed, muscling his way into the fray. ("Muscling" is probably inaccurate given my ex's anatomy, but I've never heard of anyone "flabbing" their way through a crowd.) He stumbled over Tim, ensnared himself in the folds of Clarisse's purple caftan, then skidded halfway across the dance floor before crashing into our new son-in-law and the remains of the six-tiered wedding cake.

"Mom," Tyler laughed, pulling me to my shaky feet, "aren't you and the aunties getting a little old for tackle football? How about taking up Tai Chi instead?"

In retrospect (isn't it a waste to have such brilliant hindsight and such pathetic foresight?), I know that those bizarre moments were a forewarning of the year to come. Had I known this then, I would have left the party immediately and crawled into a cave to hibernate until the following spring (or until my gray hairs overpowered my most recent application of Nice 'n Easy, whichever came first).

But I didn't. Instead, I joined Gwen, Marie, and Jessica in polishing off another bottle of champagne. Big mistake. *Really* big mistake.

Chapter 1

"Surprise!"

"Oh! Oh! Oh, my gosh!" I exclaimed. My hands fluttered up to my cheekbones and my eyes popped open wide in astonishment. I gave a tremulous smile, tears of appreciation glistening on my lashes. "You shouldn't have. Really." I held the pose for a breathless count of three. One thousand one, one thousand two, one thousand three. "Okay, what did you think of that one? Spud? Alli?"

Spud moaned halfheartedly, his hairy little face studying my performance from his prone position on the bed. Despite what you are thinking, Spud is not some tattooed trucker I picked up while cruising our local 7-Eleven the previous evening. He is one of my two ever-loyal, never-obedient beagles. Spud's female counterpart, Alli, stared at me with Beagle Look Number 56: *Surely this proves that humans are NOT the more intelligent species.*

"Too much, you think? Maybe I should skip the 'you shouldn't have' part. What the heck does that mean anyway? 'You shouldn't have.' Of course, they should have. It's my birthday, for heaven's sake, and not just one of those 'tweener birthdays. This one turns a decade."

I was rehearsing my faux surprise in the mirror in preparation for my real surprise birthday party that night. Spud and Alli had been recruited, per a bribe of seven doggie treats each, as my personal focus group to critique the performance. Obviously, I had seriously overpaid for their services.

By the way, it is not psychologically suspect to talk to your dogs. After all, dogs are sentient beings (and perhaps a lot more intelligent than we give them credit for, given the fact that they have set up a lifestyle of sitting around scratching themselves—when they are not sleeping—while we slave to feed them, house them, and provide a generous assortment of doggie toys). And all in all, canines are definitely better listeners than most husbands (which, granted, is not a very high standard). So talking to your dogs can be very therapeutic. However, it *is* weird if you think your dogs talk back to you because dogs DO NOT talk. Well, except occasionally on subjects of particular interest to themselves.

(In contrast, however, I would not recommend talking to your cats. It only reaffirms their inflated, though perhaps deserved, sense of superiority. Look, they've already conned most of you into providing indoor toilet facilities for them, and feeding them cans of stuff that stink up your house for an entire week and cost more than an equal amount of caviar. Can you imagine what they might demand if they learned your innermost secrets? Diamond-studded flea collars? Oh. They already have those, too?)

Now I know you are asking yourself (not your cat), "If it's supposed to be a *surprise* party for her, how come she knows about it?" Well, duh. Who is ever surprised by her own surprise party? If surprise parties were truly surprising, statistically, wouldn't stunned surprisees suffer more heart attacks than the rest of the population? In which case, wouldn't surprise parties show up on the Surgeon General's list of *Behaviors Dangerous to Your Health*, along with everything else that could be fun? Well, surprise parties aren't on this list (though I hear that the annual *Sports Illustrated Swimsuit Edition* recently made the cut), which goes to prove my point that no one is ever really surprised.

Anyway, isn't that an integral element of these parties? That the surprisee is never *really* surprised but is absolutely required to *act* surprised otherwise the surprisers will be hurt and disappointed (even though the surprisers know deep down in their souls that the surprisee knew about the surprise all along and therefore is only feigning surprise)? This falls within the same category as faking orgasms and pretending to like your mother-in-law's cucumber-and-cranberry Jell-O mold. (I happen to be pretty adept at both, after twenty-six years of an uninspiring marriage, which had included a mother-in-law whose cooking skills most likely killed off at least two of her five husbands.)

"Surprise!"

"Oh! Oh, my! This is so unexpected!" I tried to get my bottom lip to tremble delicately, but it looked more like the beginning of a seizure than an expression of tender emotion. (How did those fragile Victorian heroines manage to do it? And what about that graceful swooning thing? Do you suppose I could pull that off without multiple bruises and contusions? How does a good swooner position herself so that she ends up in the handsome hero's arms and not in a heap on the floor?)

You might also be asking how I could be so certain that I'd get a surprise party this particular year, since the last one thrown for me was the same year the first spaceship landed on Mars and I turned twenty-one (the two events having nothing whatsoever to do with one another). But this year was even more significant. Because this year, on this day, I officially turned Fifty Years Old.

The Big Five-O.

Five decades.

Half a century. (Maybe if you rounded up to the nearest hundred, I could qualify for a whole century.)

Wow.

But honestly, what's the big deal about turning fifty? I couldn't see that I was a whole heck of a lot different than I'd been the night before when I was a young and girlish forty-nine. As soon as I woke up on The Big Day, I had examined my body under the covers for any signs of instant decay. Nope, I still had the same tenacious clusters of cellulite (in commemoration of frequent visits to the Dairy Queen drive-through), the same undeniable stretch marks (mementos from the pregnancies for my two kids, Tyler and Jenna), the same slightly saggy boobs (the sagging was minimal since the boobs themselves had been minimal to begin with), and the same innie belly button (stuffed with a speck of lint from my flannel jammies).

And as I studied my fifty-year-old face in the mirror, I re-affirmed that my crows'-feet were still visible and my gray hairs were not (per the extraordinary efforts of my deter-mined hairstylist). My neck was still only slightly crinkly (as if I'd ironed it on too low a setting) and those little puckery lines above my lips hadn't found a new home elsewhere. Nor had they invited more of their little puckery relatives to join them.

My mental capacity? I was only on my first cup of coffee, so my intellect was not fully functioning (it takes at least three cups of serious caffeine to boot up this brain). But I felt it safe to assume that I was not any more senile, wise, perceptive, or clueless than I had been at the tender age of forty-nine.

So what's the big deal about turning fifty?

Since I had the company of other sentient beings (whose tails revealed them to be snoozing under the throw pillows—clearly maintaining the official United Beagles of North America work schedule), I said this thought out loud:

"Really, guys, what's the big deal? I mean, if any year was significant, it would have been last year, right?"

Spud said that he agreed completely. (Ha! Caught you! Dogs DO NOT talk, remember?)

Most of my adult years had been pretty sedate; I spent them raising two awesome (if I do say so myself) kids and being married to one not-so-awesome husband (everyone but his mother agrees with me on this). I was the Ameri-can cliché: working suburban mom, driving my minivan between the office, soccer games, school plays, and the gro-cery store. The most adventuresome thing I ever did during those years was to switch laundry soaps. (What a ripoff! My whites are NOT substantially whiter, and to this day I still have terminal ring around the collar.)

But the activities of the previous year, my forty-ninth, could have made Britney Spears blush. (Okay, so maybe not Britney Spears but anyone with a molecule of propriety. Michael Jackson, perhaps?) If I'd been famous enough to attract their notice, the supermarket tabloid headlines would have screamed:

Angie Has her First Fling! Did She Know He Was Married? (no, she did not—don't ask)

Angie Lands in Jail! For Singing Christmas Carols? (actually, the charge was obstructing justice—don't ask)

Angie's Daughter Ties the Knot! In a Barnyard? (Please ask! I've got 746 pictures I'm dying to show you!).

My sexy black lace thong is stolen by a blackmailer! I burglarize a judge's house in a GI Joe costume! I discover a bra that gives me cleavage for the first time in my life! Honestly, how could my fiftieth year possibly top that one?

Besides, I didn't want it to. I really liked my life. My life had settled down quite nicely, and settled down was a very good place to be. I had a new boyfriend, Tim, who gave me space. I had an old job as an asset manager that gave me stability. I had kids (Jenna and Tyler) who gave me fewer gray hairs now that they were grown, and three dear friends (Gwen, Jessica, and Marie) who gave me seasoned support during my hot flashes. Life was good, very good.

"Surprise!" I grinned into the mirror. Being fifty was great. Being fifty was having it all figured out and dialed in.

Being fifty was being able to give the best gosh darn faux surprise performance since Elliot first saw E.T.

"Oh! Oh! This is so unexpected!"

Ha! As if anybody could really catch me by surprise on my fiftieth birthday.

Chapter 2

"Surprise!"

I had just walked into the back dining room of Lucca to "meet Jenna and Tyler for a casual birthday dinner." The crowd of sixty or seventy of my friends and family stared at me with gleeful anticipation. This was my moment.

"Oh! Oh! Oh, my gosh!" I exclaimed, hands to cheek-bones, eyes popped open wide in astonishment, broad smile of wonder, touching tears of acknowledgment wetting my eyelashes—altogether an Oscar-winning performance. "I had no idea! Oh, my!" One thousand one, one thousand two, one thousand . . .

"Mom!" Jenna exclaimed, throwing herself through the crowd. Her big brown eyes were lit with excitement, her face flushed beneath the halo of her peacock blue hair. "Mom!" she breathed, flinging her arms around me, "Happy birthday! And, guess what?" she giggled, whispering in my ear, "I'm pregnant!"

"What!" My feigned surprise ratcheted up to honest-to-God, heart-pounding astonishment. "You're what? Sweetie, how did it happen? No, never mind; I know how. But when? What . . . ?" But before she could respond, the sea of merry party guests swept her away. A tiny but strong, blue-veined and bejeweled hand grasped my wrist and spun me around.

"Happy birthday, Angie dear," an elderly Southern voice cooed. "Goodness, my dear, you don't look a day over fifty!" My ex-mother-in-law grinned, reaching up to peck me on each cheek.

"Gosh, thanks, Lilah," I responded, laughing. "Of course, you realize I'm *not* a day over fifty. But did you hear that Jenna . . . ?"

"Yes, yes. I know all about that. But I have news as well," she whispered conspiratorially. "Tom and I are getting hitched, just like Tyler and Angela."

"You're what! You mean Tyler and Angela are . . . ?" But before I could absorb this latest bombshell, the crowd crowded Lilah out. I found myself facing Phil, my boss of many years. The lines around his intelligent eyes crinkled as he smiled, stepping up to give me a courtly kiss on the cheek.

"Happy birthday, Angie," he said warmly. "You look lovely tonight."

"Why, thank you, Phil." I'm not sure how he does it, but when Phil (one of my favorite men in the whole wide world) tells you that you look lovely, you really feel lovely even if you'd qualify as a "before" picture on *Extreme Make-over*. I basked for just a moment in Phil's perception of my loveliness, then noticed a slight, nattily dressed stranger at Phil's side (no, I don't normally say "nattily" either, but in this case it fit). He looked to be in his early thirties with carefully coifed blond hair that added a few inches to his five-foot-three frame.

"Russ Martin," the young man said extending his hand and smiling confidently. "I'll be taking over the business when Phil retires this month."

I turned to Phil with a stunned look, who in turn turned to Russ with a stunned look, who in turn turned back to both of us with a triumphant look of having just swept his opponent's rook off the board.

"But, but, Phil, when did you decide . . . ?" I stammered stupidly. Phil opened his mouth to reply but before any sound came out, the crowd inserted itself between us. Two warm hands gripped me by the shoulders and turned me around. I looked up to see Tim, the man whose smile always melts my toenail polish, beaming down at me.

"Angie, happy birthday." Tim gazed deeply into my eyes, and I felt the shiver that those chocolate brown eyes of his always give me.

"Tim? I thought you were out of town and . . . ?"

"I wouldn't have missed this for the world." He smiled and slowly bent down to kiss me. I sighed happily and closed my eyes in anticipation.

Let me just stop the action here to explain that Tim is an Exceptionally Talented Kisser. Okay, so you've got your Okay Kissers (who might keep you awake but never inspire you to do those things your mother warned you about). You've got your Lousy Kissers (who make you think about gooey germs, toxic microorganisms and what time you have to get up in the morning). And then you've got your Exceptionally Talented Kissers. Exceptionally Talented Kissers are the ones who make you wonder if maybe romance novels are not fiction after all. A kiss from an Exceptionally Talented Kisser ignites every cell in your body and sends your rational mind on sabbatical to Puenta Arenas. A kiss from an Exceptionally Talented Kisser is the kind that leaves you breathless just thinking about it four days later. These kisses are Belgian Nirvana truffles of chocolates, the Vilmart Coeur de Cuvée 1993 of champagnes, the Oreck XL21 of vacuum cleaners. Tim is that kind of kisser.

So I sighed happily and closed my eyes in anticipation. But while still in prepucker position, I felt another body plunge forward and break up our hug. My ex-husband shoved his belly between us and gave me a big, fat, slobbery kiss on the lips (well, actually, on just one lip because he missed his target). The lip(s)? Eiouw!

"Happy birthday, darling!" Darling? I don't recall that Bob ever called me "darling" during our twenty-six years of marriage, and certainly not in the past two years since we've been divorced. (Bob is definitely in the Lousy Kisser category: think gooey germs and toxic microorganisms, Tootsie Rolls, Manischewitz, DustBusters.)

I was stunned speechless (which is probably fortunate given that I was seriously grossed out and might have said something I'd have to pretend to regret later). Before I could reconnect my brain to my vocal cords, Bob was swept aside by a massive arm and I was encircled by the significant bulk of Bob's significant other.

"Happy birthday, Angie," Clarisse grunted. My nose was mashed against her prominent bosom and I felt her grip getting tighter and tighter. "And many!" *squeeze* "Happy!" *squeeze* "Returns!" *squeeze!*

Based on this experience, I feel confident that I grok (you may have to look up the word "grok" if you missed the sixties) the feelings of an anaconda victim during its last moments. You've seen it: when that huge African snake squeezes the little bunny to death every week on the Nature Channel? My breath was totally expelled, and I lost all sensation in my limbs. My eyes tried to pop out of their sockets (stopped only, I'm convinced, by two coats of waterproof mascara) and my tongue, losing all sense of dignity, lollygagged out of the corner of my mouth, indelicately spraying spittle on my chin. I was close to fainting but somehow it wasn't the graceful swoon I had envisioned. But then again, did it really matter? I felt myself floating into a world of blissful unconsciousness, ribs cracking, knees buckling. Just at the moment when I wondered if Last Rites would be more appropriate than a chorus of "Happy Birthday," an earsplitting shriek saved my life:

"Happy birthday, Angie!"

Jessica (one of the trio of my very best friends) may be petite, but her voice could overpower the sound of a howitzer in an echo chamber. The volume of Jessica's normal conversational tone has been compared to an Alice Cooper finale; the gusto with which she declared "Happy birthday, Angie!" undoubtedly triggered an avalanche in some faraway country. Clarisse was so startled that she released her killer grasp and I stumbled backwards. Fortunately, Marie (very best friend number two, who competed for many years in coed softball) was able to catch me before I fell to the floor in an indecorous heap. At the same time, Gwen (my third very best friend, a highly successful trial attorney whose only fear is that she might be forced to drink cheap wine) stepped strategically between me and my three hundred-pound boa constrictor. "Are you okay, Angie?" she asked sharply.

"Need some air," I croaked. Immediately, my three best friends formed a protective phalanx around me, like the Secret Service after someone takes a pop shot at the president.

" 'Scuse us! Coming through! Emergency powder-room run!" Jess shrieked, splitting the crowd like Charlton Heston parting the Red Sea. My rescue patrol whisked me efficiently through the crowd to the ladies' room, pausing only to nab a bottle of wine from the bar and a plate of hors d'oeuvres from a startled waiter. (Don't you love women who can keep their priorities straight, even in times of emergency?)

Once safely ensconced in the ladies' room, Marie plopped me down on the padded stool in front of the vanity mirror. "Good grief, Angie! You look like you've gone into anaphylactic shock. You're as pale as a sheet!" She patted my hand anxiously. Still a little light-headed, I tried to determine if anaphylactic shock was a good thing or a bad thing. Let's see, there's Shock and Awe (not good), Chaka Khan (pretty good), shock therapy (perhaps an option) . . .

"Honestly, Angie," Gwen arched an eyebrow at me in exasperation. "You're the only person I know who is actually surprised by her own surprise party." She turned and pulled out four Dixie cups from the dispenser, filling each with the wine. "I mean, think about it. It's your birthday, and you're turning fifty. Did you really think we wouldn't throw you a party?" Hand sternly on elegant hip, Gwen handed me my Dixie cup. "Drink," she commanded.

I drank, then stammered, "Yes. I mean, no, it's not . . ."

"Well," Jess inserted, "Angie has been acting a little strange ever since she opened up her root chakra last year. Maybe her kundalini is running out of control."

"No," I protested, "my kundalini is just fine. But Jenna said . . ."

"Oh, sure," Marie said simply, smoothing the long, dark curls that fell to her shoulders. "Jenna's pregnant. We know that. She's due in March. She wanted to save the news for your birthday so she made us promise not to tell you."

"You knew? All of you? And you didn't tell me?"

Jessica, making serious inroads on the hors d'oeuvres platter, looked at me innocently. "Of course. It was a secret. Besides, if you'd just paid attention to Jenna's aura lately, you would have known." Few people can end an argument the way Jessica can.

"Okay, but what about Lilah and . . ."

"Lilah and Tom getting married?" Marie interrupted, elbowing Jessica aside to nab a stuffed mushroom. "You mean you didn't see that coming?"

"Probably soon to be joined by Tyler and Angela, if I'm any judge," Gwen added smugly, wolfing down a piece of sushi. "Honestly, Angie, where have you been?"

Before I could think of a clever retort (which, in all honesty, might have taken until my next birthday), a female restaurant patron walked innocently into the ladies' room. She stopped abruptly upon seeing our animated group, eating and drinking in a part of the restaurant where normally one does not do those activities.

"Sorry," Jess declared brusquely, "private party in here. Try the facilities across the street." She shooed the poor woman out and slammed the door in her face.

"So what did you think of that guy who's taking over for Phil? Russ Martin, was it?" Gwen asked while demolishing a spray of parmesan twists. "Bit of a martinet, don't you think?"

"Now there's a classic Virgo if I ever saw one," Jess agreed, popping a spinach wrap in her mouth. "Conservative. Perfectionist. Probably a royal pain in the . . ."

"Hey, wait a minute! I'm a Virgo," I objected, trying unsuccessfully to maneuver around Marie to grab a crab cake.

"Oh, Angie, you're not *that* kind of Virgo. You're more the practical, shy, reliable type of Virgo." Jess swooped up the crab cake I had in my sights. "And, of course, that does explain why you can't make up your mind about anything . . ."

"What do you mean I can't . . . ?"

The woman who had been thrown out of our privy party thumped on the door and heaved it open. "I really need to use the facilities!"

"We're still busy in here. You'll have to commandeer the men's room," Gwen pronounced with authority, slamming the door in the stranger's face once more. "Or buy some

Depends," she muttered. "Honestly, some people have no self-control."

"Forget about Russ Martin," Marie said with a wink to the others. "I'd rather hear about Tim."

"He was looking pretty good tonight, Angie." Gwen grinned.

"Very good. In fact almost good enough to, well, you know," Jess agreed.

"But I suppose that didn't cross your mind?" Marie said, eyes wide with innocence.

The three of them stared at me expectantly until my face turned a deep, burning crimson. "Ha!" they cried in unison, high-fiving one another, each grabbing another nosh. The newest sport in my crowd seemed to be getting me to blush which, due to the onset of menopause and my recent re-entry into the dating world, turned out to be a pretty easy feat.

"But what's with you and Bob?" Gwen demanded sharply, beginning her cross-examination with one well-shaped eyebrow arched to express total disapproval. "I know you two had a reconciliation of sorts, but really!"

"But I didn't . . ." I started, sidling up to the nearly empty platter.

"You're not leading him on, are you, Angie? That wouldn't be nice." Marie had never really cared for Bob, but her kindness extended to all kinds of lowly beasts and vermin. "I can't imagine the two of you back together again." She removed the hors d'oeuvres to just beyond my reach to offer the last crostini to Jessica.

"No, I never . . ."

"Was he using the tongue, Angie?" Jess asked with a look of horror. "It looked like he was using the tongue."

"And when did you get so chummy with Clarisse?" Gwen continued.

"She hugged you like her long-lost puppy," Marie agreed.

"More like her next meal," I started weakly. "I swear she was trying to . . ."

"Speaking of food, you really should be eating if you're planning to drink tonight, Angie," Gwen admonished as she polished off the last crab cake.

"Looks like this is going to be quite a year for you, young lady"—Marie smiled—"with all the changes coming your way. Being a grandma, maybe change of job . . ."

"But I don't want things to change! I like it just the way . . ."

"Don't be silly, Angie. You can't expect life to just stand still," Gwen pronounced, with the conviction of Dr. Phil.

"But I like standing still," I whispered feebly.

There was a fierce pounding on the door. "I've got the manager with me!" screamed the woman who yearned to relieve herself.

"Oh, well, we're out of food and probably should get back to join the party anyway. Angie, are you feeling better?" Marie asked solicitously.

"Here, finish off the wine," Gwen advised, once again filling my Dixie cup, which I once again dutifully emptied. "And honestly, next time we throw you a surprise party, we'll forewarn you so you don't overreact like this. How embarrassing!"

They stood me up and brushed me off and marched me out the door. I stumbled right into the impatient woman waiting in the hall, whose bladder issues had become critical. I gave her my most apologetic smile. She glared back angrily.

"You know," Marie murmured confidentially to her, pointing at me, "our friend has these little spells. She rarely gets violent, but we're never sure."

"She hasn't bitten anyone for months," Gwen added seriously. "But we like to err on the side of caution and isolate her when she starts."

"We've all kept our rabies shots up to date," Jess contributed, "so we don't worry if she nicks us now and then . . ."

The woman gasped and fled to the restaurant, urinary urgency forgotten.

And my three best friends and I rejoined the noisy, happy-birthday throng.

Chapter 3

I have yet to meet anyone who really enjoys big noisy parties. Big noisy parties only work if you successfully subdivide them into smaller intimate parties. And if you're going to divide into small intimate parties, why don't you just start that way and spare your eardrums and vocal cords?

I maneuvered myself through the crowded room, stopping only for brief chats (brief shouts?) to make sure I could acknowledge all of my family and friends before the night was over. My determined mingling meant, of course, that I had very little to eat, though someone always made sure that my wineglass was full.

I found Tyler with his new girlfriend sitting in a quiet corner, trying to avoid the crush. Six months ago, Tyler had traded in his lingerie-runway model (a woman with the intellect of Play-Doh) for a beautiful American Indian law student. It was definitely a trade-up as far as I was concerned. They looked wonderful together: Tyler at six-one with his

blondish preppy haircut, looking every bit the young attorney that he is as he towered over Angeline's petite but
strong frame, her shining black hair falling to her waist.
Their children—my grandchildren!—would be beautiful.

"You knew about the surprise party, didn't you, Mom?"
Tyler asked anxiously as he hugged me.

"Of course, honey," I replied, based on my long-standing
policy of honesty with my children. Then, based on my
long-standing policy of encouraging them (Honesty can be
seriously overdone, don't you think?), I added, "But you
weren't the one who gave it away."

"Really?" Tyler said, looking hopeful.

"Really," I responded definitely. And in truth he wasn't
the *only* one to give it away. Though he had reconfirmed
our "casual birthday dinner" seventeen times within the
same number of days, and had come over that very morning to check that my minivan was running properly, and
to make sure all my clocks were synchronized so I could
arrive at our "casual birthday dinner" on time ("not early,
Mom, but just on time"). My son is brilliant in many ways,
but he'll never be recruited for clandestine operations with
the CIA.

"So, what's this I hear about you and Angeline?" I
beamed happily at the two of them. Angeline looked at me
quizzically; Tyler looked at me in full-blown panic. "I just
heard through the grapevine that you two are planning to
tie the . . ." Tyler's face paled and took on that deer-in-the-
headlights-of-an-oncoming-train expression. Of course I,
being particularly perceptive and always (if I do say so myself) brilliant on my feet, redirected my sentence smoothly,

". . . um, the dye. Rather that, um, you two are planning to do some tie-dyeing."

"Tie-dyeing . . . ?" I could see Angeline's bright mind whirling, trying to make sense out of the senseless. Tyler covered his eyes, waiting for the crash.

"Oh, yes. It's all coming back in, isn't it?" I continued undaunted. "You know, psychedelic colors, flower children, Tiny Tim, *'tiptoe through the tulips,'* " I trilled, grinning merrily, like a patient on a double dose of laudanum. "No? Then perhaps it was another Tyler and Angeline I heard about," I finished brightly.

Tyler groaned, rolling his eyes. But Angeline, who at twenty-three has more poise than most French diplomats (who are trained to be charmingly eloquent even while denouncing you as a complete ninny), ignored my loony rantings and kissed me on the cheek. "Well, I wish you the happiest of birthdays, Angie," she smiled sweetly. "In my tribe, you would now be considered a crone."

A crone? Instantly, my mind was filled with Disney images of old hags. I could feel my skin wrinkling up like dried apricots, my hands gnarling like twisted branches, and my nose growing to a large hooked honker with a wart on the end. Angeline caught my reaction and laughed. "Oh, no! A crone isn't what you think. It means a wisewoman, a sage. Ask my grandfather; it's actually quite a compliment." Her smile was so sincere that I couldn't take offense.

"Well, then, thank you. Honey, why don't you give me a call next week. I know quite a bit about, uh, tie-dyeing. We should talk. Angeline, I'm so glad you could be here." I gave them both a hug and exited quickly so that Tyler could resume breathing. I headed toward the tuft of peacock blue hair I spotted across the room.

"Jenna!" I enfolded my beautiful daughter in a mama bear hug. "I'm so happy for you! When did you find out?"

"Just last week. I've been nauseous for a month and a half and finally decided to go get myself checked out."

I gazed in amazement at my son-in-law, the extremely competent veterinarian, and my daughter, who had several years (and many thousands of dollars' worth) of premed on her résumé. "A month and a half of nausea and it didn't occur to either of you . . . ?"

Ryan looked sheepish and coughed nervously. "Well. Mrs., uh, I mean, moth . . . er, Ang . . ." he stuttered. After three and a half months of being my son-in-law, poor Ryan still couldn't find a comfortable way to address me. At thirty-seven, he was closer to my age than Jenna's, so "mom" seemed to be out. But his conservative upbringing prevented him from using my first name, and I refused to be called "Mrs. Hawkins" by someone who was a kid when I was still a teenager myself. But at this point, after months of his painful stammering, I would have been happy with "Toots."

"See," Ryan managed to croak, "my experience is working with farm animals. None of my cows have ever complained of nausea."

Jenna grinned impishly. "Actually, now we're thinking that we must have conceived on that trip to Bodega Bay a few weeks before the wedding."

"Jenna!" Ryan gasped, looking shocked. "You're telling your mom that we . . ."

Jenna laughed and hugged him affectionately. "Darling, I think she would have figured it out when the baby comes in February." Her confidence in my math skills was flattering but misplaced. "So what do you want, Mom? A girl or a boy?"

"I get to choose?"

"Oh, no," Ryan, looking startled, protested quickly. "I mean, the sex of the baby is already . . ."

"Yes, Ryan, I know." I smiled. "We're just kidding. I get to choose the sex of the next one though." Jenna laughed as Ryan looked even more alarmed. Honestly, would he ever relax around me?

"So, Mom, have you figured out your name?"

"My name?" Did I look like I'd had that much to drink?

"Your grandmother name," Jenna explained. "You know, Gran is already Gran. You don't want something that sounds too close to that or it will be confusing."

"How about Mother Hawkins?" Ryan said with all sincerity, obviously having watched too much *Little House on the Prairie* as a kid. My old-crone image suddenly had the addition of frizzy white hair under a starched white bonnet. And a rocking chair. And a couple of scrawny cats.

"I'll work on it," I promised, and headed back into the party's fray.

"Angie," Phil's deep baritone caught up with me as I was making my rounds. "I'm so sorry. I don't know what Russ was thinking. I never meant to announce my retirement to you like this." His face was filled with concern, Phil being the most considerate of men.

"It's okay, Phil. I was just caught off guard," I said, feigning much more composure than I actually felt. "I've known for a while you wanted to retire. I just didn't think it would be so soon."

"Well, it all happened very suddenly. Russ flew in on Friday and we've been meeting all weekend. His offer was just too good to refuse. And I made him promise to keep you on as long as you want the job."

"Thank you, Phil," I smiled a brave little smile, the one I'd learned as a kid watching old Shirley Temple movies. "I appreciate that." It was just like Phil to make sure that I was protected even in the midst of a multimillion-dollar deal.

"Besides," Phil continued hopefully, "I'm sure you'll be grateful for the change. You and I have worked together for so many years. Maybe too many. We're like some old, worn-out vaudeville act that's run its course." He smiled sadly, shaking his head. But I *like* old, vaudeville acts, I protested silently. Abbot and Costello? Hysterical! Burns and Allen? Who could be more clever than . . .

"And it doesn't do to get too contented or too settled too early in life, does it, Angie?" But I *like* being comfortable and settled and contented, like those cows who stand around all day chewing whatever disgusting thing they're chewing. I could do that! I'd be more than happy to just moo and chew and . . .

But I knew Phil was distressed and worried about my reaction so I flashed my *Littlest Colonel* smile again. "I'm sure it will be fine, Phil. Just fine."

"Good. We'll be finishing up the deal next week. Russ suggested that you take the week off, get a little R and R before starting with him."

Oh. A week off already? Maybe this wouldn't be so bad after all. "Thanks, Phil."

"And maybe this will become your opportunity"—Phil's eyes sparkled—"to share all of the wisdom and insight you've gained over the years with a younger person."

Wisdom? Insight? Did I miss something? I wasn't positive that I possessed those qualities, but I am positive that few young people actually appreciate their elders "sharing" whatever they've got. "You know, Angie," Phil continued cheerfully, "I'm really enjoying my life now. Your golden years can truly be golden if you approach them right." Golden years? Switch my rocking chair out for a walker.

I persisted in my socializing, jaw aching from my constant grinning. I spotted Tim across the room but couldn't get to him. I spotted Clarisse and Bob across the room and made sure they couldn't get to me. I ran into a bunch of The Guys from the Twenty-ninth Street Gym (men who make Conan the Barbarian look positively petite), my hairstylist Garrauch (who takes sole credit for my newly de-frumped locks), Jack (Marie's doting and adorable husband), Jonathan (my charming pediatrician friend), along with scores of others from my past and present.

Toward the end of the evening, I stumbled across Lilah and Tom canoodling in a corner. (What a great word "canoodling" is! I don't know exactly what it means, and I would guess that no one ever did. I wish I'd had that word in my vocabulary when I was a teenager: "What were the two of you doing in the gazebo last night?" the angry father demands. "Just canoodling," his sweet daughter replies. "Uh, oh. Ahem. Well, then, that's all right then.")

Lilah, my mother-in-law (though her son and I are no longer married, she refuses to give up the title), is a sparkling octogenarian. She deserves a Ph.D. in the art and science of outrageous behavior (which I'm sure they grant at Chico State), and she has dedicated much of her life to the lucrative hobby of marrying and divorcing wealthy men. To be fair, Lilah would probably have stayed with one of her five (six? seven?) husbands had any of them bothered to be faithful. But as it was, she had ended up with enough of the bums' assets to be quite comfortable.

Her newest beau, Tom, was quite a departure from her prior conquests. Quiet and ageless, Tom is an American Indian shaman with bright intelligent eyes and a long silver ponytail that flows down his back. Somehow, I doubt that he is very wealthy, but I know for sure that he is wise, ethical, and very loyal. I wondered if Lilah realized that she might have a keeper if she married this one.

"So, you two, when is the happy event?"

Tom rose from his seat and took my hand, smiling. "Happy birthday, Angie. This is quite an event in your honor."

Lilah rose and gave me another hug. "Excuse me, you two. I appear to have mussed my lipstick and must repair to the ladies' room." She smiled coyly at Tom, then whispered conspiratorially in my ear. "You keep an eye on him for me, Angie."

Tom gazed at my face intently but kindly. "So, Angie, this has been a night of surprises and revelations for you."

"I suppose so, Tom," I replied grudgingly. "But I wasn't really looking for surprises and revelations. I was thinking more of, well, just a little birthday cake."

Tom laughed. "I understand. But for the next year, here's what you need to say to yourself to give you courage: It's good. It's all good."

"It's good? It's all good?"

"A little less question mark; a lot more certainty, Angie." Tom chuckled. "Angeline tells me that you're not quite sure that you are ready to be a crone."

"Wise and insightful? Clear and confident? Nope. I gotta tell you, Tom, I haven't noticed anything like that."

"I think it sneaks up on you, Angie. Some women have it, and some don't." Tom turned to me and pierced me with his eyes. "You have it, Angie," he said seriously. "And, trust me. It's a very attractive quality."

"Attractive?"

"Yes. Attractive universally. But especially attractive to men."

"Oh, gosh, Tom, really?" I said, uncertainly. "And is that, um, why you are attracted to Lilah? Because of the wisdom and clarity thing?"

"Heck, no!" He laughed. "She's just incredibly hot!"

Chapter 4

"Hey, Sunshine," Tim breathed in my ear. "I know you showed up to this party by yourself. But would you mind some company on the way home?"

"I was hoping you'd ask," I murmured back, then promptly blushed to a shade that could appropriately be named Vibrant Maraschino. Around Tim (especially Tim breathing in my ear) I degenerated from a mature, self-confident fifty-year-old to giggly, giddy fifteen-year-old in less time than it takes to change the toilet-paper roll. (For those of you who lack the X chromosome, and therefore toilet-paper-roll-changing experience, trust me. It takes no time at all.)

The happy, noisy birthday bash was finally running out of steam. Guests started to realize that they either needed to pull out their pajamas and toothbrushes or go home; restaurant staff revved their vacuum cleaners in the background to encourage the latter. Finally, nearly all of the well-wishers at the party had finished well-wishing me and headed home.

"We're still on for lunch at noon tomorrow, Angie," Jess reminded me with a hug.

"If," Gwen added, with a significant look in Tim's direction, "you're able to get out of bed by that time."

"Jack and I will drive the minivan home and bring your gifts," Marie offered with a broad wink. "Have a wonderful evening, Tim." Tim, apparently oblivious to my friends' pointed innuendos, smiled one of his delightful smiles innocently.

Finally, we were able to leave, and Tim held my hand to walk me to his car. (Besides being a great kisser, Tim is awesome in the hand-holding department. You know that feeling when a guy holds your hand and it's warm and solid and assured? He doesn't yank at you or hold your hand upside down so your wrist gets tweaked and your shoulder strains forward. You can just slip your hand into his and his fingers cover it gently and . . .)

"Angie." Tim paused in the parking lot, smiling one of his truly extraordinary smiles (the man has an unlimited repertoire of those), and wrapped his arms around me. "I've wanted to do this all night," he said softly. "Happy birthday, Angie." He bent down and gave me one of his Truly Extraordinary Kisses. One of his better Truly Extraordinary Kisses. It took a few moments for my body to return to Mother Earth. But, of course, once it did, my immediate response was to blush—again.

Let's just get straight on this blushing thing. Blushes on young brides, small children, and that little Disney skunk in *Bambi* are charming. But at my age, my blushes look more like hot flashes or the precursors to cardiac arrest.

Like something that is being overcooked—not pretty. But it's not as if I can do anything to stop them; my blushes pop up unbidden, unwelcome, and unrelenting. Marie claims it's a menopause thing. Personally, I wonder if it isn't just that I'd found myself in some excruciatingly embarrassing situations over the prior twelve months. Whatever the cause, my blushing had become a frequent occurrence in the past year, causing me to consider changing the shade of my foundation to Mad for Magenta.

Tim was not the only factor in my blushing, but he was definitely a major contributor. Given that he and I had been dating for about six months, you would think that I wouldn't be at all nervous, shy, or blush-prone with him. You would think that he could hold my hand or kiss me or whatever, and I could be perfectly cool about it. You, my friend, would be wrong.

Tim and I drove home together talking about the party, Jenna's pregnancy, Phil's retirement. I "uh-huh'd" and "mmm'd" in all the right places, but only the teensiest part of my mind was involved in the discussion. Most of my synapses were synapping about a much more crucial issue: Would we or wouldn't we?

See, Tim and I had only been together, as in *been* together (as in get naked and mess up the sheets), once. Just once. And so it was quite possible that this night would be The Second Time. Or maybe not. In order for The First Time to take place, I'd had to enlist the formidable strategic expertise of my three best friends:

"I'm having a little problem," I had announced to them about a month ago, "with my love life."

"Oh, well, that's a surprise," Jessica said, looking suspiciously unsurprised.

"See, Tim and I have not, uh, haven't yet, um well, we've not . . ."

"Well, spit it out, Angie. What on earth are you sputtering about?" Gwen asked impatiently.

"By her blushing and stammering," Marie speculated, "I'm guessing they haven't had sex yet."

"Yes. That. What Marie said," I confirmed. "And I think part of the issue is that even though Tim and I have known each other for six months, we've only actually dated fourteen times and spent, oh, by rough estimate, fifty-three hours and forty-seven minutes in each other's physical company."

"That's a *rough* estimate?" Jess rejoined peevishly. She was taking notes, still miffed that I wouldn't let her set up her flip chart.

Fifty-three hours and forty-seven minutes may sound like a lot. But when you string it out over six months, it's just slightly more time than you spend within that same period cleaning your house (depending on your level of domestic hygiene) and much less time than you would spend walking your dog (or, as in my case, letting your dogs walk you).

"But that's because Tim travels a lot for business, right?" Marie pointed out. "And he does keep in touch, right?"

"Sure, he calls about every other day and e-mails me a lot. But I've seen his ;-) a lot more in the past few months than his actual face."

"So?"

"So, though he keeps in touch, there hasn't been much actual touching lately."

"Give the guy a break, Angie. Unless he's into astral projection, how can he be touching you from halfway across the country?" Jess gave up all pretense of taking notes and folded page one into an origami crane.

"But technically, even if he's out of town, fourteen dates is still fourteen dates," Gwen, whose successful law career depended on such technicalities, noted. "If he was going to make a move, he would have done it by the third date at least."

"Uh, well, I think that's the real problem," I admitted. "He did."

"And?" my three friends demanded in unison.

"Uh, I told him I wasn't ready." My confession was followed by three incredulous looks and four pained groans (even I had to join them in the groaning). "He's been a perfect gentleman and, except for good-night kisses, he hasn't laid a finger on me since then."

"You're telling us that you leaped into bed on a first date with that married scum bucket, Ben, but you told wonderful, sweet, eligible Tim that you weren't ready?" Marie lamented in exasperation.

"Honestly, Angie, sometimes I wonder about you." Gwen shook her head in frustration, and I'm guessing that "sometimes" was an understatement.

"How can you be nearly fifty years old and still so totally clueless?" Jess crumpled up her paper crane and threw it at me. "Do you know nothing about the opposite sex?"

"Hey, I was married for twenty-six years and . . ."

"Well, she does have a point there. Bob only marginally qualifies for the opposite sex." Gwen shuddered in disgust. "Being married to him would destroy anyone's natural instincts."

"All right, all right. But the critical issue is that now that I *am* ready, Tim doesn't make a move. I think he's waiting for a signal."

"Then give him one. Shave your legs . . ." Gwen counseled.

"Wear your sexiest undies . . ." Marie interjected.

"And make sure the sheets are freshly laundered," Jess weighed in. "And that the pillows are turned at a forty-five-degree angle to the north . . ."

"But I do all those things every time I see him. And he still doesn't get it."

"Well, then you'll just have to make a very blunt and blatant first move to get things going," Gwen declared firmly.

"But I can't do that!"

"What do you mean you can't do that?" Marie countered. "Women have been taking charge since *The Graduate*. Remember when Anne Bancroft grabbed Dustin Hoffman's hand and put it on her breast? Or did she grab his crotch?"

"Gwen, I'm not going to grab anybody's . . . or put Tim's hand on my . . ."

"Okay, what about using that Mae West line? 'Why don't you come up and see me sometime . . . when I've got nothing on but the radio,'" Jessica quoted throatily.

"Jess, I could never say a line like that with a straight face!"

"Oh, for heaven's sake, Angie! Then just be straightforward. Tell him that you weren't ready before, but you're ready now." Marie, whose patience was infinite, sounded like she was losing it.

"But, Marie, I'd be too embarrassed. I can't just come out and tell him!"

"Yes, you can, Angie. And let me tell you why in just one word: bikini wax," Jess said firmly.

"But that's two words."

"This is no time to get technical, Angie," Gwen, the queen of precision, announced. "Jessica is absolutely correct. If you go to the trouble of getting a bikini wax, there's no way you're going to let it go to waste."

"They're right. The experience itself will be just the motivation you need," Marie agreed adamantly. "It's the ultimate sacrifice."

"Sacrifice? I'm not sure I'm ready for . . ." But my protests were too little, too late. The squad had moved into action.

"Your date with Tim is tonight, right?" Gwen confirmed. "Jess, do you have the number for Maxine's? Tell Maxine that it's an erotic emergency. I'm sure they'll fit her in." Jess grabbed the phone and dialed (from memory, I might add).

"I've got a Maxine's coupon at the house," Marie declared. "I'll be right back."

And this is how we all ended up that afternoon at Maxine's Exfoliation Palace and Depilatorium. The four of us climbed into my minivan, and everyone seemed quite enthusiastic about the excursion. Everyone but me, that is. I'd never had a bikini wax, nor had I worn a bikini since Lady

Bird Johnson's Beautify America campaign (I figured that my cellulite-laden rump would not contribute positively to that cause). So I felt it legitimate that I expressed some concern and trepidation regarding the procedure:

"But don't I need to actually own a bikini to get a bikini wax?"

"Isn't forty dollars a lot to pay to remove hair that's just going to grow back anyway? Uh, it will grow back, right?"

"How do we know that Maxine is fully licensed to do this kind of work? Even the woman who plucks my eyebrows had to go to school for two years to be certified. Waxing personal areas should be at least a four-year degree, right?"

"Why do they use wax? Where do they get that wax? Do you suppose they recycle the wax? Wouldn't that be unsanitary? Aren't there some pretty awful diseases you can catch from other people's wax leavings?"

For some odd reason, when we arrived at Maxine's, my three best friends bolted out of the minivan; they seemed a little annoyed with me.

"So, this is her first time?" the young woman behind the counter, whose tongue stud gave her a slight lisp, inquired. "Shall we do just a little upper thigh touch-up then?"

"Well, I'm certainly not going to pay forty dollars for 'just a little touch-up'!" I huffed.

"No, you're not," Gwen confirmed, teeth grinding. "Let's go for the Brazilian."

"Yes," I said with haughty authority to the young woman whose studded tongue was now hanging out in surprise. "The Brazilian. Of course."

Ah. Well. For those of you who are as innocent as I was

before entering the tiny treatment room at Maxine's Exfoliation Palace and Depilatorium, a Brazilian bikini wax turns out to be, um, *everything*. I'm not quite sure what kind of bikinis Brazilians wear to require so much hair to be removed. Their bikini bottoms must be the size of semicolons. (I wished we'd ordered the Italian wax. The only hair real Italian women bother removing is their split ends.)

And the pain? Ah, yes, the pain. Let's just say that childbirth without drugs has nothing over bikini waxing. Those countries who regularly use torture for interrogation? They should stop importing bamboo and electric-shock equipment and simply purchase the $39.95 Brazilian wax special at Maxine's. The next time I need a root canal, I will laugh—ha-ha!—at my dentist for offering me Novocain. "I," I will say to him with a sneer, "have endured a Brazilian bikini wax."

But my friends were absolutely right. That evening, when Tim started to break away from our good-night kiss at the door, I grabbed him by the collar and announced in no uncertain terms, "Hold it, buster. I'm not through with you yet." Without going into detail, let me just say that Tim's response was extremely enthusiastic.

So my friends (and the unforgettable experience of a Brazilian bikini wax) had gotten me over the first hump, so to speak. But since that First Time, Tim had been out of town and I hadn't actually seen him face-to-face since The First Time. So whether this time would be The Second Time was still unknown. Or was it? If you've had a First Time, is it then a foregone conclusion that you'll have Another Time *every* time? I mean, ever since the first good-night kiss, he's *always* given me a good-night kiss. So now that we have, um, you know what, do I assume that we will always . . . ? You would think that a wise, mature, sophisticated fifty-year-old would know these things. She might—I don't.

Maybe if I'd known that he would be back in town that night, I would have gone back to Maxine's for inspiration. (Do you suppose a Bulgarian bikini wax would be less invasive?) Then when Tim and I got to my door, I'd have the nerve to fling myself at him passionately and . . .

No, wait. I shouldn't *always* be the one to make the first move, should I? No, I'll just wait and gaze up at him sweetly as he puts his arms around me passionately and tells me that he can't bear it any longer, that he must have me right then and right there and . . .

"Did you just say something?" Tim said as he stopped the car, startling me back to reality from my erotic reverie. I was embarrassed to notice that I was breathing heavily; my blush lit up my face like a stoplight.

"Oh, nothing. Just thinking about, uh, how hungry I am."

"Hungry?" Tim, smiled, raising an eyebrow. He drew my hand to his lips and kissed it gently. "Hmmm. Me, too."

Oh, my gosh! Was that a signal? Had we just agreed to . . . ? Or had he, like me, missed out on all the food at the party? And if he did just hint at what I thought he hinted at, would he be disappointed because I was not recently waxed? Should I forewarn him that, after three weeks, I was more bouclé than Brazilian?

When we got to the door, Tim bent down and kissed me. It was one of his Truly Fantastic Kisses that made my bones go floppy like overcooked spaghetti. "Well," he said huskily, "it's late and I suppose you're tired."

Uh-oh. Does that mean he *wants* me to be tired? Would he rather go home and not . . . ? "Um, no. Not especially tired." Was that too forward? Will he think I'm trying to talk him into . . . ? "Well, I mean, I'm a little bit tired. But maybe you're tired." Okay, that was better. Open it up so he can decide.

"No, I'm not tired."

"Good." No! Too pushy again. "I mean, it's nice to not be too tired." Please note that during this entire brilliant interchange, Tim and I were still kissing and nuzzling; my verbal skills and mental capacity had their bags packed, ready to abandon ship, and my breathing was as even as the stock market when the Fed hikes interest rates.

"Unless you're ready to go to bed," Tim continued, nibbling on my ear. "I mean, to sleep."

"Right. To bed. To sleep."

"But it *is* your birthday."

"And laundry day."

"Laundry day?"

"Hmmm. That means clean sheets."

"On the bed?"

"On the bed."

"I really love laundry day," Tim said, with an enthusiasm that could have sold truckloads of fabric softener. We headed inside.

I won't get into specifics about the next couple of hours. (Surely, you have enough imagination to fill in the detail.) But I was strongly reminded that once Tim and I get past the awkward "should we or should we?" phase, we move forward into the activity itself with absolutely no hesitation or awkwardness at all. The term "wild abandon" comes to mind (though, truth be known, absolutely nothing else comes into my mind once we've started).

Afterward, we wrapped ourselves comfortably around each other, pleasantly spent. On my cheeks, I could feel the subtle sting of beard burn from his five o'clock shadow and the tickle of his breathing on my neck. Tim snuggled in close, and I heard his breath getting deep and even. I matched my own breathing to his and started the sweet descent into slumber. Deeper, more relaxed, floating downward. My mind and body feeling heavier, fuzzier, looser as I drifted toward deep sleep.

"You know, Angie," Tim mumbled sleepily into my hair. "I guess we probably should get married sometime, don't you think?"

"Hmmm," I murmured drowsily, slipping finally into sweet unconsciousness.

Twenty minutes later, my eyelids zinged open like roll-up blinds on too tight a spring. Oh, my gosh! Did he just say "married"? Or had I been dreaming?

Tim's breathing was still deep and even, his arms wrapped tightly around me. We were now locked into our spoon position by Spud and Alli who had sneaked up on the bed and claimed mattress space on either side of us. I nudged Spud over a few inches, careful not to disturb the trio of gentle snorers. I turned over and studied Tim's face. It was perfectly relaxed, perfectly innocent. Wouldn't he look different if he had just proposed? No, wait; it wasn't a real proposal. More like a suggestion, wasn't it? If he actually said it, that is. Which maybe he didn't. And if he did, maybe he was just talking in his sleep. Was he already asleep? Or was I already asleep and dreaming this?

My mind churned along this totally unproductive line of thought for several minutes before it collided into the truly important question:

And if he did ask me to marry him, should I say yes?

Chapter 5

"Oh, my Gawd! A Turn Over and Snore Proposal!" Jessica exclaimed to the entire Western Hemisphere.

Jessica and I were the first to arrive for lunch at the restaurant that following day. I had just confided to her what Tim had said to me (or maybe didn't say?) in bed the night before. Note the word "confided." I did not say "Jessica, please announce this, one of my innermost secrets, to the entire world" nor did she ask my permission to announce this, one of my innermost secrets, to the entire world. But Jessica's normal speaking voice has a kind of announcing-to-the-entire-world quality to it. And when she is excited (as apparently she was, hearing that Tim—maybe—proposed to me, then fell promptly asleep)? Well, it is believed that the pitch and volume of her voice may have contributed substantially to the continental drift (most continents choosing to drift as far away from Jessica's voice as possible).

"Jess, I'm not absolutely sure he . . ."

"Gwen!" Jess screeched across the restaurant as Gwen entered the door, "Tim gave Angie a Turn Over and Snore Proposal last night." This, of course, ensured that the four or five people in Greater Sacramento who had missed the news the first time were now fully informed.

"No kidding?" Gwen yelled back, making her way to the table. "How did she respond?" Gwen, assuming correctly that Jess had already disclosed my private life to the entire restaurant, apparently felt no need for discretion herself.

"Haven't gotten that far," Jess hollered back.

"But I'm not positively sure he actually said it. What if I just dreamed the whole thing?"

Gwen arched an eyebrow as she settled herself at the table. "Oh, come on, Angie. Even you have enough imagination to dream up a more romantic proposal than that."

"Well, maybe he was just talking in his sleep, and I misunderstood."

"Ha! That's exactly what they want you to believe when they pull a Turn Over and Snore!" Jess exclaimed. "I saw it on *Oprah*."

"Sorry I'm late, everybody," Marie said breathlessly, joining us. "The maître d' says Angie got a Turn Over and Snore last night. I would've given Tim more credit than that."

"But . . ."

I was interrupted by the arrival of our waiter who, according to his nametag, should be addressed as George. "Good afternoon, ladies," he smiled at each of us, shuddering ever so slightly upon recognizing Gwen, the scourge of the restaurant world. Gwen, to put it very mildly, is known within the restaurant community as a "high-maintenance patron." After an encounter with Gwen, many waitpersons have opted for less stressful careers, choosing to retrain themselves as air traffic controllers or dental-drill testers.

"Madam," George said turning to her, with more courage than sense, "shall we begin with your order?"

"No, not today. I've just started my new diet and the first step is to eat exactly like a very thin person. So," Gwen eyed the three of us carefully. Marie, a curvaceous size twelve, was out of the running, but Jess and I are both size fours. The difference between us is that Jessica wears her size four like a light and lilting sonata; mine fits more like a stubby John Phillip Sousa march. Gwen made her decision: "Jessica, what are you having?"

"I'll have the Italian sausage sandwich with extra mozzarella cheese, fries, onion rings, and a Coke to drink. Oh, and a dinner salad with extra blue cheese dressing."

"My God, I felt my cholesterol count rising just listening to that order," Marie exclaimed.

"Jess, I thought you were a strict vegetarian," I said.

"I am, and I don't eat fried foods," Jessica responded matter-of-factly. "But I feel it's important to consume a meal of disgusting toxins every once in a while to reaffirm my dietary choices."

"Okay. I'll join you then," Marie said agreeably.

"Hmmm. Disgusting toxins," Gwen murmured, looking slightly squeamish. "Perhaps I'll order with Angie. What are we having, Angie?"

"Well, I'm thinking about the broiled salmon."

"Good choice. But you don't want it too well done, do

you?" Gwen asked. "You want the very center to still look deep pink, like a Mexican sunset, don't you Angie?"

"Uh . . ."

"A Mexican sunset?" George gulped, his Adam's apple throbbing nervously.

"And you want it cooked with extra virgin olive oil, don't you, Angie? The kind from Greece, not Italy? Not just regular virgin olive oil, right?" George and I nodded numbly. "With baby asparagus rather than broccoli, just the tips, of course, not the stalks. And you like the asparagus broiled with a touch of lavender sea salt and a dash of tangerine juice sprinkled over them. Right, Angie?" George and I continued nodding mutely like those bobble-headed dolls in rear windows of cars. Over the next three minutes, Gwen re-created all of the ingredients of the menu's selections and finalized her, uh, my order. "Okay," Gwen smiled sweetly up at George. "Then I'll just have the same."

George's sigh was barely noticeable as he turned to re-educate the kitchen staff on food preparation. "By the way," he said as he turned to leave, "the gentlemen over on table five told me to inform you that a Turn Over and Snore is not a binding contract. Something about the incapacity of the contracting party given the prejudicial activities directly proceeding the offer."

"Well, George," Gwen huffed, "you just tell those gentlemen that the offering party entered those prior 'prejudicial' activities willingly and therefore the offer was not tendered under any form of duress."

"So, Angie, what are you going to do about this Turn Over and Snore?" Marie asked.

"She says she's not even sure that it happened," Jess proclaimed to the world at large.

"Hmmm. That's awkward," Marie noted.

The busboy came by to fill our water. "Dees womens by the window wants to know how come you don't jes' ask heem," he said in heavily accented English. "You know, jes' ask eef he said it or eef he don't said it."

"Well, that's a lame idea!" Jessica sputtered. "If she asks him, and Tim didn't propose, then it'll look like she's fishing for a proposal. And if she asks him, and he did propose, then she's got to respond. A Turn Over and Snore does NOT deserve the dignity of a response!"

"Besides," I broke in meekly, "I'm not even sure if I want to marry him."

"Ha! See?" Jess demanded of the busboy. "She's not even sure she wants to marry him." The busboy nodded and trotted over to report to the ladies by the window. "What do you mean you're not sure if you want to marry him?"

"Well, I . . ."

George returned swiftly with our salad course. "Table twelve wants to know if the sex is good. And if so, why doesn't she just keep sleeping with him and forget about marriage? If the sex is not good, they say she shouldn't even consider marriage."

"Which one is table twelve?" Marie asked.

George pointed to a group of four well-dressed octogenarians giggling and talking in the corner. They wore similar ensembles of bright purple suits and flamboyant red hats. And they looked like they were having the time of their lives.

"That's us in thirty years." Jess sighed admiringly.

"I'm sure those ladies have a wealth of experience in these matters," Marie agreed.

"And they do make a good point," Gwen conceded.

"George, you can tell them that, yes, the sex is good," Marie stated confidently. "Probably very good."

"Marie!" I gasped in protest. "Just how would you know whether the sex is good or not?"

"Oh, Angie! It's so obvious! Whenever he's been with you, the next day you're all glowy and you have a little bounce in your step." Marie turned to Jessica and Gwen and confided, "She actually whistles!"

"What tune?" Gwen asked.

"Remember that Rod Stewart song? 'Do Ya Think I'm Sexy?'"

"Ah-ha!" Gwen and Jessica exclaimed in unison with matching knowing nods.

Now at this point, you just might be asking yourself: Why hasn't Angie simply died of embarrassment by now? Well, the thing is that you don't actually die from embarrassment. I know; I've tried. Especially over the prior year, these very same friends had embarrassed me so thoroughly, you would think it would have been fatal. But, alas, it was not. Despite forcing me to bounce on mattresses with complete strangers, dressing me in exotic, barely visible underwear, and dragging me through the Sexual Dysfunction section of our local bookstore—still, the embarrassment was only sufficient to paralyze me and leave me temporarily speechless.

That afternoon, however, had hit a whole new level of

humiliation, even for me. My friends were now banded together to mortify me, and as it turns out, they are very, very good as a team in this regard.

"The ladies on twelve said that if you decide you don't want him, they would like his phone number," George informed us as he delivered our entrées. "They seem to be working out some kind of time-share arrangement on him."

The manager came up to our table. "The gentlemen on five are asking if there was a handshake or any other physical signal that the Turn Over and Snore was not just a passing comment but delivered as a contract." This brought Gwen to her feet.

"George," she demanded, "show me to table five."

"I'd better go calm down the ladies on twelve," Marie said, rising.

"Dose ladies by the window says only a coward don't ask the question directly and . . ."

"Take me to them!" Jessica fumed.

And so this is how I came to be sitting all by myself at my post-happy-birthday lunch, talking to my wilting salad (a salad with exceptional listening skills, I might add), watching the extra virgin olive oil (Greek, not Italian) congeal on my salmon. "Honestly, they're my very best friends. I don't think they intentionally mean to humiliate me in public; it just seems to come naturally to them when . . ."

My cell phone rang stridently in my purse and, though usually I'd be too embarrassed to answer it in a restaurant, my mortification meter was already reading at Beyond Human Endurance level. So I answered it.

"Hello?"

The restaurant buzz muted to a gentle hum.

"Hey, Sunshine."

"Hey, yourself, Tim."

The news spread quickly from table to table: *"It's him! On the phone right now!"* The restaurant became silent except for the squeak of chairs drawing nearer.

"I'm calling for two reasons, Angie. First and foremost, to tell you that last night was really special, one I'll never forget."

"Me, too," I blushed. "I mean, me neither."

I heard a faint murmur, almost a chant: *"What did he say? What did he say?"*

"And also that I've got to head out of town this afternoon. The meeting went well, and it looks like they want to buy all of our music stores. But I've got to go around and make presentations to all of the partners separately. They want to wrap up the deal by the end of the year. Looks like I'll be on the road for a few weeks."

"Oh, Tim, that's wonderful! No, not that you'll be gone for a few weeks but that they might buy you out."

"He's leaving town!"

"He'll be gone for a few weeks."

"Where's he going?"

"Angie?"

"Yes?"

"I'll miss you."

"I'll miss you, too, Tim."

"He said he'll miss her."

"And about what I said last night?" Tim paused with a sigh.

56

Oh, no! The moment of truth! I could hardly breathe, and my hand shook so that the phone bobbled against my cheek. "Uh, yes? What you said?"

"I didn't mean it," he said softly.

"You, uh, didn't mean it?" I replied weakly.

"He didn't mean it!" "He didn't mean it!" The whisper undulated through the restaurant like a well-choreographed wave at Arco Arena.

"Yeah, that crack about your grandkid having blue hair? I was trying to be funny. I didn't want you to think I was criticizing Jenna. I think she's great and . . ."

"Oh. Of course. Blue hair. Uh, don't worry about it, Tim," I said shakily. "I didn't take offense."

There was a moment of silence after I ended the call. Then the buzz began again in earnest.

"Blue hair? Who has blue hair?"

"So, not only is it a Turn Over and Snore Proposal," I heard Jessica inform the ladies by the window. "It's a Turn Over and Snore, followed by a Leave Town."

"Doesn't sound good," one of her new friends opined.

"I don't even know what I wanted him to say just then," I confided to my wilting salad. "I don't even know if I want to marry him." The restaurant buzz wound down to an eerie quiet. "I mean, I care about him. Maybe I'm even in love with him," I confessed to the salt and pepper shakers. "But I like the way things are. I don't know if I want to marry anyone," I continued to the bread and butter plate. "I've spent more than half of my life being married, and I think I'm just starting to find out who I am, just myself." My three friends returned to the table. "Not defined as somebody's mom or

57

someone's wife. Not based on what I do for a living or the kind of car I drive . . ."

"Thank God for that," Gwen mumbled, reseating herself next to me. "I mean, really, Angie! A minivan?"

"I know Tim is a wonderful man . . ." I acknowledged to my iced tea.

"An extraordinary man. Steady yet charming. Funny yet deep," Jessica added.

"He's good-looking with a great smile," Marie chimed in.

"And he obviously loves you," Jessica asserted.

"Obviously," Gwen agreed. "He even likes your dogs."

"And he likes your kids, and they like him," Marie continued.

"And," Jessica's voice rang through the restaurant, "we've already established that he's great in bed and . . ."

"Enough!" I shrieked, silencing not only my best friends but the entire restaurant.

"Angie!" Jessica whispered, loud enough to rattle the glassware. "For heavens sakes, for a Virgo who's supposed to be modest and demure, you're certainly making a public spectacle of yourself."

"Me? I just . . ."

"She's right, Angie," Marie said, shaking her head. "What's gotten into you? Mumbling to yourself, then yelling like that?"

"Honestly, Angie," Gwen declared in all seriousness. "You're becoming quite the exhibitionist."

"I . . ." I sputtered as our waiter came back to the table.

"The elderly gentleman on table six says that he'll marry you," George reported as he dropped off our check. "But he asked if you'd mind waiting until the end of the month when he's had his cataract surgery. He wants to be able to see what he's getting first."

My next words are not fit to repeat. In fact, most people would be surprised that I even knew some of them.

Chapter 6

"So, what's with this Turn Over and Snore Proposal I heard about?"

"Lilah?" I unwound myself from my blankets to look at the clock—6:14 A.M. Thinking to take advantage of my few days off before I started my old job with my new boss, I had planned to sleep in. This, of course, ensured that Lilah would call at hours when neither the early bird nor the worm had yet surfaced. "Where are you?"

"Back home in Macon."

"So, how on earth did you hear about . . . ?"

"Oh, Bob called to tell me," she responded nonchalantly.

"Bob?"

"Yes, dear. He seemed quite agitated about it. He's acting kind of strange lately, don't you think? Not that he wasn't a little strange before," Lilah mused.

Despite the fact that I had not yet gathered all my brain cells into a unified caucus, I was sharp enough to make no comment to Lilah's critique of her one and only child. Lilah could call Bob a buffoon (as she did frequently) or "an addlepated nitwit with the common sense of a tub of margarine" (no one could have said it more eloquently). But others who criticized Bob within her earshot were not likely to live long enough to repeat the error.

"Lilah, I'm not even sure if the proposal really happened. I was half-asleep at the time. And even if it did happen, I don't know what to do about it," I sighed as the whole sticky dilemma came back to me. "Have you ever been in this situation?"

"Of course not. I'd never sleep with a man I intended to marry."

What? Lilah had been extremely vocal about me "getting back in the saddle," as she put it during one of her many pep talks. (She had also told me to "get jerky with the beef" and "find a six-shooter before the holster dries out"; I believe that she was on a Western theme at the time.) "But I thought you told me I should . . . ?"

"Of course, Angie dear. It's only healthy that you fool around. But not with a man you plan to marry down the road. It's like letting a child open up all his Christmas presents before the big day. Takes all of the fun and anticipation out of it. The kid might even decide to skip Christmas altogether, if you know what I mean."

"But, Lilah, what if you marry someone and find out that you're not compatible in bed?"

"Sexual compatibility is highly overrated, my dear. You are much better advised to rely on verification of proper equipment and training."

Now, I really should know better than to encourage Lilah in conversations like this. But it's too irresistible, like the urge to scratch at your poison ivy or peek between your fingers just when those zombies are about to eat the bad guy. "Uh, equipment and training?"

"Absolutely. First, you must inspect his package, as they say, and verify that it is in good working order. You can do this with a dry run, if you know what I mean."

"Gosh, Lilah, we can probably skip the details here. I think I . . ." Tell me, does your ex-mother-in-law talk to you like this? I hoped my phones weren't being tapped.

"Then, naturally," Lilah continued, "every man needs specific training to fully grasp your particular requirements in the bedroom. Do you remember my third—or was he my fourth?—husband, Oscar?"

"Uh, the Hungarian who looked like a miniature Walter Brennan? I think so . . ." Though I can honestly say I have no recollection of Oscar's package.

"Well, Oscar was not great in the sack in the beginning. I believe they call it 'a bum lay.' " Okay, now I'm *certain* your mother-in-law doesn't talk to you like this. "But within a few months, I trained him to be an excellent lover by rewarding him with little treats."

"Like doggie treats?" I asked weakly. My vision of Oscar perched on his haunches, tail wagging, was almost enough to transform me into a cat lover.

"No, silly girl! I had a treat using leather straps, then the one with whipped cream and . . ."

"Never mind, Lilah," I interrupted quickly. "I get the picture." And a very bizarre picture it was. "But I think expectations about sex before marriage are a little different nowadays."

"Expectations? Pish tush!" Lilah scoffed. "Do you clean your teeth with a toothbrush before you've paid for it? Do you take a shower in a new house before you've closed escrow on it?"

Sensing we were on a hygiene theme, I chimed in, "Do you wash your hair with a shampoo before you've bought the bottle?"

"Well, you might do that."

"What?"

"From those little samples. You might wash your hair with one of those free sample packets before you buy the whole bottle," she clarified. "Anyway, what does that have to do with sex before marriage?"

"I don't know, Lilah," I groaned. "I feel like I don't know much of anything anymore."

"Angie, do you suppose you're in one of those midlife crises they talk about on *Dr. Phil*? You did just turn fifty, after all."

"Oh, I don't . . ."

"Let's see, Dr. Phil had a test for it: Can you see your shoelaces when you stand up straight and look down?"

"Uh . . ."

"No, wait that was obesity. Maybe it was, do you know your multiplication tables up to the twelve timeses?"

"Well, I . . ."

"No, that's not it. That was the No Kid Left Behind test. Was it something about hair in your ears? Or hearing voices that other people don't hear?"

If, sometime in the future, I am ever haunted by strange voices, I'm pretty sure they'll sound a lot like Lilah. "So did you have a midlife crisis when you turned fifty, Lilah?"

"I don't really remember. I was stoned during most of that year."

"You were what?"

"Stoned. It was the seventies. Don't you remember that song. 'Everybody must get stoned!'" she sang merrily. "Well, I was part of everybody."

"Wow."

"Yes, wow. We said that a lot in the seventies. Usually after ingesting certain substances. Maybe," she continued thoughtfully, "that's what you need. A drug experience."

Hmmm. At that point, the only drug experience that sounded even vaguely enticing was a month's supply of Sominex.

"Maybe. But enough about me, Lilah. What ideas do you and Tom have for your wedding?"

"Well, I've not yet discussed it with Tom. But I was thinking we could do a sweat lodge theme. All of the wedding guests could get naked together in one of those steamy yurts and . . ."

Perhaps it is not good to have too much time off. Because I spent 90 percent of the next few days (all those hours when I would have at least pretended to think about work) thinking about Tim. Thinking about marriage. Thinking about Tim plus marriage. Thinking about me plus Tim plus marriage. Analyzing every single word, action, and breath that ever happened between us. (I spent the other 10 percent practicing my twelve timeses table and checking for ear hair.) I did not do this all by myself, of course. I sought the assistance of my most loyal alter egos: Analyzin' Angie and Fantasy Angie.

The two of them had entered my life about the same time I started my Barbie collection. I remember hearing Analyzin' Angie's voice during my very first encounter with a member of the opposite sex, Bobby Therrell in preschool. She popped up to reveal The Underlying Meaning of Bobby's very first words to me:

"Hey, Angie! Get off the swing or I'll tell! You're hogging it! It's my turn."

"Oh, boy!" Analyzin' Angie whispered in my ear. *"I bet that means he wants to be your boyfriend . . ."*

She followed me faithfully through the years. When Peter Van Luden stole my sandwich in the third grade, Analyzin' Angie said that *he obviously had a crush on me.* But when Phillip Winoski asked me to the senior prom, she warned that *he probably was just trying to make Melissa Hardwicky jealous.*

Analyses from Analyzin' Angie got even more intricate as years went by. (Look me in the eye, ladies, and tell me that you do not have a similar little voice. If men hear something from a woman that is not precisely clear, they simply toss it off with a shrug and a "Huh. Never understand women." We women, on the other hand, listen to every word with two sound tracks: what he said (often boring) and The Underlying Meaning of what he said (usually much more fascinating).)

So, when Tim said, "How about those Kings? I thought about giving up my season tickets, but now I'm not so sure . . ." Analyzin' Angie was ready with several possible interpretations: *A) Season tickets? That spells commitment. He's trying to tell you that he's a guy who can commit. B) Is this a test? If you tell him you know nothing about basketball, will he think you're cute or clueless?*

Obviously it took the two of us several hours that afternoon to review and decode each interaction of my brief history with Tim.

Discussions on this same topic with my other alter ego, Fantasy Angie, were lengthy but simpler. Fantasy Angie was the one who embellished all ordinary moments in my relationship with Tim (and, oh, how much of the rest of my life?), reinventing them as heroic and romantic scenes in full Technicolor. Of course, she didn't cast the *real* him and *real* me for these scenes; she created a me who was a tiny bit (okay, quite a bit) more eloquent, alluring, and sophisticated, and paired that me with a him who was just a bit (by 200 percent?) more romantic, enamored with me, and, well, psychic. I admit these scenes were entertaining, but since we were considering a (maybe) marriage proposal that (maybe) happened in the real world, it was time to extricate the real him and me from the fantasy him and me. Fantasy Angie and I negotiated this glasnost carefully:

"*Well, you really did go on that picnic in William Land Park . . .*"

"Okay, but I'm pretty sure we never stood out on a windswept hilltop . . ."

" '*The delta and I will never change, Angie. Don't you.*'

" '*No matter what I ever do or say, Heathcliff . . .*' "

"His name is Tim."

"Oh, right. 'No matter what I ever do or say, Tim, this is me now, standing in this ragweed beside you. This is me forever. Tim, when you left, where did you go?'

'I went to Livermore. Then one night, I was headed to Nevada but I was held up in a traffic jam on I-80. I sat there for hours, thinking of you, and the weeks and weeks ahead without you. I made an illegal U-turn and rushed home to you.'

'I think I'd have died if you hadn't.'

'Angie, we're not thinking of that other world now.'

'Smell the goldenrod, Tim. Fill my arms with goldenrod, all they can hold.'

'Angie, you are still my queen.' "

"Okay, great scene. But it never happened, right?"

"You can be so picky! Okay, but what about that day cruise down the American River?"

"I'm fairly certain we never met at the fo'c's'le decked out in formal attire. Heck, I don't even know what a fo'c's'le is!"

" 'Hello, Jack. I've changed . . .' "

"It's Tim!"

"Okay, okay! 'Hello, Tim. I've changed my mind. The woman at the Delta Queen Deli said you might be out here.'

'Shhh. Give me your hand. Now close your eyes. Go on, step up. Do you trust me?'

'I trust you, Tim.'

'Then open your arms and . . .' "

"Nope. Didn't happen. And I'm afraid of heights, remember?"

"You are irritatingly pedantic at times, you know?"

(Do men have a fantasy world like this? I know they frequently undress women in their minds, though I've always hoped that they exclude nuns, congresswomen, and ladies over ninety years of age from this activity. But do their imaginations ever go beyond the inevitable conclusion? Do they ever script dialogue more complex than "Yeah, baby, do it to me"?)

"And Tim didn't rush in on New Year's Eve to tell me that he loves the way I order sandwiches and the crinkle in my nose. '*Bella Notte*' was not playing in the background when we ate at the Spaghetti Factory, and he never bellowed desperately for me that time we were separated by the crowd at Arco Arena."

" '*Adrian!*' "

"That's Angie."

" '*Angie!*'

'*Tim!*'

'*Angie!*'

'*Tim!*'

'*Angie!*'

'*Tim!*' "

"And that scene at the Mexican restaurant?"

"*Oh, the one where Tim said: 'Angie, I was told you were the most beautiful woman ever to visit Casa Burrito. That was a gross understatement'?*"

"From *Casablanca*, right?"

"*Well, maybe but . . .*"

"He never said that. He asked if I wanted the bean or beef burrito. That's it."

"*But what about when he climbed up on your balcony with a rose in his teeth and . . .*"

"I don't, in fact, have a balcony."

"Spoilsport. Okay, let me ask you: If we delete all of the fantasy scenes and just stick with the real stuff, how boring is that?"

Fantasy Angie had a point. By the time I'd stripped away those Cecil B. DeMille scenes of her/my fantasy world, the history of my relationship with Tim started to look, well, almost mundane. It's not that Tim is not romantic. He is. Sort of. In a typical American guy kind of way. In other words, not very. But he often says nice things like, "Angie, you look great" or "I had a great evening" or "Wow, that was great."

"But does he ever say, 'Angie, you are the most delectable, delicious woman I have ever met. How did I exist so long without you?' "

"Uh, no, not lately . . ."

"But if he did, Angie," Analyzin' Angie chimed in, "that may or may not be a good sign. I mean, any guy who uses a line like that . . ."

The three of us hit an impasse. I was getting tired of talking to myselves, and was ready for some outside counsel. So I sent Fantasy Angie and Analyzin' Angie on a prolonged time-out and sought objective third parties for my analyses going forward. My best friends were only too glad to help out:

I consulted Marie after Tim's call Monday night:

"Repeat what he said, word for word," Marie insisted.

"Well, he said that after the business sells, he wants to settle down."

" 'Settle down'? Wait a minute. Jack!" Marie hollered. "Tim said he wants to settle down! What does that mean?" I could hear Jack's deep baritone murmuring in the background, then Marie came back on the line. "Did he just say settle down, or did he say settle down with you?"

"Just settle down."

"Jack! He just said settle down!"

"But then he asked if I thought that was a good idea."

"But he asked her opinion about it!" she yelled. We remained silent as Jack determined his ruling. "Sorry, Angie. Jack says that's inconclusive."

Tuesday night, I conferred with Gwen:

"So he said 'I love you'?"

"Not exactly, Gwen. It was more like 'luv ya.'"

"'Love you'?"

"No, not so clear. More like 'luv ya' or even 'lub jya.'"

"'Luv ya'? Like when those drunks say 'I luv ya, man'?"

"I think so. Only without the 'man' on the end."

"But did Tim sound drunk?"

"No, I don't think so."

"So what did you say in response?"

"Nothing. He hung up too quickly."

"But the whole 'luv ya' came out before the connection went dead?"

"Yes."

"Hmmmm." I could hear Gwen's brain whirring. "I'm afraid it's still inconclusive, Angie."

Wednesday night, I reported to Jess that Tim had left his toothbrush at my house:

"What kind of toothbrush? Does it have one of those little rubber toothpick things at the end of it?"

"Hang on, Jess. Let me get it. Yes. Yes, it does have one of those rubber toothpick things on it."

"Well, that certainly isn't a wild fling kind of toothbrush. It's a more stable, more committed kind of toothbrush, don't you think?"

"I guess so."

"Angie, when he asked about it, did it seem to be his only toothbrush . . . ?"

But it took all of us, gathered on a four-way conference call, to dissect the meaning behind his belated birthday gift:

"A watch? Well, that's technically jewelry. Wouldn't you agree, Gwen?" Jessica asked.

"Depends," Gwen mused. "It could be a subtle criticism. Has he ever complained about your being late?"

"Uh, no."

"Good," Gwen ruled. "But then watches could also be classified as a practical gift, like a blender or toaster oven."

"Which is not a good sign, Angie," Marie noted.

"No? So how do I . . . ?"

"What kind of band does it have?" Gwen asked.

"Uh, it's gold and silver."

"Good." Marie sighed with relief. "Metal moves it closer to jewelry."

"But is it one of those stretchy, twist-o-flex bands?" Jess inquired.

"Nope."

"Good. And the face? Roman numerals or Arabic? Does it have a second hand or . . . ?"

We cross-examined the watch for another twenty minutes. The final determining factor was that the numbers on the face (Roman, not Arabic) were so miniscule as to be unreadable—definitely jewelry, not a timekeeping device.

By the end of that phone call, all of us—me, my alter egos, my high-powered interpreters, even Spud and Alli—were completely sick of the whole subject.

"Look, everybody," I said with a sigh. "I appreciate your help, but I think it's time we moved on to other topics."

"Hallelujah!" Gwen exclaimed. "No offense, Angie, but I think we can come up with more important, more thought-provoking issues."

"We are, after all, multifaceted women," Marie chimed in.

"Our love lives are only a small part of our lives," Jessica concurred. "We have many other interests."

"Absolutely. Just because Tim asked me about the movie *Bambi* last night . . ."

"He what?" Jess exclaimed excitedly. "He asked about a children's movie? Angie, that might be very significant . . ."

I needed a diversion to stop my obsessive, monothematic mind churning. But who could provide such diversion? Who in the world can possibly be more self-absorbed than a woman thinking about a man who might (or might not) have proposed to her? A woman who is pregnant, of course. I called Jenna.

Chapter 7

"Mom! I can't stand this! I'm the size of an oversized hippopotamus! A bloated water buffalo! An obese sea cow with severe water-retention issues!" Jenna, sitting across from me in the sidewalk café, had been whining (with much drama and creativity) for the past several minutes. According to her calculations, she was now seventeen weeks pregnant. Within that time, she had exploded from her normal size one to a gigantic! gargantuan! enormous! size two.

"Sweetie, I hate to break the bad news, but your weight gain is just starting. You'll probably grow to a size six, maybe even an eight, before you're done."

She looked at me, horrified. "Tell me you're kidding."

"Not."

"But what do people wear when they get that big? There's absolutely nothing in my closet that would fit that size!" she wailed.

I guess body size is relative. Most of my friends would

forswear their remote controls (and the husbands who operate them) to be a size eight. But from Jenna's perspective, the new little roundness of her tummy must have looked as big as the Astrodome.

Jenna had never had to be conscious of her weight before. She's one of those naturally slim people who snarf down bowls of nachos followed by half a Super Supreme Three-Cheese Double-Stuffed Pizza with Extra Pepperoni and top off the meal with mountains of Häagen-Dazs—and never gain an inch or a pound or even a single centimeter of cellulite. This is, of course, totally unfair. But life is known for its unfairness. (Is it fair that 1 percent of this country's population owns nearly 40 percent of its wealth?) However, life is also careful to provide humbling experiences to ensure balance. For naturally skinny women, the great leveler is pregnancy. (For The Donald, it's that awful haircut of his.)

"Look at this, Mom. My hair is falling out, and it feels like straw. And Ryan is afraid there might be toxins in my hair dye. So he wants me to go natural!" Jenna hadn't been "natural" since she was fifteen. Her hair has been more colors than a Sherwin-Williams showroom.

"I've got permanent black circles under my eyes," she moaned. "And I'm getting zits! Where the heck is that 'glow' everyone talks about? All I'm getting is acne!"

Jenna has never been particularly given to whining. But for someone with very little experience, she was pretty darn good at it. However, my patience was tapped out so I decided to put an end to her grousing. "That 'glow,' Jenna," I said in my best maternal I-know-whereof-I-speak voice, "comes from the inner happiness of a grateful mother-to-be who is carrying a precious child. A woman who recognizes what an incredible gift it is to be able to give life to another human being." I gave her my most formidable parental frown, one eyebrow slightly raised.

There was a pregnant pause. Jenna took a deep breath. "Uh, Mom? Is this the beginning of one of your lectures?" she asked anxiously.

"Well, it might be if you don't knock off your whining." I maintained my eyebrow raise and scowl externally as, internally, I gleefully outlined the sermon I was about to deliver.

It had been quite a while since I'd given either of the kids one of The Lectures. From the very beginning, I had used The Lectures sparingly to preserve their dramatic impact. (Research in torture and torment methodology indicates that overuse of any particular technique can dull its effect. For instance, in the seventies, college students were exposed to screechy nails on chalkboards for hours at a time. The result? The subjects learned to tolerate, ignore, and even enjoy the sound, finally setting it to a beat. Hence, the birth of Heavy Metal.)

Though themes may vary from culture to culture, The Lecture, done properly, is structured in four essential movements:

Introduction: *Establish Ingratitude.* The classic favorite, "After all I've done for you!," remains a popular choice for proclaiming the child's thanklessness. However, many parents prefer the more subtle "When you've been blessed with such talent/health/beauty/brains/ adoring family/etc.!" During the present administration, many parents have adopted a patriotic tone: "You, who have the privilege of being born in this great nation of ours . . ."

Section Two: *How Could You Possibly Do* **That?** The *That* should be described with as much detail and drama as possible. However, if the parent is certain that an infraction has occurred, but is not yet clear about the exact nature of the crime, the phrase "such a thing" can be used very effectively. "How could you say/do/ think such a thing?" accompanied by tears and/or wailing will often elicit the missing information from the guilty party.

Section Three: *Invoke a Higher Power.* Here the parent invokes the imaginary opinion of a culturally relevant Higher Power. "What would the Pope/Buddha/the neighbors/Grandpa Moskowitz (God rest his soul!) say?" Personally, I prefer to summon the individual child's Personal Conscience. My reasoning is that the child may assume that the neighbors or Grandpa Moskowitz (God rest his soul!) may never be aware of their wayward behavior. But their very own Personal Conscience is like an ever-vigilant Jiminy Cricket, ready to tsk and finger wag at the drop of a hat (or the dropping of any forbidden substances).

Conclusion: *It's Up To You.* The parent must conclude The Lecture by throwing all responsibility for salvation of the situation on the child's shoulders which, if the rest of The Lecture has been delivered successfully, should be quivering by now. An additional and totally acceptable conclusion may include the promise of "Or Else."

I took a deep breath, frown and eyebrow still in place, as I prepared to deliver my opening statement.

"No! Please, Mom, not The Lecture!" my daughter begged. She waved her napkin in capitulation and grinned her familiar impish grin. "Okay, Mom, you win," she said. "But now that I'm going to be a mom myself, will you teach me how to do that lecture thing?"

"Of course, Jenna," I replied sweetly. "And you can even start now. Surely if you can teach a kid to play the violin while it's still in the womb, you can teach it to fear The Lecture. Invaluable tool for every parent."

"Speaking of parents, Dad called and was asking about you."

"Really? That's odd."

"So, Mom, you haven't said anything about Tim's proposal. Aren't you excited?"

"How did you hear, sweetie? Your dad?"

"No, Tyler. He said some attorneys in his office went out to lunch and . . ."

"Never mind." I sighed. "Jenna, it's kind of an odd situation. I'm not sure it was an actual proposal. We were, uh, kind of asleep at the time."

Jenna raised an eyebrow, unconvinced. "Sleeping. Yeah, right. But even though you were, um, sleeping, you said 'yes,' right?"

"I didn't actually say anything."

"Well, do you love him?"

"I think so."

"You just think so? You're not sure?"

"Well, I love him in some form. I'm just not sure it's the kind of love to get married on."

"Oh." Jenna looked pensive. "But if you've been, uh, asleep together, it's not just a buddy kind of love, right?"

"I suppose so," I conceded. "But that doesn't mean he's Mr. Right."

"Just Mr. Right Now?"

"Jenna!"

"Well, what's Mr. Right supposed to be like?"

"I haven't a clue," I admitted. "I hadn't really thought about it. And even if Tim is Mr. Right, I don't know if I even want to get married again."

"Why not? What's wrong with marriage?" Jenna, happily married now for four whole months, was like a reformed smoker ready to stub out every cigarette (or every single person) who came across her path.

"Oh, nothing in general. It's just that I'm wondering if marriage isn't only for certain stages of life."

"What do you mean?"

"Well, sweetie, you're in the childbearing and -raising stages. It's definitely a plus to have a partner during that stage."

"So, you're promoting the theory that marriage is mainly a practical, societal arrangement."

"Uh, I suppose."

"How romantic." Jenna looked at me dubiously. "Mom? Do you really believe that?"

"Well, actually, probably not."

"Okay, so let's organize your thinking."

"Jenna, I've done way too much thinking about this already. I've been analyzing every little thing that Tim has ever said or done for the last week. I'm sick of it!"

"Like what?"

"Oh, every dumb thing. Like he asked me last night whether he should buy a regular waffle maker or a Belgian waffle maker."

"Well, that's pretty obvious, Mom. Any conversation with a guy that references breakfast issues means . . ."

"Jenna!"

"Okay, okay. But I think you've been looking at this from the wrong angle."

"I have?"

"Yes. You're apparently trying to figure *Tim* out, how *he* feels and what *he* intends. Shouldn't you be figuring your*self* out first?"

"Good point, sweetie. But how?"

Jenna reached into her purse and pulled out a pen and pad. "Let's make out a list of pros and cons first about marriage in general."

"Okay."

"So, aspects of marriage," she started efficiently. "Number one. Let's see. Well, you get to live together twenty-four/seven. Pro, right, Mom?"

"Uh, no, sweetie. I'd say that's a con. After twenty-six years, I finally get to have a place all to myself. I really like it for a change."

"Oh, okay." Jenna looked at me doubtfully. "Con then. What else about being married is there to consider?"

"Okay, how about this one? You aren't out dating other people anymore. So that would be a . . ."

". . . Con, right?" she finished confidently.

"Definite and absolute pro, Jenna." She sighed and shook her head. "Really, sweetie. Being 'out there' at my age is no picnic."

"Okay, but what about the fact that when you're married, you always have an appreciative audience when you parade around in your underwear?"

"Oh, I don't know if . . ."

"Mom, you've got all that new, sexy underwear. And you've been getting into shape. It should be a pro, right?" As Jenna started to write, I stopped her hand.

"Sweetie, no configuration of underwear can cover up my saddlebags and saggy rear end. So, it's only a pro if the lights are dim."

"So then it's a qualified pro?"

"Let's make it a qualified con."

We tried a few more: sharing financial decisions (her pro, me con), someone to cook for (me pro, her con), someone to do the "guy" things around the house (me con, her pro based on her inexperience with the incessant whining that usually accompanies a guy doing those guy things). But invariably my pros were Jenna's cons and vice versa. The only ones we agreed upon were filing joint tax returns and "someone to have regular, uh, sleep with": both of us gave those items, especially the latter, enthusiastic pros.

"Mom, maybe we should move on to the pros and cons of Tim himself. Our perspective on marriage may be in different stages, but a good guy is a good guy at any age, right?"

"I suppose. So, Tim himself? Well, he's had a vasectomy."

"Mom, I'm not even touching that one."

"Right. Just put it in the pro column. And Tim snores, especially if he falls asleep on his back."

"Ugh! Definite con!"

"Oh, no, Jenna. That's a pro. It's very soothing. You know that someone you care about is sleeping safely beside you."

"If you say so." Jenna reluctantly wrote snoring under Tim's pro list.

"And he knows the words to every Moody Blues song ever sung."

"The who?"

"Well, maybe."

"Maybe what?"

"Maybe he knows The Who."

"The Moody Blues?"

"No. Look, Jenna just put that as a pro. And he calls his mother every day."

"No, really? He calls his mother every single day? Isn't that a little . . ."

"He even accompanies her to her annual colonoscopy."

"Mom," Jenna groaned. "Perhaps you'd better finish this with one of the aunties."

"Good thought, sweetie. Let's go shopping."

Technically, the purpose of our get-together was to shop for Jenna's maternity clothes. Truthfully, neither of us was very eager to do so. For one thing, I had never been Jenna's first choice as a shopping partner. As a shopper, I am undecided, unfocused, and totally out of it fashion-wise.

Jenna, on the other hand, is relentless, discriminating, and at the cutting edge of style. But our main problem was that we were shopping for—ugh!—maternity clothes. Jenna seemed grimly determined about the mission.

"Mom, if I'm going to explode like this," she explained, "I definitely want to look pregnant. Not just fat."

I clearly remember the maternity fashions of my day: sweet little Peter Pan collars with sappy-looking bows, and cutesy baby animals leaping and dancing across every inch of fabric. The only colors available were baby blue and powder pink; the clothes were so sickeningly sweet and cute that even Shari Lewis and Lamb Chop would have gagged. Now tell me: What grown woman—one who is old enough to be having a baby, for gosh sakes!—would choose to wear that stupid stuff? Unless she had no choice which, in my day, we didn't.

And then there was the polyester. Yards and yards of polyester. Polyester pants, polyester skirts, polyester belts on polyester dresses that were shaped like Quonset huts. It was as if the Surgeon General had personally decreed polyester as necessary for a healthy pregnancy. (Didn't medieval women start their "confinement" months ahead of actually going into labor? They were probably hiding out so they wouldn't be seen in hideous medieval maternity outfits.)

And maternity underwear? Don't get me started. I'm no underwear aficionado; until recently I didn't know that many undergarments are designed to *expose* and *enhance* body parts rather than modestly conceal and contain them. But even *I* could barely stand to wear maternity panties which had all the sex appeal of a canvas car cover. And maternity bras? They weren't apparel; they were structural support systems. Normal underwires had been replaced with heavy-gauge steel, and the ugly straps were wide enough to support the national debt. (Did I warn you not to get me started?)

Of course, I did not tell Jenna any of this. But I think she had some inkling because both of us approached Mimi's Maternity with a certain amount of trepidation.

"You go in first, Mom," Jenna said nervously. "Let me know exactly how hideous it is so I can steel myself."

"Okay, sweetie." I took a deep breath, walked through the doors and straight into a highly animated salesclerk.

"Hello! I'm Chrissie!" the young woman exclaimed with a delight that surely came from inhaling nitrous oxide. "And how are we today?" she enthused. "And exactly how far along are we?"

"Oh, well, gosh," I stammered, blinded by her exuberance. "We are about four months. But, um, Chrissie, I don't mean *me* we. It's *her* we." I pointed at the tip of Jenna's head as she ducked around the corner again. "Yes, that her is we. Oh, heck! Jenna, get in here."

Jenna approached the door sullenly.

"Hello! I'm Chrissie!" our very own sugar plum fairy announced brightly. "Welcome to Mimi's and welcome to motherhood!"

Jenna and I waited three beats to see if Chrissie would burst into song. When she didn't, Jenna asked stiffly, "And where would I find, um, maternity clothes in my size, or the size I will become."

"Here!" Chrissie chirped cheerfully, flinging her arms

wide to encompass the whole store. *The hills are alive* . . .
"Just let me know if I can help you!"

After Chrissie had floated off, Jenna and I looked around
very cautiously. To my surprise, I saw absolutely no polyester, no bunnies or chickens, and very few bows. Colors ran
the spectrum: bright yellows, passionate purples, serious-
looking grays. We saw jeans in real denim, cleverly cut
business suits, sexy strapless dresses, and even . . .

"Miniskirts! Mom, these aren't half-bad," Jenna proclaimed,
ratcheting up to an almost Chrissie level of enthusiasm.

"When you are ready to try things on, I'll bring you the
pillow!" Chrissie trilled.

"The pillow?" We shrugged and kept looking. Sassy two-
piece bathing suits, jaunty sweats and capris, even the underwear wasn't awful.

"Oh, my gosh, Jenna! A thong! They make a thong for
pregnant women!"

"Makes sense to me, Mom. If your tummy is going to
poke out that far, it would probably yank regular panties
into a wedgie anyway."

We wandered around the shop until we had an armload
of clothes for Jenna to try on. Chrissie escorted us to the
dressing room and showed Jenna how to put on "the pillow," a small heart-shaped throw pillow with two Velcro
straps on either side.

"Pointy side down," Chrissie chirped. "This will add four
to six months to your tummy."

Jenna dutifully fastened the pillow around her still-tiny
waist and slipped a beautiful blue sweater dress over her
head. The effect was astonishing.

"Oh my God," Jenna whispered in awe, staring at herself in the mirror. "I'm pregnant."

I couldn't speak at all. Wasn't it just yesterday that I looked at myself in a mirror and came to the same mind-boggling realization? Of course, the dress had been much uglier (as I recall, it had a baby hippo plastered on each hip). But the wonder of the moment, the incredible sensation of the miracle of it all, was exactly the same.

We stared at Jenna's reflection, mesmerized, for a few moments. Jenna was the first to snap out of our mutual trance. "This is really fun, Mom." She giggled. She grinned at me and grabbed for a denim miniskirt to try on. "I wonder if there's a store like this for grandmothers-to-be."

"Grandmothers?"

"Sure, grandmothers. You know, clothes that will make you look wizened and wise and ancient, like a real grandma," she teased. "Better get prepared, Mom. The big day is coming!"

I looked back into the mirror, but at my own reflection this time. I definitely felt more shock than awe. "Oh my God. I'm a grandmother."

Later that evening, as I was studying my face for signs of grandmotherly wisdom and/or deterioration, I got a call from Tim.

"So, Tim, do you think of me as a mature woman?"

"Sure," he replied innocently. I groaned. "What? You want me to think of you as an immature woman?"

"No, of course not. It's just that . . . did you realize that I'm about to become a grandmother?"

"Oh, I see. So, you're saying that I'm lusting after a senior citizen?"

"Lusting?" I'm sure he could hear me blush over the phone.

"Unh-huh. And you're particularly cute when you blush." See? I knew he could hear it. "But did you realize that you've been dating a grandfather these past few months?"

"Well, yes, but . . ."

"But what?" Tim chuckled. "What's the big deal?"

Yeah. What's the big deal?

Chapter 8

The next night was Thursday night and Thursday night is my night to work out with The Guys. The Guys are all serious weight trainers; I am not. All of them are huge and muscular, and all of them are male; I am none of those things. Most of them are under the age of thirty; they make me feel like the foster mother of a string of collegiate linebackers. So what the heck am I doing there? Put simply: It's a lot gentler on my psyche to work out with The Guys than working out with the Angelina Jolie look-alikes who show up on other nights.

"Here, Angie," Ralph leaped to the heavy door as I arrived at the Twenty-ninth Street Gym, barely disturbing his tattooed biceps as he opened it for me. "Let me get this for you."

A small group of The Guys surrounded me as I entered. Each held a kazoo, and at Ralph's signal, they kazooed a spirited, if slightly off-key, version of "Here Comes the Bride." I, of course, turned the color of spaghetti sauce.

"So, we hear you got a special kind of proposal," Bobby said, blushing (even at 270 pounds, he had a cuter blush than mine).

"Let me guess. Tyler told you, right?"

"No, Keith heard it from one of the other cops on his shift."

"No, I heard it before Keith," Ralph insisted. "The congressman from Contra Costa County was talking about it with the lobbyist from the Dental Association."

All I could do was groan. Well, and blush. Again. (Or was I merely continuing the blush I'd already started?)

"Can I carry your gym bag, Angie?" Keith offered.

"Why don't you set up over here, Angie?" Bobby suggested, moving his weights aside. "It's a little chilly tonight, and you'd be right under the heater."

I eyed my muscle-bound training mates suspiciously. "What on earth is this all about? Do I look incapacitated somehow?"

"Uh, no," Bobby replied, nervously studying his shoelaces carefully for signs of life. "But we were at your birthday party last Sunday. And, um, we heard that you're going to be a grandmother."

"Yeah," Keith chimed in. "And we didn't realize that you were turning"—he paused reverentially—"fifty."

"Are you sure that a woman of your age should be working out like this?" Ralph continued anxiously.

"So, help me out here, guys," I asked. "Five days ago, when I was forty-nine, it was okay that I was working out. But now that I've officially turned fifty and my daughter is giving birth, you think it might be hazardous to my health?"

"Yeah, exactly." All three of them nodded seriously.

"We just didn't know that you were that old," Keith continued. "You're just so, um, so . . ."

"Well preserved?"

"Yeah, that's it!" Keith responded enthusiastically.

"So how old did you guys think I was?"

"Um . . ." This had the three of them stumped. "Maybe, like, forty-seven?" Ralph offered tentatively.

"And, Angie, we had a question, if it wouldn't embarrass you too much," Bobby asked carefully.

"Shoot." Heck, how could I be any more embarrassed than I'd already been? At least half of Sacramento knew that I'd gotten an almost-proposal and the circumstances under which I'd received it. What could possibly be more embarrassing than that?

"Well, the three of us were wondering if, that is, do people your age, I mean, you and the guy who proposed, do you actually, you know, *do* it?" Bobby looked at me with sincere curiosity. And yes, my embarrassment meter hit new highs, or lows depending on your point of view. Fortunately, just then a familiar, welcome voice interrupted from across the room.

"You don't have to answer that, Angie," my friend Jonathan called, laughing. Jonathan is one of my favorites of The Guys. He and I had developed an easy friendship probably because, despite the fact that he is around my age, good-looking, single, and "just my type," he is also gay. After the initial heartbreaking discovery of this fact, being with such an attractive gay guy turned out to be very relaxing. Our only conflict ever came when we found ourselves flirting with the same guy. Jonathan, still laughing, beckoned me to join him at the mirrors across the room. "Here's where the senior-citizen set hangs out."

But before I could join Jonathan, I was hailed by an oddly familiar and not-so-welcome voice.

"Yoo hoo! Angie!" Bob trotted up to our little group from the far side of the gym. His shiny spandex outfit and brand-new tennies made quite a contrast to the tattered T-shirts and baggy boxers most often sported at the Twenty-ninth Street Gym. The one commonality between my ex and The Guys was the bulging—only Bob's bulges gathered around his tummy and rear end area rather than at his biceps and pecs. My mouth opened to speak, but the sight of him sent me to a country beyond speechless, perhaps Catatonia. "Hi," Bob said, turning to The Guys. "I'm Bob. Angie's husband."

That inspired my vocal cords. "Ex! Ex-husband," I squeaked with conviction.

"Yeah, whatever," Bob continued. "So, I figured it was time for ol' Bob to get back into shape. Are you surprised to see me, Angie?" Surprised did not begin to express the way I felt seeing ol' Bob squeezed like steamed bratwurst into his tank top and bicycle shorts. "I was thinking that maybe we could work out together. You know, we've got a lot to discuss now that we're going to be grandparenting together."

Excuse me? Now here was a man who had just barely shared the parenting duties of our two kids while we were married. As I recall, his most major contribution parenting-wise was in 1989 when he slapped together a peanut butter and jelly sandwich for Tyler's lunch box. What exactly were we supposed to share as grandparents?

But before I could come up with something to say, Frank, head trainer at the Twenty-ninth Street Gym, arrived.

"Ready to go, Mr. Hawkins? Let's get started on your orientation." Turning to me, Frank chided, "I'm surprised at you, Angie. You never told me you're married."

"But I'm not married," I cried desperately to their retreating backs. "I'm divorced!"

"Whatever," Bob threw over his shoulder.

"Angie," Jonathan said quite seriously as I stomped over to join him, "you never told me about your wild drug experiences."

"What wild drug experiences?"

"Surely you were on strong hallucinogens when you married that guy," he said, with a mischievous grin.

"Cute, Jonathan, very cute." I slugged him in the arm, wishing I could be slugging Bob instead.

"Ow! Your workouts are starting to pay off. Especially"—he grinned again—"for such an old broad." As I wound up my gym bag to let him have it, he sidestepped quickly. "Hey, I'm just kidding! I'm older than you are."

"You are?"

"Turned fifty last year."

"Fifty? Really? You don't look it."

"Well, you don't look fifty either, Angie."

"Listen to us, Jonathan. If I'm fifty and I look like this, and you're fifty and look like that, what the heck did we think fifty was supposed to look like?"

"I figured it would look something like Archie Bunker."

"Or Aunt Bee on *The Andy Griffith Show*?"

"But it turns out that it looks like us."

"Weird, huh?" We looked at ourselves in the mirror as we pumped our weights in silence.

"And now I'm going to be a grandmother," I said, with a sigh, visualizing myself in a little gray bun with wire-rimmed spectacles. "I've always wanted grandkids. I love being with little kids . . ."

"Yoo-hoo! Angie!" Bob called from across the gym. "Look at me! I'm on the treadmill! See me? I'm almost jogging!"

"Uh, well, most of them anyway." I sighed again and looked at the rapidly aging me in the mirror. "But frankly it never occurred to me that in order to have grandkids, I'd have to become a grandmother. 'Grandmother' just sounds so, so, um . . ."

"So old?" Jonathan offered.

"Yeah, old. And I don't feel old. Heck, I hardly feel grown-up. I figured by the time I hit this age I'd feel more mature, more settled, that I'd have all the answers, and know my purpose in life."

"And?"

"And I don't."

"Good. Me neither. I'd hate to be the only one."

"Jonathan, I feel like an adolescent girl, like I'm no smarter or more together than I was at fifteen. My own daughter seems more mature than I am."

"Angie, it's probably just the halftime blues. You know, you're in the locker room, thinking about the prior two quarters, what you did right, what you did wrong. And you're deciding whether you want to play the next two quarters the same way."

I hate it when guys use sports analogies. I know nothing about sports. (I get particularly lost when they choose sports like j'ai alai or rugby. During college, a British boyfriend once told me that "in every bloke's life, there's a time when a free kick should be played as a scrum." I've wondered ever since what that meant.) I've never actually played football and therefore never experienced the deep halftime contemplation the team apparently goes through while the cheerleaders are shaking their little hearts out on the field. So I couldn't say I really knew what Jonathan was talking about. But I do know my math.

"So you think that fifty is the halfway point of our lives?"

"Maybe," Jonathan mused. "I intend to take it a quarter at a time. Maybe even make it to overtime."

"Bet you won't look like you're one hundred when you get there, Jonathan. Bet you won't look a day over ninety-nine."

"Angie! Look, look!" Bob yelled, panting nearby. "I can bench press 150 pounds!" Ralph and Bobby grinned at me, each holding an end (and at least seventy-five pounds each) of Bob's weights.

"Uh, but you know, Angie," Jonathan said seriously with a nod in Bob's direction, "it's pretty critical not to make the exact same mistakes you made in the first two quarters. Know what I mean?"

"If I'm going to make them, make new ones?"

"Exactly." He chuckled. We continued our reps in silence for a few more minutes, then Jonathan started with surprise. "Angie, my eyes must be going bad," he said, staring out the storefront window. "I could have sworn that I saw a bright yellow Volkswagen parked outside the gym. It just got up and walked into the bakery across the street."

Chapter 9

After my workout, I had arranged to meet Tyler at La Bou, the bakery/coffeehouse across the street from the gym. As I rushed through the door, I was nearly bowled over by a familiar figure.

"Clarisse! Gosh, what a very, um, sunny dress you're wearing." We stared at each other awkwardly. "So, what are you doing here?"

Clarisse looked at me belligerently and puffed up furiously, a steaming hot-air balloon ready to burst at its seams. "In this country, Angie" she huffed, "a person has the right to go wherever she chooses." And with that, she slipped her moorings and flew angrily out the door.

Huh?

"Hey, Mom!"

Tyler filled the space Clarisse had just vacated. (To be precise, it would have taken three Tylers to fill that space entirely.) He kissed me on the cheek and we moved to the counter to order our coffee. Actually I ordered coffee; Tyler ordered a "double-shot nonfat caramel latté, extra hot, no foam, with a sprinkle of nutmeg."

"I don't really want that," he confided. "Auntie Gwen wants me to practice techniques for harassing witnesses on the opposing side. She advised me to start with coffee orders and work up to restaurants. She said if I can get a maître d' to cry, I'm probably ready for the courtroom."

"Honey, I'm not sure all of Auntie Gwen's advice should be taken literally." And I wondered if, in all fairness, I should warn the waiters' union that Gwen was grooming an apprentice.

"So, Tyler," I said, as we took a seat by the window. "What was the deal with you and Angeline at the party the other night? Had I said something wrong?"

"I don't know, Mom." Tyler, my cool, confident son, squirmed uncomfortably in his seat. "See, I know that everyone thinks Angeline and I are great together and that we should get married."

"But you don't agree?" I asked, carefully keeping the neutrality of the Swiss in my voice.

Several months before, I had been determinedly diplomatic when Tyler was dating a female who made my nostrils flare and my blood pressure rise to record levels. I figured that I should now practice the same neutrality regarding his new young woman: Angeline, the intelligent, warm daughter-in-law of my dreams, the perfect loving mother for my yet-to-be-born grandchildren, the sweet succor of my old age, the . . .

"You don't think that you and Angeline should get married?" I inquired nonchalantly.

"No. I do. I think everybody is right. I think we should. Get married, that is." Tyler, my calm, unflappable son, looked absolutely panicked.

"I'm sorry, honey. I'm not seeing the problem. Doesn't Angeline want to get married?"

"I don't know. I haven't asked."

"But why not? Are you afraid she'll say 'no'?"

"No. I'm afraid she'll say 'yes.' "

"Uh, which would be bad because even though you think you *should* marry her, you don't want to?"

"No! I do want to marry her! As much as anything I've ever wanted," Tyler, my ever-cheerful son, said miserably. "But then, if we get married, we'll probably have kids within a few years."

"Oh, I see. And you don't want children?"

"No! I really want children! And I especially want children if I could be fortunate enough to have them with Angeline. She would be the most awesome mother imaginable and I would be the luckiest man alive!" And with that, Tyler, my unexcitable, self-possessed son, looked at me desperately, ready to weep.

Okey-dokey.

Isn't exercise supposed to increase your endorphins? Get your blood pumping and your brain lobes functioning at peak performance? I had just spent an hour and a half sweating, grunting, and endorphin building. How come I couldn't follow this conversation? (Maybe I should have stayed on the Stair Stepper.)

Now I'm female, which means I'm allowed to admit out loud when I don't understand something. But I'm also a mother. And I wasn't quite ready to relinquish that mystic maternal aura I'd crafted over the years. You know, where your kids think that you are all-seeing, all-knowing, all-powerful? And heck, I was about to become a grandmother; who is more omniscient than a granny?

So I gave Tyler my Universal Mother gaze of deepest empathy and complete comprehension, and said, "Ah. I see." Then, nodding wisely, I remained silent.

"I knew you would, Mom!" Tyler cried with obvious relief. "You always understand!" Yeah, right. "So, what should I do?"

Do?

"Well, honey, we should start by verbalizing the issues, maybe jotting them down on paper." I pulled pen and pad out of my purse. "I mean, I know they are obvious, but it always adds clarity to put the issues in black-and-white."

"Good idea, Mom," Tyler said excitedly. "I mean, not only do you understand me completely, but you also have the female perspective, right?"

"Uh, right." My discussion with Jenna the prior day had made it obvious that I had the perspective of an *ancient* female. I threw my mind back to my twenties before I'd married Bob. What were my concerns back then?

I had worried about whether I was choosing the right man (no comments, please). I had wondered if his mother would like me, whether I'd look beautiful at my wedding, and whether our wedding night would be any better than that night in the backseat of his '65 Chevy. I don't remember much beyond that. Somehow I doubted that these were the concerns bothering Tyler.

"Okay, Mom, so the first issue is that marriage is obviously such a huge responsibility."

"Of course." Responsibility?

"I mean, for the first time in my life, I'll have to take care of someone else."

"Uh, well, Tyler, Angeline seems pretty able to take care of herself."

"Oh, I know that, Mom. But she'd be my *wife*. As her husband, I'll need to look after her, protect her, you know?"

Hmmm. Like most of us, I had mothered Bob from day one, a kind of Pavlovian response. I had scheduled his dentist appointments, monitored his food groups, and made sure he always had clean boxer shorts. But did I feel "responsible" for him?

"And then there's the possibility that Angeline might change. To me, she is absolutely perfect exactly as she is. But will she stay like this over the years?"

The answer is, of course, no. Had I feared that Bob would change before we married? Nope, in fact I had prepared a mental list of the few small improvements, maybe a hundred or so minor adjustments, that I planned to help Bob make through the years (for his own good, of course). And as perfect as my son is, I'd bet Angeline had a similar list prepared already.

"Then, of course, I'll be sacrificing my career."

"Uh, Tyler, I think statistics show that most highly successful men *are* married." Whereas most highly successful women are not.

"But that's the old paradigm, Mom. Why would I marry a wonderful woman like Angeline, then mess it up by putting my career ahead of her?" I don't know. Maybe we

101

should ask Newt Gingrich or The Donald. "And I won't be able to just focus on my own dreams anymore. I'll have to consider hers as well, right?"

"Sure, honey." I wrote "career sacrifice" down. Had I ever even worried about giving up my dreams to be married? Nope. I just dropped them with no thought at all.

"Then there's that communication thing."

"Of course. That communication thing. But could you be a little more specific, honey?"

"You know, women always want to talk about things. Like feelings and what you're thinking. It's okay every once in a while, but to live with it all the time? I don't know if I could handle that."

I thought of telling Tyler that he could do what his father always did: turn on the TV and ignore all attempts at conversation. But I didn't want to give him any ideas. Do we women like to communicate? Yes, we do. But, oh, how quickly we learn to give up on our mates and talk to our girlfriends instead. Maybe Angeline would be one of the persistent ones who . . .

"And what about all the compromises? What if she doesn't like my car? Or my sheets? Or my Tupperware?"

"Uh, Tyler, you have Tupperware?"

"Some."

"I see."

"And what about my time with the guys? Just hanging out? Watching sports?"

"Doesn't Angeline like your friends?"

"Sure. But when she's around, we don't get to act like, well, you know, like guys."

"Ah, of course." In other words, they're required to be civilized.

"And, of course, there's the Little League thing."

"Right. The Little League thing." The Little League thing?

"When kids come along, I'm sure my career will suffer even more. I can't be just an absentee dad. I'll need to get involved, coach the kids' sports teams, help them with school projects." Tyler looked at me helplessly. "But what's even worse, Mom? What if I'm no good at those things?"

Had I worried about this? About what I'd have to sacrifice to attend PTA meetings or go on field trips? Had I been concerned that my cupcakes wouldn't be up to snuff for the preschool Halloween party? Nope.

"And kids are really expensive. How do I know I'll be able to make enough money to take care of a family? There's orthodontics and college and . . ."

When I had thought about having kids, all I saw was happy, healthy babies in cute outfits. I didn't foresee the 12 A.M., 2 A.M., and 4 A.M. feedings. I didn't anticipate those nasty diapers, toddler tantrums, and the inevitable adolescent angst. And I certainly didn't think about the zillions of dollars it would take to raise those healthy, happy babies. If I'd known those things were coming, perhaps my birth-control regime would have been a bit more rigorous.

"And then there's the sex issue," Tyler continued self-consciously. He heaved a heavy sigh. "You know, the monogamy."

"Right. That *is* a problem," I said gravely, with absolutely no idea why it would be.

"Of course, it's not a problem right now, Mom. I'm crazy

about Angeline and we, uh, do very well together." I did not ask Tyler to elaborate on this subject. "But what about in ten years? Thirty years? Should I be sowing more wild oats now so that in fifty years I'll still be happy being with only her?"

I thought of telling Tyler that, in fifty years, he'd be lucky if his equipment could sow any kind of oat. The question of "with whom" would probably not be the focus. But I figured this wasn't the time to give him more to worry about.

Had I ever worried about being monogamous? All I remember was my (definitely naïve) expectation of happily ever after. And even though I had never been giddy in love with Bob, it never occurred to me, especially not before we got married, that I was martyring myself to monogamy. It must be a guy thing.

"Maybe it's a guy thing, huh, Mom?"

"Hmmm. Have you talked with your dad about this, Tyler? Maybe he'd have a better male perspective."

"No. Dad's been acting pretty strange lately, Mom." Tyler turned to me with trusting eyes. "So what do you think I should do?"

Do? We were back to that again? I took a deep breath, a Universal Mother of Wisdom breath. "I think you should do what your heart tells you, Tyler," I said, knowing his own heart had to have a lot more answers than I did. "And then maybe check out some of the concerns we just listed with Angeline. I'd start with the Tupperware . . ."

As I drove home, I thought about Tyler. He was definitely more conscious of the potential pitfalls of marriage than I had ever been. Was this a good thing? Probably. It might help him avoid some pain. But then again, if I'd not made some of the foolish blunders I'd made in my life, would I have learned as much as I'd learned? And by the way, what *had* I learned?

I ran into Jack as I walked through my (our) back gate and told him about my conversation with Tyler.

"Sure, Angie, every young man thinks about those things."

"Um, but what about older men?" I asked, thinking once again about Tim. "Are they concerned about the same things?"

"Well, no, not so much. Little League and orthodontics are usually nonissues." Jack chuckled.

"But the others?"

"Worries about career? Most of us have got that figured out by our forties or fifties."

"The relationship concerns?"

"Well, let's see," Jack mused with a smile. "If a man has been married before, he probably has experience handling compromise and communication." He paused, then continued thoughtfully, "But then again, prior experience can be an issue in itself."

"It can?"

"Sure. My divorced friends worry that, if marriage didn't work out for them the first time, it might not work out the next time. And my widowed friends, if they had a great marriage, are afraid that nothing could ever be so good again."

Interesting. It seems to me that women are a bit more

optimistic (intentionally naïve?) about "the second time around." "So what about the monogamy, Jack? Is that still a problem?"

"Angie," Jack said quite seriously, "for any single adult male over forty, regular sex is the miraculous answer to his most fervent prayers. Unless he's an idiot, monogamy is a moot point."

"Even if that regular sex is with an older woman?"

"Depends on the older woman, I suppose." Jack grinned, then abruptly excused himself. "My apologies, Angie, but I think I hear Marie calling."

Ah.

I was still thinking about all of this when Tim called me later.

"Tim? Do you get enough time to hang out with the guys?"

"What guys?"

"You know, your guy friends."

"I suppose. Why do you ask?"

"Just curious. What about Tupperware?"

"Tupperware? What about it?"

"Um, do you have any? Any that you especially like?"

"Angie, have you been drinking?"

"No. I've just been, well, thinking about things."

"Tupperware?"

"Yeah. Among other things."

"Hmmmm. Sounds to me like you've got a little too much time on your hands. Maybe you need to get back to work."

Chapter 10

Tim was right. By Monday morning, I was really ready to get back to work. My minivacation had involved way too much thought and not enough action. It was time for me to lace up my bootstraps, head out to center field for the next quarter, slam that pigskin over the net and into the cup! Enough moping around and analyzing my love life, or worrying about how grandmotherly I was becoming!

I just needed to get back to work, to feel productive and vital again. I was even eager to find out what the ownership changes at work would bring. After nearly twenty years of much the same, this would be new. And new (as everyone kept reminding me) was exciting. And exciting can be fun!

I am so stupid.

After spending six hours in the office with my new boss, Russ Martin, I could state definitively that he is short. Very short. And that every preconceived notion I'd ever had about short men having a short man's complex is true. Absolutely true.

I did not like Russ Martin.

I do not believe I had ever met anyone—male, female or alien life-form—that I have disliked more completely and more instantly. I have several—no, make that many—adjectives that I could use to describe him and his character. The list would begin with "supercilious," "vain," and "pompous." Then it would wrap up, several pages later, with "Booger Brain." ("Booger Brain" was a term Jenna had coined in the second grade. This was the first time I'd ever felt moved to use it.)

And Booger Brain was my new boss.

It started when I, excited to be back to work, back to the land of the productive and vital, walked in that first Monday morning. Booger Brain, aka Russ, was standing in my office looking irritated and impatient. Had I mentioned before that he was a natty dresser? Actually, his fashion statement should be described as Fastidious Fascist; his trousers were pressed to a dangerously sharp crease, and his shoes were polished more brilliantly than the mirrors of the Hubble telescope. His sunflower blond hair had been sprayed so heavily it could qualify as protective gear and it added at least two inches to his ramrod-straight stature of five-foot-three (and I'm pretty sure he got that tall by adding lifts to his shoes). As I walked in, Booger Brain, with no preamble, asked where I had been.

"Uh, well, you and Phil told me to take the week off while you finalized your contract. So I took the week off."

"Yes," Russ replied sharply. "But I assumed you would still be available by pager."

"Uh, but I don't actually own a pager."

Russ stared at me as if my lack of a pager was an act of the most insidious mutiny. "You don't own a pager?" he said icily.

"No." Why did I feel so apologetic? "It's never been needed. I mean, the property managers know how to reach me in an emergency and . . ."

"You will have a pager by tomorrow," Booger Brain, the new god of property management, declared. "And where were you this morning?"

"Well, I stopped at the office building on Greenback this morning on my way in and . . ."

"I wasn't told that you were going to the office on Greenback this morning," he said, his beady little eyes narrowing.

Let me set the stage here. I had worked for Phil for nearly twenty years, overseeing his property and his business. I was pretty much a one-woman show for many of those years. My schedule and my actions were determined by common sense and my loyalty to Phil. Granted, I was pretty much self-trained, but managing property is not neurosurgery: A) You make sure that buildings do not leak, do not smell, do not collapse. B) You make sure spaces are rented out to tenants who pay rent on a regular basis. C) You make sure that A does not cost more than the revenues from B. That's it.

"Angie," he said (due to the fact that he was my same height yet attempting to look down at me, the N got stuck in his nose and was drawn out painfully), "there will obviously be some changes now that a new regime is in place." I swear to God on my Miracle Bra, he said "regime." Just like the Ayatollah Whatsoever or Slobadon Milwhatshisface.

Russ slammed a binder, twice the size of the Sacramento yellow pages, in front of me. "Here is the company handbook" (Who in the world has a hand that size?) "of policies and procedures. I expect you to familiarize yourself with it over the next couple of days. We'll discuss it in depth at our staff meeting on Wednesday."

"Uh, Russ, there are really only six of us in the office. Do you really think this, uh, type of structure is necessary?"

He paused, then took a very deep breath into his scrawny little chest. "Angie, there's a right way to do things and a wrong way. We will be doing things the right way around here for a change." He rotated with military precision and headed toward the door. "By the way," he said, turning back with a sneer, "your husband has been calling here. We don't allow personal calls during office hours. You'll find that in Section 27A."

"Who called?"

"Your husband. Bob."

"He's not my husband; he's my ex-husband."

"I'm not interested in discussing your personal affairs, Angie. Just see that he doesn't call again."

And this was the most pleasant part of our day together.

I flipped open my new "handbook" to a passage that turned out to be fairly representative of the rest:

Section 33.B: Coffee Procurement in Coordination with Bathroom Breaks: Employees may obtain coffee (if desired) on the hour and the half hour only. Bathroom Breaks shall be precisely fifteen minutes after such Coffee Procurement. Employees who waive their Coffee Procurement Privileges for any particular time slot automatically waive the immediately subsequent Bathroom Privileges. However, should an employee continue to waive Coffee Procurement Privileges throughout the day, Substitute Bathroom Break Privileges shall be granted to coincide with the schedule of Regular Bathroom Break Privileges that would normally have been granted. (See Section 33. C in reference to Tea (Hot and Cold) Procurement Privileges.)

But as delightful as it would have been to continue my reading, Russ called me into his office so we could "work on a few important projects collaboratively." The first urgent tasks on his list were to redesign 1) my filing system (Apparently, alphabetical organization is no longer de rigueur in the world of filing—who knew? Russ insisted on implementing the Dewey decimal system.); 2) my budget spreadsheets (We would no longer calculate only Most-Likely, Worst-Case, and Best-Case scenarios for budgets. Russ insisted that we also create Slightly Worse Than Expected, Not Quite Best Case But Better Than Average, Cataclysmic, and Apocalyptic versions as well.), and most importantly; 3) my fax cover sheet.

" 'TO' is not aligned properly with 'FROM' and their corresponding lines are too thick. It's very unsightly. And we should be using the European system of delineating area codes within the phone number. Periods, no parentheses," he instructed firmly. We spent nearly two hours on this very critical document before we reached fax-cover sheet perfection. Then we moved on to the crucial issue of Proper Placement of House Plants within a Professional Office Setting. We owned two plants; this matter took an hour and a half to resolve.

To describe Russ as a micromanager is to describe the Pope as slightly religious. He watched my every move as if I were a wayward preschooler under clinical observation. Toward late afternoon, when Russ was on one of his sanctioned Bathroom Breaks, one of my property managers sneaked into my office.

"Angie," she whispered nervously, "are you still my boss? Russ says I'm supposed to report directly to him about everything."

"Don't worry about it, Donna. Just do what he asks right now, and we'll figure this out over time." I gave her a reassuring smile that I did not feel.

By the time I left the office that evening, my self-esteem was battered and bruised, and I was exhausted after a day of getting absolutely nothing accomplished. All the way home, I tried convincing myself that: It's good, it's all good. But myself didn't believe me.

When I got home, I immediately climbed into my jammies, poured myself a glass of wine (not a short, ugly, supercilious one, but a *very* tall, handsome, intelligent one), and answered the phone on its first ring.

"So, Sunshine," Tim said. "How was the first day with your new boss?"

"Not so good. I don't know if this is going to work out. I feel like . . ."

"Sure it will, Angie," Tim interrupted. "You can handle him."

"But I . . ."

"Angie, this company has been your baby, and Phil has trusted you completely all these years. So there's a little change in the winds; so what? Don't give up the ship now. Don't let a little ripple in the stream throw you off-balance."

"But he . . ."

"You can roll with the punches, Angie. That's what the business world is all about. Don't let them see you sweat, and never give up."

"But I'm not . . ."

"You're a team player, Angie. Maybe there's a new quarterback, but you can adapt. Give it your best can-do efforts. And if, in a year or so, it isn't working, you can look for something else."

"But a year is so . . ."

"And then you can leave with your head held high because you'll know that you gave the team your all, right?"

"Uh, yeah. Right."

"Good. Well, then g'night. Lub jya."

"Yes, and I . . ." Click.

Sigh. Somehow, the perspective that Tim (aka Vince Lombardi) had on my work issues was less than emotionally satisfying. I dialed another number.

"Gwen!" I wailed piteously. "Russ is awful! He . . ."

"Angie," Gwen said calmly, twenty minutes later after my detailed tale of woe. "Clearly, he's setting you up to fire you."

"He is?" I gulped.

"Of course. What he doesn't know is that you have the best employment attorney in the state on your side. I'm not sure that we have a case for harassment yet. But keep careful notes."

Fired? Gwen's interpretation was certainly not very soothing. So I dialed for a second opinion.

"Marie!" I wailed piteously. "Russ is awful! He . . ."

"Angie," Marie said calmly, twenty minutes later after my now-perfected tale of woe. "Obviously, he has the hots for you."

"He does?" I gulped.

"But what he doesn't know is that we are women of sophistication and a wealth of experience in these matters."

"A wealth?"

"Yes. We've been around the block and have seen this type of adolescent male posturing before."

"We have?"

"Yes. So we aren't going to stand for it."

"We're not?"

"Absolutely not. So when you are ready to start networking for another position, let me know."

After the call with Marie, I brooded over which was worse: Getting fired and thrown out on the street or having that hideous little man have the hots for me. I sought a third perspective.

"Jess!" I wailed piteously. "Russ is awful! He . . ."

Jessica cut me off immediately. "Well, what did you expect? Angie, the guy is a Virgo. A short Virgo. Worst kind. So either put up with it or move on. Your choice."

Oh.

"Jess?" I started tentatively, "move on to what?"

I heard her sigh heavily on the other end of the phone. "Angie, how many years of life do you have left?"

"Well, gosh, I can't really say. I . . ."

"Ballpark, Angie. Don't make a federal case of this."

"Well, maybe, then, say, thirty years?"

"Okay. Thirty years. So let me ask you: Do you want to spend the next thirty years doing exactly the same thing you did for the last thirty?"

Wow. Now *that* was a significant question. I quickly reviewed the last thirty years: a truly tedious marriage, endless PTA meetings, chartreuse bell bottoms, stinky diapers, that disastrous Dorothy Hamill haircut in the seventies, waiting up for teenagers who've missed curfew, waiting in orthodontists' offices, waiting in grocery lines, waiting for my divorce papers to come through, waiting for . . . "Uh, well, gosh, probably not. Especially not those chartreuse bell bottoms."

"The what? Oh, never mind. So, you know what you don't want, Angie. But do you know what you *do* want?"

"Uh, no. Not really."

"Well, then perhaps you should determine that first," she said matter-of-factly. "Then you'll be able to answer questions like whether you want to get married or whether you want to keep this job."

"But how . . . ?"

"Look, I'm afraid I can't talk right now. That PBS special on the origin of the universe is about to start. I need to find my notepad and plug in my lava lamp. So figure it out."

Oh. Okay. Right.

"So, Spud, it looks like these are my options: Roll with the punches. Wait to get fired. Respond to Russ's backhanded

115

sexual advances. Or sit down and figure out exactly what the heck I'm supposed to do with my next thirty years." Spud looked up at me, then opened his jaws in a mighty yawn. "Right. We'll hit the sack early, sleep it off, and hope it all goes away." So we did.

Chapter 11

But it didn't.

Through the next week, my work life continued to be painful, awkward, discouraging, and demoralizing. Russ intensified his nanomanaging. He corrected the way I answered the phone; "Hi, this is Angie" was replaced with "Universal Properties, where real estate and real people come together! Good morning. This is Angie Hawkins. How may I assist you on this beautiful Sacramento day?" He clocked my lunch hours to the minute and installed some software called The Vigilant Remote Monitor to scan and report all Internet activity on my desktop. (I think he was sorely disappointed when Lay It on Thick, Hot and Steamy turned out to be a site that compared asphalt techniques.)

During this period, my fantasy life took on a new dimension. Fantasy Angie still entertained me with romantic Tim scenes:

> " 'Last night we said a great many things. You said I was to
> do the thinking for both of us. Well, Ilsa, uh, Angie, I've done

117

a lot of it since then, and it all adds up to one thing: You're getting on that plane to join me in Schenectady where you belong!' "

But now Russ showed up as my costar in a few of them:

"Angie comes back to the office unexpectedly to find Russ rearranging my pencil drawer. 'We're not just going to let you walk out of here, Booger Brain.'
'Oh, yeah?' he says belligerently. 'You and who else?'
'Smith, and Wesson, and me.' Russ moves as if to reposition her paper-clip holder. 'Go ahead,' Angie says, eyes narrowing, finger on the trigger. 'Make my day.' "

Finally, after two weeks of long-distance phone calls and endless e-mails, Tim came back into town. And on the day he was to arrive, I received a huge bouquet of flowers in the office. (It's fortunate that Russ was not around because I'm certain this would qualify as a serious infraction per Section 42.D: Unwelcome Personal Business in the Office.) I ripped open the card which read simply, "From You Know Who."

"From You Know Who"? A quick survey of my buddies revealed that the message, though certainly not highly passionate, could be interpreted as cozily familiar with a hint of devotion behind it. And though the flowers, carnations and daisies, were not particularly extraordinary, according to Marie they were . . .

". . . flowers, for God's sake, Angie! The guy sent you flowers! Stop overanalyzing and go see him!"

And so I did. The specific nature of my relationship with

Tim might have been nebulous, but my eagerness to see him was not. I slipped out of work early (by fifteen whole minutes!) and drove over to his work to surprise him.

Rushing through the door of Tim's music store, I nearly knocked down a woman standing on the other side.

"Oh, my gosh! I'm so sorry!"

"Well, I should know better than to stand right in front of the entrance," she smiled pleasantly. "But most of our customers are not quite as enthusiastic as you seem to be." She was an attractive woman, probably about my age.

"You work here? You must be new. Nice to meet you. My name is Angie."

"I'm Liza." She held out her hand and gave me a nice firm handshake. Not one of those dead-fish handshakes that lie slimy and floppy in your hand. Liza's handshake was warm and solid, a handshake that created a genuine person-to-person connection. Recognition spread over her face. "Oh, you're Angie! I've heard so much about you."

"You have?" I blushed, but only to candy cotton pink.

"All good things," she reassured me. "So I'm very happy to meet you."

You know how you can instantly connect with some people? As much as I had instantly disliked Russ, that's how much I instantly liked Liza. Her eyes were clear and intelligent with tiny crows'-feet revealing that she'd been around the block a few times and had probably laughed a lot along the way. Her makeup was casually pretty, not plastic or perfect, and her unpretentious haircut was slightly mussed. She wore a simple skirt and blouse, not at all fussy, and I especially liked her shoes.

"Naturalizers?"

"Yes, and very comfy. I got them on sale." See what I mean? We were definitely soul sisters.

"Tim should be back shortly. Why don't we sit down and get acquainted?" Liza ushered me to Tim's office in back. "I don't actually work here," she explained. "I work for the conglomerate that's buying out these stores. I'll be in and out over the next few months to help out with the transition."

"What an interesting job that must be," I commented.

"Most of the time it is. I get to meet really interesting people, like Tim for instance. He's a great guy." She smiled at me knowingly. She made me feel as if the compliment was directed at me, that there must be something special about me to have attracted a special guy like Tim. It made me (oh, are you surprised?) blush once more.

"But sometimes the work can be rough," Liza continued. "Few people accept change easily, and my job is all about change: changing systems, personnel, reporting structures." We talked a little longer about her work, then wound around to mine.

"Oh, it's not nearly as interesting as yours," I said self-consciously. "And frankly, I'm on the receiving end of change, and I'm having a horrible time with my new boss." I proceeded to describe Russ and my agonies in detail as Liza listened sympathetically.

"Have you considered creating a Russ voodoo doll?" she asked, a small smile starting at the corners of her mouth.

"Stick a few pins in and see if I could pop that overinflated ego of his?" I chuckled.

"Of course, it would have to be a very, very, very tiny voodoo doll," she offered, grinning. As we proceeded to describe just how tiny certain parts of the Russ doll's anatomy would be, we collapsed into peals of schoolgirl giggles. Tim came in just at that moment, looking a little disconcerted to find two women doubled over in laughter.

"Angie!" he exclaimed, hugging me awkwardly. "I thought I was meeting you at your place."

"I know, I know," I said still giggling. "But the flowers were so beautiful that I had to . . ."

"The flowers? What flowers?"

"The flowers that came to the office from 'you know who.' I . . ." Tim showed absolutely no sign that he knew what I was talking about. What was going on? Had I embarrassed him somehow?? "I, uh, always get excited when I see flowers, so I thought I'd just drop by."

"Will you excuse me?" Liza said, rising from her chair. "I think I heard a customer come into the store." She exited discreetly.

Tim seemed to recover himself and wrapped his arms around me. "I'm so glad you came, Angie." He nuzzled my hair and gave me a quick kiss. "I've missed you."

"I've missed you, too, Tim."

"Then I'll see you tonight around seven?"

"Oh, okay, sure." I felt a little awkward, like I was being dismissed. But Tim bent down and kissed me again—ah, yes, one of his Truly Extraordinary Kisses—and whatever I had been feeling was replaced with breathlessness.

I ran into Liza on my way out and felt a little guilty that my new buddy would be spending her first night in Sacramento alone. "Why don't you join Tim and me for dinner?" I offered with mixed emotions.

"No, Angie," Liza replied. "I wouldn't dream of being a third wheel." She smiled at my obvious relief. "But let's get together soon, okay?"

"That's a deal."

By the time I got home and fed the pups, I had just a few minutes to get ready for Tim. I agonized over which outfit to wear.

"He really liked the blue sweater dress, but he's already seen that," Analyzin' Angie reminded me.

"She walked in through the French doors," Fantasy Angie enthused, *"in a lovely gown of lavender . . ."*

"I don't own a gown of lavender."

"Pity."

"What about the brown? No, too businesslike. He's been gone for two weeks. It needs to be something . . ."

" 'Angie,' Tim says huskily, 'I've been gone for two weeks! Do you think I care what you wear? We don't need any clothes to . . .' "

"Right, she shows up to dinner wearing nothing at all. That must be one of your X-rated fantasies."

While the two of them argued, I went through my entire closet, discarding every possible choice. Except for the deep rose red sleeveless dress that I had stashed in the back of my closet. Did I dare?

"Angie, are you sure? The woman who did your colors said this color would absolutely guarantee you a proposal."

"Tim sweeps her into his arms . . . no, Tim falls at her feet on one knee and . . ."

"But we haven't even figured out if you want to marry him, right? What if the dress works and . . ."

While myselves discussed the merits and risks of the dress, I remembered the advice I'd once been given about job interviews:

"Do everything you can possibly do to get the job offer," my anemic college counselor had counseled. "That way, you'll have the choice whether to accept or not. If you go at this tentatively, you may not get an offer, and you may regret it." She sniffed into her handkerchief. "So give all you've got," she wheezed. "Go in determined to win the battle and figure out if you want the spoils later."

"You know what? I'm going for it. And you two," I announced to myselves, "can just stay home." I bravely slipped into my deep rose red, guaranteed-to-get-a-proposal dress.

Tim obviously appreciated the effect when he picked me up at seven. He wound his arms around me and gave me one of his toenail-curling kisses. "Angie," he whispered huskily, "we'd better get out of here before I try to convince you to skip dinner altogether." Though I wouldn't have minded missing a meal, I let him walk me to the car.

Tim had made reservations at Slocum House, arguably the most romantic restaurant in the Sacramento area. It's an old mansion, hidden in the winding tree-lined streets of old Fair Oaks. We chose to sit outside on that still-warm October evening to gaze at the lush garden and the hundred-year-old maple. Small white lights twinkled from the trees; a jazz trio played softly, and wild chickens wandered confidently beneath the tables. (And if you don't think wandering chickens can add to a romantic ambience, you're obviously not from Sacramento.)

Tim took my hand as he ordered us a bottle of wine (*"Chardonnay? Not sexy. The Pinot would have been more passionate."*) and told the waiter that we weren't in a hurry. (*"because we have the rest of our lifetimes to be together . . ."*)

"It's so good to be home, Angie," he said. (*" 'Good to be home, Angie, but wherever I am, my only true home will always be with you . . .' "*)

"You've been on the road a lot lately," I said sympathetically (*"Ack! Angie, that was too desperate sounding!"*). "But the transition is almost over, right? And it's going well?"

"Very well. Liza's very sharp (*"Liza? What's he bringing her name up for? Is he trying to tell us something?"*) and the new systems are fairly compatible, so . . ." and Tim launched into an animated (and quite detailed) discourse on the ins and outs of the sale of his business.

Analyzin' Angie continued to dissect every word (*"Accrual basis? Does that mean he's the kind of guy who takes his fun early and pays his dues late?"*) while Fantasy Angie got impatient (*"Who cares about stock options? Tell us that 'the only option that would make my life worthwhile is the option of having you now and forever!' "*) But me? I was just enjoying the simple pleasure of watching his face, listening to the sound of his voice, feeling the squeeze of his hand whenever he made an important point.

"I'm boring you, aren't I, Angie?"

"No, not at all. (*"Yes! Yes, you are boring us! I want to hear about how much you . . ."*) I'm very happy for you, Tim. You seem ready to move on to something new." (*"Oh, no! Wasn't that a little too suggestive?"*)

"I am." Tim hesitated, smiled and took a deep breath. "You know, Angie, after my divorce ten years ago, I just threw myself into my work. (*"Is he telling us that he's a work-aholic?"*) I guess I felt like I'd failed at the marriage and I needed to prove to myself that I could succeed some-where." (*"But I know I could succeed with a wonderful woman like you!"*)

"I've been there, too, Tim. When Bob left, I felt stupid, and my self-esteem was down the drain." (*"Don't tell him that! It sounds so pathetic!"*)

"But you bounced back pretty quickly." (*"And he sweeps her into his arms and . . ."*)

I smiled, remembering those difficult days. "I have some extremely determined friends."

"Women are good that way." Tim sighed. "My buddies took me out drinking. But when I really want to talk, I'd rather talk to women friends (*"Friends? Plural?"*). Like you." (*"He thinks of us as a friend?"*) Tim closed both of his hands over mine. "I really trust you, Angie." (*" 'Do you trust me, Angie? If so, close your eyes and . . .' "*)

"Thanks."

"Angie, can I ask you a question on a different subject?"

"Sure. (*"Uh-oh! Here it comes! I warned you about that dress."*) Ask away. (*"Then carry me away! Carry me to the Kas-bah and . . ."*)"

"Angie, what type of toothpaste do you use?"

Excuse me? All three of myselves were stunned into silence.

"Angie?"

"Uh, I'm sorry, Tim. Did you say 'toothpaste'?"

"Yeah. See, I forgot to bring any with me. That appetizer had a lot of garlic. I know I'll want to brush my teeth after we eat. But I hate that toothpaste with overwhelming wintergreen taste. I can't remember the name, but there's one toothpaste that makes me gag."

"Uh, toothpaste? Honestly, I'm not sure what I've got at home. Aren't they all pretty much the same?"

"Oh, no, not at all. The one I'm talking about tastes like Skol."

"Skol? Like the chewing tobacco? They make a toothpaste that tastes like chewing tobacco?"

"No." Tim laughed. "They made a chewing tobacco taste like wintergreen. Ever since I got sick on Skol in junior high . . ."

As Tim continued his story, myselves threw ourselves into overdrive. *"Does that mean he wants us to buy another brand of toothpaste?"* Let's see. I know the tube is white, but what kind . . . ? *"How romantic! He wants his breath to be fresh so when his lips press against . . ."* Does it have a strong wintergreen taste? What's the difference between wintergreen and peppermint? *"Is he testing us to see if we would change for him?"* *"He must be seeing himself happily ever after, brushing his teeth at our bathroom sink . . ."* Maybe I've got a different brand in my travel bag . . .

Ack! Enough!

"Tim, would you excuse me for a moment?" I dragged all of myselves to the sacred feminine sanctuary, the restroom.

"All right," I said firmly to myselves in the mirror. "This is making me nuts, and I've had it with both of you. Only one of us is coming out of this bathroom alive." I heard a small noise, like someone dropping something, from one of the stalls.

"Look, you need me to figure out exactly what's going on here. Like when he ordered the Chardonnay? That combined with the trust speech means . . ."

"Enough!" I bellowed, and heard a gasp from the closed stall.

"So, are you willing to give up all of those delicious fantasies," Fantasy Angie taunted. *"Like the one where Tim drops a ring into your champagne glass and . . ."*

"Yes! I am willing to give it all up!" I yelled. "Now, you two have a choice: you can either be washed down the sink or flushed down the toilet." The person in the stall made a tiny whimpering sound.

"Well, neither option sounds particularly . . ."

"Choose!" I hissed menacingly.

"In that case," myselves said meekly, *"we choose the sink."*

As I ran the water (and my alter egos) down the sink, I heard a toilet flush and the stall door creak open. A vaguely familiar face peered through the opening. "Oh, my God! It's you!" she screamed, and ran out into the restaurant (without, I might add, washing her hands). Gosh, I know I'd seen her somewhere before but . . .

When I returned to our table, I surprised Tim with an enthusiastic kiss.

"Wow." His smile lit up the entire patio. He took my hand again. "This is turning out to be a terrific evening!"

And from that point on, it was.

In fact, the evening would have been absolutely perfect except for one small (but hugely frustrating) hitch: When we got home, we walked hand in hand through the moon-light to my door, and both of us were happily anticipating the upcoming pleasant activities on my newly laundered sheets. Neither of us was anticipating the portly figure that emerged from the shadows.

"Ack! Bob? You startled me."

"Sorry about that, Angie. But I've been waiting for you for quite a while."

"But why?" Bob had shown up at some strange times and places lately. But after midnight on my porch?

"We need to talk."

"Talk? Now? Look, it's late. Couldn't I call you tomorrow and . . ."

"Angie," Bob said sternly. "It's about the children. It's nothing life-threatening *yet*. But it should be addressed." He turned and looked pointedly at Tim. "And it needs to be addressed in private."

Tim shrugged and looked at me wistfully. "Well, if it's important, I'd better . . ."

"Tim, I'm so sorry. I . . ."

"It's okay, Angie. I'll call you tomorrow." He kissed me quickly on the forehead—the forehead!—and left.

"Bob," I said with clenched teeth. "All I can say is that this better be pretty important."

"It is. It is!" Bob stuttered nervously. "Well, it's about, well, you know Jenna's pregnant, right?"

"Of course I know that Jenna is . . ."

"And that she's married to Ryan, right?"

"Bob, you'd better get to the point pretty quickly or I'll . . ."

"Well, you realize that they haven't come up with a name for the baby, right?"

"So? The baby isn't due for another five months! They don't even know if it will be a girl or a boy, so they're just calling the baby Bubba for now."

"Bubba! Oh my God, that's terrible! But do you know what's worse?" Bob asked significantly. "Did you know that Ryan has some Basque in his family background?"

"No. Bob, that's very interesting but what does that have to do with . . . ?"

"So!" Bob pronounced dramatically. "If they haven't decided on a name yet, and Ryan has some Basqualian heritage, can't you see the danger we're in?"

"Uh, no."

"Pay attention, Angie! If we're not vigilant, we just might end up with a grandchild named Agurtzane, or Uftzi, or Gurutz."

"Gurutz?"

"Yes, Angie. Gurutz. Would you want that? Would you? Huh? Huh?" Bob demanded frantically.

"Arrrgh!" I slumped to the porch in a heap ready to weep with frustration. One of the most romantic nights of my life (in my *real* life this time, not just my fantasy life) and my half-crazed ex-husband has to ruin it with his half-baked "Basqualian" baby-name-conspiracy theories.

"See, Angie? You're as upset as I am. We need to intervene before it's too late and . . ."

"The only thing that needs to happen before it's too late, Bob, is that you need to get out of my sight before I . . ."

"But, Angie . . ."

"I'm counting, Bob! One! Two! . . . " Bob ran out the gate before I got to three. Pity. I was seething with Rambo intensity and certainly would have inflicted substantial damage.

Spud and Alli were waiting patiently by the door when I opened it. Alli ran out and over to a large shrub by the fence, barking at it ferociously. "Great guard dogs you two are," I said grumpily. "That's simply too little too late, Alli. Next time Bob shows up, bite him. Come on, you two; get into bed. It's just the three of us. Again."

Chapter 12

But despite the tragic ending to that particular evening, Tim and I were able to make up for it over the next couple of weeks. I restrained Fantasy Angie and Analyzin' Angie, allowing them to speak only when spoken to, and my new predate ritual was to firmly flush my bothersome alter egos down the drain. (If they were particularly stubborn, I used the garbage disposal.) Without my disruptive chaperones, I found that I enjoyed just being with Tim, and the simplest things were romantic and relaxing.

We watched fireworks at Raley's Field (and I never once compared them to fireworks in the Roman Coliseum) and walked along the bridge over the American River (without my trying to pretend it was the Seine). I didn't worry that Tim never used the M word and just let myself feel good when he mumbled "lub jya" (whatever the heck that meant) before we fell asleep—often together. So by the time Tim had to hit the road again, I felt very content about where we seemed to be with each other, the unspoken but comfortable understanding. As Tom had said, it was good. It was all good.

But as soon as Tim (my favorite distraction) left town again, I became more intensely aware of how miserable I was at work. It was definitely not all good. Each day was as aggravating and demotivating as the very first day. I did get a pager, and Russ used it generously:

Tuesday evening at 10:00 P.M.: "Angie, you left an unfinished contract on your desk. Very unprofessional, and probably a security breach." (The contract was for our annual purchase of restroom supplies. I'm sure every terrorist in North America was dying to get his hands on the stats for toilet-paper consumption in Sacramento.)

Sunday morning at seven: "Angie, in looking at your budget variance report, I noticed that the columns on page one do not align exactly with the columns on page two. When you hold it up to the light or against the window, it's obvious that the left-hand margins are different by at least half a space." (I was unaware that one should read such reports with backlighting.)

In the middle of a charity luncheon: "Angie, have you compared the water bill on the Madison Avenue building with the same period last year? I notice that there was a forty-two-cent increase. I want you to research this right away." (The total increase amounted to $4.37 annually. I'm sure that customer service rep is still laughing her head off about the crazy woman who called demanding justification for such a huge leap.) The petty minutiae that this man found to occupy his time and mine would have made the US Census Bureau proud.

Between the pagings and reprimands, Russ invited me out to coffee for team-building chats. I came to look forward to these little chats with the same sense of eager anticipation I have before my regularly scheduled PAP smear.

"So, Angie, when exactly did you start in property management?"

"I guess it was about 1986 or '87."

"No kidding? Heck, I would have been in the seventh grade that year."

Russ lost no opportunity to point out my advanced age. But, since this was a team-building event, I tried a little team-building humor: "Don't worry, Russ. I promise not to make your youth into an issue during the campaign."

"What campaign?"

"Uh, I was just paraphrasing Ronald Reagan." Russ looked blank. "You know, Ronald Reagan?"

"Of course I know Ronald Reagan. We studied him in high school." Russ looked at me pointedly. "And didn't he die of Alzheimer's?" Why that little son of a . . . ! "You know, Angie, this work requires a lot of energy and stamina." Energy and stamina? Ha! Just try giving baths to two toddlers at the same time, presiding over a slumber party for a gaggle of twelve-year-old girls, being the late-watch chaperone at the high school prom.

"Property management is not easy. A person has to be assertive, aggressive even," he continued. Aggressive? To get flats of petunias planted? Ha! Try the semiannual sale at Nordstrom if you want to see pure bloodletting aggression.

"And it takes an eye for detail and accuracy and extraordinary organizational ability." Oh? Have you ever typed a term paper on a real typewriter, little man? Why don't you try organizing thirteen five-year-olds in a game of Pin the Tail on the Donkey? Think you could pull it off without some kid getting fatally punctured?

"You're probably a little overwhelmed," he continued. The truth was that I was underwhelmed to the point of comatose. After nearly twenty years of feeling vital and competent on the job, I now felt as useful as a toothless comb and as productive as a session of Congress. I dreaded walking into the office each morning and developed an unsightly eye twitch every time my pager went off.

I sure was getting grumpy. Very, very grumpy.

"Angie," Marie declared clearly, buttering her scone, "you are getting grumpy lately. Very, very grumpy." She, along with Jessica and Gwen, had just shown up at my tiny studio on a Sunday morning for some treats and lattés. We'd all been busy over the past several weeks (me polishing my paper clips, the others pursuing worthwhile careers), and this was the first chance we'd had to get together in a while.

"I know," I grumbled. "I'm sorry."

"No need to be sorry, Angie," Gwen commented, sipping her latté. "When you get like that, we all just ignore you."

"But what's wrong?" Jess asked, curious. "Is it Tim again?"

"No, Tim's great."

"Whatever happened about that proposal?" Gwen stopped her munching and looked at me pointedly. "Did you ever get closure on that?"

"No." I sighed. "But actually right now, I don't really care. I mean, I care about Tim, but I'm happy with where we are."

"So then what's wrong?" Marie pursued.

"Work. It's awful."

"Still?" Jess queried, looking very unsurprised. "It hasn't gotten any better with the little Hitler?"

"His name is Russ. And, no, it's gotten worse."

"Then you need to decide what you want to do about it," Gwen declared matter-of-factly. "Like maybe start a new career."

"Aren't I a little too old to think about a new career?"

"What do you mean?" Marie said, scone in mouth. "Grandma Moses didn't even pick up a paintbrush until she was in her seventies. Then she painted for another thirty years."

"Yeah, but she obviously had some latent talent; I don't."

"Hillary ran for the Senate at age fifty-three," Gwen noted, munching on an oatmeal muffin. "It was her very first political office."

"Well, maybe if I had forty-one million dollars to launch a . . ."

"What the heck has gotten into you anyway, Angie?" Jess sipped her chai and looked at me accusingly. "Six months ago, you were ranting and raving about how great it is to be our age. Now you're whining about it."

"I don't know," I confessed miserably. "It's hard getting beat up day after day by that little runt Russ. But I probably just need an attitude adjustment." My friends eyed me skeptically. "No, really! You know Tom? He says that, in the midst of change and trouble, we just have to remember that it's good. It's all good."

"It's good. It's all good," Jessica chanted. "Well, I suppose it couldn't hurt."

"Okay," Gwen argued, tapping her muffin for emphasis, "you're telling us that if, say, you're stuck in traffic behind a dump truck loaded with manure, and its bed starts to lift and its gates open to dump manure all over your car, you're supposed to smile and say . . ."

"It's good. It's all good!" Marie and Jess chirped like Disney woodland creatures.

"Or if you're stranded in a high-rise elevator," Marie posited, "which happens to be loaded to capacity with a crowd of punk rockers with questionable personal hygiene, you just hold up your head and announce . . ."

"It's good. It's all good!" the three of them sang out like the Pollyanna chorus.

"How about if you're traveling out of town and walk into your hotel room," Jess continued, "to find Johnny Depp lying across the bed waiting for you?"

"Is Jack with me?" Marie wondered.

"No," Jess declared.

"Did Johnny bring his wife?" Gwen inquired.

"No," Jess confirmed.

"Is Johnny Depp nearsighted enough that he won't see my saddlebags?" I asked.

"Yes!" Jess announced.

"Then it's good! It's all good!" we shouted gleefully. Of course, we had to spend the next several minutes making sure we had the Johnny Depp seduction scene just right.

(We decided to let Mel Gibson join the party, just in case Johnny couldn't keep up the pace.)

"This is great," I said happily. But then I looked over at the pager staring malevolently at me from the kitchen counter. "But tomorrow is Monday," I remembered gloomily. "And it starts all over again."

"Angie, you need to focus on something else," Marie decided.

"I know," Jess said, excitedly. "We need to plan a party!"

"What for?" I groused, now back into my full grump.

"Well, obviously to get you out of your slump," Gwen replied impatiently. "But what can we use as an excuse?"

"How about a baby shower for Jenna?" Marie suggested enthusiastically. "As the baby's godmothers, I think it's our duty."

"Isn't it too early for a baby shower?" I countered petulantly. "Besides, who said you would be the . . ."

"Angie!" Gwen retorted. "When is it ever too early for a party?"

"We could have a Halloween theme!" Jess exclaimed.

"Yes! And have everyone come in costume, like"—Marie bit her lip in deep party planning concentration—"um, maybe like their favorite children's book character."

"How about their worst childhood nightmare?" Gwen offered.

"Halloween?" I protested peevishly. "Orange and black? Baby showers are supposed to be pink and frilly and sweet and . . ."

"I've got it!" Jessica screeched with eardrum-bursting enthusiasm. "Everyone comes as a famous mother!"

So over my grouchiness (which was completely ignored) and my ineffective protests (ditto), the four of us spent the morning planning Jenna's baby shower. Our invitation list included Lilah (who would be in town that week), Angeline, some of Jenna's young friends from the UC Davis veterinary department, and (after a phone consultation with Jenna) a couple of Ryan's cousins. "They're a little straight, Mom," Jenna warned. "But I suppose the family should be exposed to the genes this baby is inheriting."

"Can't honorary uncles and brothers be included?" Jack and Tyler had pleaded.

"Only if you dress as famous babies," Marie decreed. "Oh, and serve the food."

The following Saturday, we all showed up to decorate Marie's house with orange and black twinkle lights, baby bats, ghosts made out of diapers, and black cat's cradles. Marie made a cake shaped like a pregnant witch, and Gwen brought a spiked fruit punch which we voted to drink out of sipper cups.

The guests started arriving around noon. Ryan's cousins had chosen pretty tame costumes: Mother Hubbard, Mother Teresa, Mother Goose. But the rest of us were a bit more eccentric:

Mother Earth: I wore one of Jenna's maternity smocks and smeared my hair and all exposed parts of my body with mud.

Mother of Invention: Gwen's Einstein wig was topped with a big pink bow. Her earrings were made from test tubes, and a frilly apron covered her lab coat.

Virgin Mother Bloody Mary: Marie looked resplendent

in her slinky bright red dress with celery sprouting from her hair.

Mother Nature: Flowers and twigs and leaves, intricately entwined, covered Jess charmingly from head to toe (which, unfortunately, caused major difficulty when Mother Nature had a call of nature).

Jenna's school friends came as Mother Ships (blinking lights and ethereal beeps), Motherboards (a cunning bodysuit of electronic circuitry), Mother Country (all forty-nine states with Hawaii trailing behind), Whistler's Mother and Mother Tongue. Angeline's Mother of Pearl outfit, a sleek tank dress wrapped in strands of fake pearls, looked sensational. And Lilah was a stunner as Mother Lode in her gold lamé bodysuit.

But, Jenna, as Mother Hood, was the hit of the party. She wore black stiletto boots and black-leather pants. Her top was a black Harley Davidson muscle shirt (with a pillow underneath to add to her pregnant tummy), and her arms were covered with fake tattoos. She had slicked her hair back into a ducktail and tucked a switchblade into the waistband of her apron. Ryan's cousins looked a bit shocked and aghast.

"Well," Jessica said to comfort them, "at least no one came as Mother F—ker."

"Ssshhh, Auntie Jess," Jenna giggled, pointing at her own growing tummy. "Baby Bubba might hear you!"

Jack and Tyler had recruited Ryan to join the service staff and our boys looked great as babies. We had Baby Ruth (a diaper-clad Ryan with baseball hat and mitt), Baby Boom (Tyler as a stick of dynamite wearing a baby bonnet and sucking on a pacifier) and Beanie Baby (Jack came as a can of garbanzos carrying a rattle). It took maybe thirty-two seconds before the party was in full swing.

Mother Ship approached me early in the festivities. "Ms. Hawkins?"

"Please call me Angie."

"Okay, Angie. I'm Emily, by the way. Jenna says that you have a pager. Would you mind if I give the number to some colleagues of mine?"

"Sure, Emily, but why?"

"I've been caring for a female donkey who's about to give birth. I didn't want to miss the party, but I really want to stay in touch."

"Oh. Okay, sure." The pager that Russ had given me was one of those two-way radio affairs. We set it up as a speakerphone in the middle of the room. When it buzzed, anyone close by could flip it on to hear the latest status report on the mama donkey:

"The donkey has gone off into the far corner of the paddock. She's pawing and pacing. Looks like her tummy has dropped."

"The donkey is getting pretty agitated. She might be going into labor."

"Okay, we've put the donkey in the birthing pen. She's calmed down a little. She's sweating. Oops! Looks like she's going to lie down."

As the afternoon progressed, we developed a group chant every time my pager went off: "So how's the little ass doing?" we hollered, laughing hysterically, appreciating our collective wit (fueled by our collective punch consumption).

The party was, of course, a great success. Honestly, how could it fail? With seventeen slightly inebriated women of various ages in outrageous costumes being served food and wine by scantily dressed men?

Marie won the belly-measuring game hands down ("It was easy; those are *my* leather pants Jenna's wearing."), Jess had no competition on the speed-diapering race ("I've had five kids and three grandkids. There's not a safety pin, sticky tape, or Velcro strip I've not mastered."), and in the slippery-baby relay, Lilah coached her team to victory ("Just like a slippery husband, you've got to grab them where it counts.")

Later, while Jenna was opening her presents, my pager went off again. I flipped the "on" switch. "So how's the little ass doing?" we screamed gleefully at the phone.

"Angie? Is that you?" Russ's pompous, self-important, obnoxious voice squawked through the receiver, instantly (and unfortunately) deflating the merry mood of the entire group. "What on earth is going on?" he demanded.

"Well, I'm at my daughter's baby shower, and . . ."

"Angie, I don't care where you are! We have a crisis at the office building on Madison Avenue. A sprinkler in the flower bed is broken. It's drowning the petunias and squirting cars in the parking lot, and I expect you to . . ." Russ ranted on for another five minutes, describing in detail what he expected me to do. The group was completely sober and silent as his harangue crackled through the pager. He finally finished. "And I expect you to report in to me when you've taken care of the situation."

"Uh, okay."

"And, Angie. You'll have to fire Donna first thing Monday morning."

"Donna? But why? She's been with me for . . ."

"I've been trying to reach her all weekend to get a copy of the Bremerton budget. She won't answer her pager."

"But maybe she's . . ."

"No 'buts,' Angie. Just take care of it." And he disconnected.

"Uh, I'm sorry everybody," I said miserably. "So what were we talking about?"

"Angie?" Jack said with concern. "Your employer talks to you like that?"

"Geez, Mom," Jenna added. "You said it was bad but that's just . . ."

"Why that vulgar, pretentious, repulsive, little . . ." Lilah sputtered angrily.

"Gosh, Ms. Hawkins," Mother Ship said sorrowfully. "You're such a nice lady. I'd rather have my arm up a donkey's ass than let somebody . . ."

"Angie?" Angeline said with concern. "This situation sounds very extreme. Do you have someone who can advise you?"

I looked at my three buddies, sitting in shocked silent solidarity. "Yep. I've got the best counselors in the world."

After the party broke up, Gwen, Jess, Marie, and I headed to a nearby Italian eatery to discuss my whole ugly work situation. We were still in full costume, which is perhaps why the hostess chose to seat us in a far, dark corner of the restaurant. As we started walking toward our far, dark corner, I heard a voice call my name.

"Angie! Over here." It was Liza, sitting in a booth by the door. She stood and gave me a hug.

I introduced her to my three friends; Liza apologized for her uninspired attire. "When did you get in town? I thought you weren't due until the end of the week."

"Tim and I finished with Cincinnati early and caught an earlier flight. Didn't he tell you? Maybe he didn't have time to call."

"No, he didn't say anything about . . ."

"Angie!" and the aforementioned Tim stood beside me. He gave me a quick, awkward hug. "Wow, you all look, um, interesting. Angie, I meant to call but . . ."

"No problem," I said, feeling accountably uncomfortable.

"Why don't you all join us?" Liza offered graciously. "We haven't ordered yet."

"Oh, gosh, well, no, thanks," I stammered. "We've got some business to discuss, as, um, I'm sure you do."

My three friends and I settled in at our table in the dark corner at the far end of the room. Gwen, Jess, and Marie situated their chairs strategically to get a good view of Tim and Liza, and I carefully placed my chair so that I could not. We were silent for several minutes as my three buddies cross-examined me with their arched eyebrows.

"What?" I finally said defensively. "I've told you about Liza. She's his business associate. They have every right to have dinner together."

"Sure, Angie," Jess said skeptically.

"But you know what's funny?" Marie chuckled.

"What?" I said, not finding much humor at all in the past couple of hours.

"Who do you think she looks like? Her mannerisms, her voice, everything." Marie's eyes twinkled, and she winked at Gwen and Jess who smiled in return.

"Who?" I asked numbly.

My three friends burst out laughing. "You!" they gasped. "She could be your twin sister." Marie giggled.

"Or your clone!" Gwen chortled.

Or my replacement, I thought glumly. "Forget about them. We're here to figure out what I can do about Russ."

"Okay," Jess said, grabbing her pen and a stack of paper napkins. "First we need a project charter . . ."

"Well, the purpose of this project is to get Angie out of that hellhole," Marie asserted.

"With her dignity intact," Gwen added.

"Honestly, Angie," Jess said seriously, "no affirmation in the world will fix that horrendous situation or change that awful, nasty man."

"And perhaps," Marie, queen of kindness mused, "we need to inflict a bit of pain on that despicable little creature."

"A good deal of pain," Jessica agreed.

"An extreme, acute, severe, excruciating amount of pain," Gwen concluded.

"Okay," I said with a sigh. "So how?"

Chapter 13

They totally put me up to it.

I am a reasonable person, a mature adult. In the workplace, I have always been professional, respectful, and circumspect when dealing with the opposite sex. I started my career in suits with collared blouses accessorized by small scarves or bright bow ties at the throat. In the seventies, having just clamored for the right to be treated equally as professionals, we were careful to appear androgynous, avoiding all sexual innuendos and any action that might mark us as mere sex objects.

So on my own, I never in a million years would have done what I did. Without the goading encouragement of three women who should have known better, I never would have stepped so far over the line of political correctness. And if I hadn't? I would have missed one of the most memorable and guiltily pleasurable moments of my life. And it was good; it was all very good!

I strode into work that next morning. (Marie had coached

me on the striding thing: *Okay, Angie, it's a sensuous three-beat walk—ba-ba-boom, ba-ba-boom. No, not boom-boom-ba. That's how truckers walk. Try again.*) It took all of my concentration to keep that sensuous stride going, but the effect on the maintenance guys gathered for a meeting was palpable. They whistled a few wolf whistles (Can wolves really whistle?) and hooted the equivalent of "hubba hubba" in several different languages. (Of course, the sheer black stockings and stiletto heels I had borrowed from Jess—remnants from her brief Boy Toy phase—might have added to the overall effect.)

Gwen had dressed me in a slim black suit that I had hidden in the back of my closet because it's always hugged my hips much too ardently. (*Perfect! Now, wear that lacy camisole under the jacket, no blouse. Leave the top button of the jacket unbuttoned. Now roll the waistband under until the skirt is a few inches above the knee. Here, let's open up that slit on the side.*)

I strode (ba-ba-boom, ba-ba-boom) to Russ's office door and leaned languidly (*No, Angie, keep your chest out, head slightly back. Drop your elbow. Remember to lick your lips.*) "Russ?" I said throatily (*Just like Lauren Bacall after a heavy night of smoking.*). "You wanted to see me?"

He looked up and, I swear, the man bounced a couple of times in his seat. He blinked twice and swallowed hard, searching for his voice. I remained silent and arched a Gwen-like eyebrow (*Easy with the arch, Angie. You don't want your nose to go into spasm.*) Russ blinked again and cleared his throat. "Ahem, yes, I did. Have a seat."

Per my coaches' instructions, I closed the door (*Make sure he hears the click.*), leaning with my back against it for just a moment before I strode (ba-ba-boom) to the chair in front of his desk (ba-ba-boom). I nearly tripped mid-ba-boom. But Russ was so flustered by that point, he didn't seem to notice. I sat down very slowly (*Now, keep your back straight and chest out. Look him right in the eye. Okay, now down on a slow three count.*), crossed my legs (*Hitch that skirt up ever so slightly.*), and flipped my hair (*Angie, always flip to the side or back; if you flip to the front, you won't be able to see.*).

"Er, Angie, I wanted to discuss your attitude based on our interaction yesterday," Russ started, fingers under his collar to loosen it.

"My attitude? Our interaction?" I breathed, sounding now more like Marilyn Monroe. I recrossed my legs and hitched my skirt up another notch.

"Well, yes," Russ gulped, staring at my legs, his face reddening to a dangerous color. "Yes, it's that, well, company policy is that all employees keep their pagers with them at all times. It's in Section, uh, Section, er . . ." His eyes bugged out as he watched me draw my middle finger down my neck to my collarbone, then just below the vee of my jacket. (*Slowly, Angie, everything very slowly.*) "Uh, some section or other. It's so, er, you can respond to all emergencies."

"And," I drawled (I drawled! Just like Liz Taylor in *Cat on a Hot Tin Roof*!), "the drowning petunias were an emergency?" I re-arched my eyebrow, recrossed my legs, then licked my pinky and used it to moisten my lower lip.

That did it. The poor man turned the color of overripe plums, his breath was ragged, and his chest heaved.

It's true that revenge is actually quite sweet, delicious in fact. But Russ looked like he was ready to go into cardiac arrest. I fleetingly wondered whether, in good conscience, I should give him mouth-to-mouth resuscitation if that should become necessary. (My good conscience voted a resounding no.)

"Well," he squeaked, "perhaps we have gotten off on the wrong foot. Perhaps we could get you some training and . . ."

"Training?" I leaned in toward him. "Personal training?" I purred. Having now lost all color and the ability to speak, Russ merely nodded rapidly. "Well," I said, rising slowly, "I'm afraid that just won't do because I quit."

"You what?"

"I quit," I said in my own, outraged Angie voice. "I've had it with your micromanaging and your pagers and your red pencil! I've had it with that manual, Sections 33.6 and 49.7 in particular. And I've especially had it with you! I quit!"

"You, you, you can't quit!" Russ blustered. "Because I'm firing you!"

"You can't fire me, little man, because I already quit. And," I said with as much menace as I could muster, "if I hear that you're bullying Donna or any of the other property managers after I leave, I'll hit you with an age discrimination or sexual harassment suit so fast it'll make your pompadour melt." I reached in my purse and pulled Gwen's card and slammed it, along with my pager, on his desk. "Check with my attorney if you don't believe me. And you know exactly where you can put that pager!" And with that, I stomped (no more sensuous striding!) out the door.

The guys in the lobby had apparently heard the final moments of our interaction because they applauded quietly and gave me high fives on my way out. Yahoo! I was free! Ding dong old Booger Brain is dead!

I streaked out of the office and rushed over to Tim's store to tell him the big news. I had done it! I was totally free! I found Tim working with Liza in his office in the back.

"Angie? I don't know what you're dressed up for, but the effect is worth it." Tim grinned appreciatively. "So what's the news? You look like you just won the lottery."

"I did! Well, no, I didn't really. But I just quit my job, and it feels like a million bucks!"

"You what?" Tim's sunny smile faded to dusk.

"Uh, I quit my job. I told that odious little Russ guy that I wouldn't work for him anymore."

"Just like that?" Tim said. Was there a hint of disapproval in his voice?

"Well, not just like that. I mean, I tried to make it work with him, but it didn't. And I . . ." I wondered why I was making excuses. This was not going as I had planned.

"Why don't I leave you two alone?" Liza said, exiting quietly.

"It just seems a little extreme, Angie," Tim said, shaking his head. "What are you going to do? For work?"

"I don't know," I said exasperated. "But I thought you'd be happy for me. I thought you knew how miserable I was, and . . ."

"Uh, well, of course. If this is what you want. I just think it's awfully sudden."

"I've been thinking about it for a long time, Tim. You haven't been around a lot, so maybe you missed out on some of the thinking. Or maybe you just weren't listening."

"Or maybe I've got other things on my mind besides your dramas at work," Tim retorted.

"Oh, I see," I responded angrily. "So when you've wanted to talk about work, I'm supposed to pay attention, but when I want to talk . . ." We stared at each other, both breathing hard, realizing that we were about to enter very dangerous territory. I took a deep breath to calm myself. "Wait. No, Tim. I didn't mean that."

"Oh, Angie, I'm sorry. I didn't mean it either," Tim said, wrapping his arms around me. "Of course I support you in whatever you want to do. It just took me by surprise, that's all."

"I'm sorry, too. I'm still all revved up from this morning. Let's go out and celebrate tonight. We could have dinner at . . ."

"I'm sorry, Angie. I'd love to. But I've got a working dinner scheduled tonight."

"With Liza?"

"Yes, with Liza. Why?"

Analyzin' Angie had apparently escaped from the garbage disposal. She grabbed me by the throat and yelled into my ear:

"Again? They're going to dinner again?"

I batted her away. Liza is my friend. This is work. Men and women can work together without . . . Fantasy Angie joined the party:

"Ah, conducting business at night? Over candlelight? 'Oooo, Tim, those strategic plans of yours are so manly!' "

I swatted at the little devils. What are you talking about? There's no candlelight.

"Don't be a fool, Angie. Call him on it!"

And sound like a suspicious shrew? Not on your life!

"Your funeral, toots!"

"Angie? Are you okay?" Tim asked, looking at me strangely.

"Yeah, sure."

"Look, why don't you track down the girls and celebrate with them tonight. You and I can go out later in the week."

"Uh, sure. Fine." I left feeling shaky and uncertain.

But I didn't have to "track down the girls." When I got home late that afternoon, they were perched on my porch, champagne in hand, dying to get a blow-by-blow account of the entire event. I reenacted the entire scene for them with (relatively) little exaggeration, much audience participation, and a good deal of champagne.

"Angie, you're a mythic hero!" Jess raised her glass in toast.

"Not one of the ones who die a ghastly death at the end, right?"

"Of course not, Angie! Don't you feel proud of yourself? Empowered?" Marie encouraged.

"Well, I suppose. But I also feel unemployed. I'm fifty years old and who . . . ?"

"Don't be silly, Angie! Relax! You've got lots of skills and experience," Gwen said. "Just bask in the knowledge that today you struck a blow for all womankind!"

So I relaxed, basked, and drank a little more champagne.

Chapter 14

By the next morning, however, I was definitely not basking or relaxed. (Perhaps some of my foul mood could be attributed to the champagne hangover I happened to have; even the sound of my own blinking was painful.) I was no longer in the euphoric soaring phase of leaping off a cliff. I was at the stage where you've landed in whatever the heck it is below, and I couldn't yet figure out if I'd landed in mud or on sharp, neck-breaking boulders or into one of those bouncy things they use for stunt people.

What on earth had I done? Quitting had made so much sense at the time when my thinking was fueled by righteous indignation. But now that I was facing "what now?" the whine of my meager bank account was deafening. Maybe Tim was right. Maybe I should have waited a little longer until I had something else lined up. Maybe I was just being melodramatic. Do you suppose if I just showed up to the office and pretended it never happened . . . ?

I called Gwen for support.

"I'm sorry. Ms. Winsor will be in court all morning."

I tried Jessica.

"Ms. McIntyre is in LA giving a PowerPoint presentation today."

I tried Marie.

"Ms. Fenner has a meeting out of the office this morning, then a luncheon at twelve-thirty, and another . . ."

Tyler would certainly be at work. Jenna was probably on some farm somewhere doing who knows what to cows or pigs. Even Jack, retired for two years now, was busy with a regional conference of miniature train aficionados. I was the only one I knew with no meaningful occupation, no life, no purpose, no raison d'être. I felt unproductive and unwanted adrift and useless.

And it was only 9:15 A.M.

When the phone rang, I leaped for it.

"Angie, I called because I heard what happened yesterday." It was Bob, the only other unemployed and worthless being on the planet. "Are you okay? Shall I come over?" Huh? Bob's concern would have been touching if it wasn't so weird. Was this the man who, during the entire twenty-six years of our marriage, never once offered to pick up the dry cleaning or his socks? The same guy who thought "being there" for me meant showing up for the next meal on time? "Should I come over and keep you company?"

Eiouw! The thought of seeing Bob further depressed my already dismal mood. "Uh, thanks, Bob, but I'm pretty busy right now."

"Oh, really? What are you doing?"

Doing? Doing, what am I doing? "Oh, you know. Exactly what you'd be doing if you were in my shoes." Swigging down a six-pack and watching cartoons?

"Oh. Updating your résumé? Looking through the want ads?"

"That's it! That's exactly right! I'm up to my ears doing, uh, those things."

"Well, if you need some help just . . ."

"Absolutely. Thanks for calling."

Okay, that call was definitely strange. But it was nice of Bob to call. He was certainly being more supportive than Tim. Oh my gosh! Had I just compared Bob with Tim—and Bob came out ahead? I was obviously in worse shape than I'd thought. But at least my ex had given me some action items. I couldn't let the blues overtake me now. I had to get moving.

I hunted through my file drawer and found my old résumé. When I say "old" I am not exaggerating in the least. I had prepared it for my interview with Phil on a real, live typewriter sometime back in the roaring eighties. To say it was sparse would also not be an exaggeration: It showed my high-school retail experience, my part-time job at the library during college, my "efficient homemaker" phase, then a brief stint as an Avon lady. My position with Phil, which had lasted nearly twenty years, wasn't even on it yet. So I spent the next two hours roughing out a draft for a new one. My first draft was pretty well finished when I heard Jack at my door.

"Angie? Are you decent?"

I looked down at my tattered flannel jammies. Perhaps

not acceptable for future job interviews, but in the eighteen months that I'd lived at Jack and Marie's, he'd seen me in much worse shape. "All embarrassing body parts are covered, if that's what you mean. Come on in, Jack."

"I just popped in to see how you're doing before I head off to my railroad convention."

"Um, okay, I guess. I decided to get to work on a résumé. Would you like to see the rough draft?"

"Sure." Jack adjusted his reading glasses. "Let's see. 'Objective: To make enough money to support my modest lifestyle'?"

"Yes. Well, I want to be honest and I think that makes me sound modest and practical. What do you think?"

"Ah, well. Perhaps we needn't be quite so honest. Let me keep reading." He hmmm'd and mmm'd for a few more minutes, nodding his head every so often. "'Key Accomplishments: Halloween 1989'?"

"I made all of the costumes for Tyler's entire Boy Scout troop."

"'Budget Variance reports of 1993'?"

"It was an awful year, but Phil said my reports always emphasized the bright side and kept him positive."

"'Evictions of 2001'?"

"Yes. I evicted an average of 1.5 tenants a month that year. I think it's a county record."

"I see. And your summary of attributes: 'Self-motivated, flexible team worker with strong detail orientation'? What does that mean exactly?"

"I have absolutely no idea, Jack," I confessed miserably. "But the résumé Web site said I needed to have those words in there." I looked at Jack, who had his most neutral judicial mask firmly in place. "It's not very good, is it, Jack?"

"Angie, I think the most appropriate way to describe it is that . . ." Jack paused to gather his thoughts and find the exact right wording, "it sucks."

"I was afraid of that," I sighed.

"Your résumé sucks, Angie, but *you* don't. You are a very bright, capable woman with so much to offer any prospective employer."

"I am?"

"Of course," he confirmed reassuringly. "I think you might be approaching this résumé thing from the wrong angle."

"I am?"

"Yes. I think you should determine exactly what jobs you want to apply for. Then tailor a résumé. Highlight your skills and assets with that particular job in mind."

"Oh, okay."

"And, Angie?" Jack said with a hint of embarrassment. "I hope Marie made it quite clear that we certainly will accept no rent from you until you've found yourself solvent again."

"That's very sweet of you, Jack," I said. And I meant it, though in truth, the $150 per month I paid them was the least of my worries.

"Look, I know you don't get the newspaper, so I brought you the classifieds. Maybe that will give you some ideas."

I felt a bit deflated after Jack left. But I brushed my teeth (which always perks me up), all the while repeating the mantra Tom had given me: "It's good. It's all good." Then

I took a deep breath and a new approach. I opened the classifieds and scanned quickly through the Help Wanted section. Several of the listings meant nothing to me (*Bioflex Firmware Engineer? Senior Fluvial Geomorphologist?*), but a couple caught my attention:

Bookkeeper: A/R, A/P, P/R exp; F/C w/ GL and P&L pref; FT ASAP (After I had filled in the missing consonants and vowels, I realized that I was qualified to do all of those things. I also realized that I hated doing them.)

Hotel Front Desk: Smiley faces, peppy demeanor, gung-ho spirit, can-do attitude, positive team builder (Were they hiring a front-desk clerk or a high-school cheerleader? Should I bring out my old pompoms?)

Driving Instructor: Calm, mellow adult to retrain clients with poor driving records. Extensive DUI exp. a plus (I suppose it would be a plus to find instructors who can drive while under the influence. It might help them to stay calm and mellow, but wouldn't that set a bad example?)

Activity Assistant for Primrose Day Center: Alzheimer's exp pref. (Hmmm. I probably wasn't qualified for this one. I've had several senior moments, but no full-blown Alzheimer's.)

At around noon, I was still trying to figure out how they might interview for *Dancer/Topless* when I heard a knock at the door. With just my scruffy jammies and my bleary morning face still in place, I opened the door to find Phil, my old employer, standing self-consciously on my porch.

"Angie? Oh my goodness! Are you all right?"

Phil, never having seen me first thing in the morning without makeup, did not know that I always start out looking that bad. To him, I undoubtedly looked like I'd started my downward slide to depravity and ruin. Appreciating his sympathy, though, I did not bother to correct his impression.

"Hi, Phil. What are you doing here?"

"Russ called and told me what happened. Actually," Phil said thoughtfully, "knowing you as well as I do, I doubt that it happened exactly as he described it but . . ." Phil's voice faded, and he looked distinctly uncomfortable. Uh-oh. I wondered what Russ had told him. But what did it matter? I had already burned that bridge along with the toll booths on either side.

"Oh, don't worry, Phil. It just wasn't . . . I just couldn't . . . I needed to . . ." I stammered. Then, seeing Phil's concerned look, the kindness and caring for me that lay beneath it, I broke down, flopped on the porch in a muddled heap, and started to cry.

Phil and I had known each other for over twenty years. And though we'd been through some pretty rough times together, I don't think Phil had ever seen me really weep, and he had certainly never been the cause of any of my tears. Not that I didn't cry during those years; I cried plenty. But at the office, I've always kept tears to an absolute minimum; my blubbery, red-eyed, sniffling-nose tears were reserved for private.

But with the floodgates opened, it was hard to stop. I told him everything: the pager, my fax cover sheets, the drowning petunias. Phil listened with fatherly kindness and concern, getting angry only when I mentioned that Russ had removed his favorite stuffed moose head from the office.

"My nyati from Mozambic!" Phil cried, outraged. In truth, removing that ugly head with staring eyes and huge nostrils had been the one thing about which Russ and I agreed. But I was enjoying Phil's outrage, so didn't comment.

Finally, all cried out, I calmed down enough to offer Phil some coffee. I made two cups and sat down beside him.

"So, Angie, shall I demand that he give you your job back?"

I contemplated this for a full seven seconds; should I swallow my pride for the sake of a paycheck? The image of Russ reorganizing my pencil drawer kept my resolve firm. "No, Phil. Thanks anyway. But I can't go back."

"What will you do then?"

"I was just looking through the want ads. Do you think I would be a good toll booth collector?"

Phil laughed and put his hand over mine. "But Angie, we don't have any toll booths in Sacramento."

"It just seemed like something within my skill set . . ."

"Angie," Phil interrupted enthusiastically, "this is your chance to explore. Expand into new territory. Discover totally new talents and interests." My main new interest was being able to pay my monthly VISA bill. But Phil, whose personal accounting was done with many more zeros than mine, probably couldn't grasp how even a small increase on a utility bill could throw your personal P&L firmly onto the L side. "You might take some trips, Angie. Relax and enjoy life for a while."

"That's a thought, Phil. But I really think I should get back to some kind of work." If I want to eat, that is.

"Of course, if you are motivated to do so. But you don't

have to make up your mind right away." Phil obviously hadn't had a good look at my latest bank statement. "I mean, your severance should carry you for a while."

"My what?"

"But, I can understand that you might be eager to get your teeth back into something. To find new . . ."

"Phil, did you say 'severance'?"

He looked at me puzzled. "You didn't know? That, under the contract to sell the business, I negotiated a twelve-month severance package for you? No matter what the circumstances of your departure?"

After a few moments of stunned, incredulous joy, I threw my arms around Phil's neck (another first in our twenty-year relationship). "I had no idea! Phil, thank you, thank you, thank you!"

"Uh, you're welcome." Phil's voice was muffled under my enthusiastic embrace. "But, Angie, I can't believe you quit like that when you didn't even know about . . ."

After Phil left, I floated into the shower, washed my hair (and that nasty Booger Brain out of it), threw on some makeup and a cheerful purple sweater with my jeans. My jeans! On a Tuesday afternoon! A workday—ha-ha! I rushed over to Tim's store to see if I could catch him for a late lunch.

I found Tim wrestling with the front cash register, odd parts lying all over the counter. As I recall, this is exactly where Tim had been when I'd met him the very first time. But this time, he didn't beam his thousand-watt smile at me as he had then. He just seemed frazzled and frustrated when he looked up and spotted me.

"Angie?" Oh, hi." He continued pulling at wires and mumbling under his breath.

"Guess what?" I gushed. "I just saw Phil. I get twelve months' severance."

Tim gave me a brief smile. "That's great, Angie. Something to put away for a rainy day."

"Well, actually, I thought I'd use it to take some time off. Maybe explore a bit, develop some new interests, spend sometime thinking about . . ."

"Seems to me you've done plenty of thinking lately," Tim said, still focusing on the register.

"Well, I've got some more to do," I replied, feeling a little irked.

"Okay, fine then." He studied me briefly. "I just think you might be wiser to put most of it into your 401(K). You said you don't have much there."

"What's my 401(K) got to do with you?" I countered defensively.

"Apparently nothing," he snapped, and turned back to the mess on the counter.

I took a deep breath and remembered why I had come. "So," I said more cheerfully "why don't we go out and grab some lunch and celebrate?"

"Angie, I can't just go running off in the middle of the day," Tim replied impatiently. "I'm still a responsible adult, and I work."

"And I don't, so I'm not? Is that what you mean to say?" I said fuming.

"No!" he said in exasperation. "Look, Angie, you bounce in here when I'm right in the middle . . ."

"Right. So whatever you're doing is important but . . ."

"I never said you aren't important, but my life doesn't revolve around the ins and outs of your . . ."

"Obviously, it doesn't," I threw back, nearly shouting. We stared angrily at each other for several uncomfortable moments. Just like the day before, we were hovering on the brink of some dangerous territory. But this time, I took a step into it. "You know, Tim, maybe you're right," I finally said, shaking inside. "Maybe I need to go away and let you concentrate on your work."

"Angie, I didn't mean . . ."

"And maybe we need to stop seeing each other and get some breathing room."

Tim stared at me, a mixture of anger and misery on his face. "If that's what you want."

"Yep, I think that's exactly what I want."

Of course, that isn't what I wanted! What I wanted was for Tim to apologize, for him to protest and fight for me, to argue with me and tell me that I was too important to him to lose because of a silly disagreement. I wanted him to come out from behind that stupid counter and put his arms around me and tell me that he loved me and that everything would be all right.

But that's not what happened. So I turned and left.

Of course, the first thing I checked when I got home was my answering machine to see if Tim had left a message. And, of course, he hadn't. Was I going to spend the next several weeks pining over him? Driving past his store? Racing to reach the phone every time it rang? Replaying every word we just said to each other and wondering . . . ?

No, I was not.

"No, we are not," I announced emphatically to Spud and Alli. "We have a full life and much to be grateful for," I continued, pacing the floor of my tiny studio with the pups at my heels. "So," I declared forcefully, "we will now only look on the bright side. For instance, the good news is that I no longer have to work for that nasty little Russ."

Analyzin' Angie slipped out of the disposal to whisper, *"Though he's done such a number on your self-esteem that you'll have trouble forgetting him."*

I ignored the whispers. "And the good news is that I am totally free to pursue a new, fulfilling career."

"Though you don't really have any burning desire to do so . . ."

"And," I continued vigorously, "the good news is that I'll have a grandchild soon and . . ."

"And you'll have to face the fact that you're a grandmother and getting on in years and . . ."

"And," I shouted, startling Spud and Alli, "the good news is that I've got a wonderful family and great friends who . . ."

"Who are probably sick of listening to all of your troubles and . . ."

"And," I hollered, "the good news is that I've got twelve months of severance and I'm free to do whatever I want and . . ."

"The bad news is that you have no idea what you want to do, and now you don't have Tim to do it with . . ."

"Enough!" I shrieked. "Toilet or disposal?"

"I think toilet this time, please."

I flushed her. Twice. Then I sat down and cried.

Chapter 15

Over the next few weeks, I tried to think positively, on the bright side, or not at all. ("Not at all," aided by frequent naps, turned out to be the easier option.) I operated my garbage disposal frequently and told my friends that I just didn't want to talk about "it."

"What do you mean, you don't want to talk about it? You want to talk about everything! And the hours we've spent on Tim shouldn't go to waste if you'll only . . ."

"Gwen, I don't want to talk about it."

"But, Angie, maybe you were a little hasty. Don't you think that maybe you just caught him at a bad time, and . . ."

"Marie, I don't want to talk about it."

"So, I heard this great NPR special about native Alaskan tribes who speak Yupik and use whistling to . . ."

"Jess, I don't want to talk about it."

"About what?"

"You know, *it.*"

"Yupik?"

"No, Tim."

"Who's talking about Tim?"

But on the bright side, the distraction of all distractions was upon us: We were approaching the holidays.

I don't know about the rest of the world, but in these United States, "approaching the holidays" is practically a year-round activity. The retail community insists that bright red Santas and twinkling ornaments pop up as soon as ghosts and goblins of Halloween are displayed. (Am I the only one who thinks that red and green clash horribly with orange and black?)

So we start "approaching the holidays" in mid-October. Private businesses slow their operations down to the speed of overfed slugs, and government offices (prevalent in Sacramento) match their hours to our local preschools.

Don't get me wrong; I love the holidays. However, it's amazing to me that our economy can remain strong when most of the country turns itself off from October 15 until it sobers up on January 3. (Of course by then, we are moving into several presidents' birthdays, Martin Luther King Day, the Super Bowl, Valentine's . . .). But, honestly, this year I was thrilled to have the diversion.

Jenna had volunteered to host her first Thanksgiving.

Hosting one's first Thanksgiving is a critical rite of passage. It may not get as much recognition as bar mitzvahs or graduations or funerals or baptisms, but it probably should. Not only is the planning nerve-racking (Do we own twelve plates without cracks? Does anyone actually eat yams anymore? Do we serve canned cranberry, which is edible, or homemade cranberries, which is historically correct but totally inedible?), but there is the distinct possibility that the virgin host or hostess might unintentionally kill some of his/her dinner guests through food poisoning. (When this happens, it typically puts a real damper on the celebration.)

Jenna was very excited about her first Thanksgiving. Thirty days prior to the event, the phone calls started:

"Mom, can I borrow . . . ?" Plates, glasses, napkins, and folding chairs.

Fifteen days prior, the phone calls centered around:

"Mom, should we have . . . ?" Corn bread or plain stuffing? Yams or sweet potatoes (who the heck knows the difference?) And that all important question: How big a turkey?

"So. Sweetie, how many people will be there?"

"Fifteen."

"So figure around a pound and a half for each. Say, twenty to twenty-four pounds, right?"

"Uh, I've invited Dad and Clarisse."

"Ah. Then add another ten, fifteen pounds and you'll be fine."

At two-thirty on the morning of the event, the frantic phone call started:

"Mom! Do you have a roasting pan large enough for a thirty-five-pound turkey?"

"Uh, yes, sweetie. But it's in storage."

A long pregnant pause. "Is it a twenty-four-hour storage?" Sigh. And this is how I came to be on the road at 3:15 A.M. Thanksgiving morning.

Everyone arrived at Ryan and Jenna's around two o'clock Thanksgiving afternoon. When I say everyone, I mean *everyone*. Jenna had decided that we should all be one big happy family. So Clarisse and Bob were invited (representing the "big"). Lilah was told to bring Tom, and Tyler was instructed to bring Angeline (as prospective "family"). And the "happy" was ensured by inviting the aunties and their spouses/significant others.

Of course, I was the only one in the crowd to show up solo, the honorary spinster. It had never bothered me before, but somehow . . . Oh, well. Maybe it was just time to get used to it. It was good. It was all good, right?

As soon as I came through the front door, Ryan grabbed my arm frantically. "Ang . . . uh, moth . . . uh . . . Mrs. Haw—"

"Spit it out, Ryan," Gwen said from behind me. "What's wrong?"

"Jenna. In the kitchen. Really upset," he managed to say.

Gwen and I motioned to Jess and Marie, and the four of us headed to the kitchen. There we found my baby girl, my now obviously pregnant baby girl, crying.

"Oh, Mom," she wailed. "It's just not coming together! I think I've ruined it."

"Jenna, the Thanksgiving meal was designed to test the limits of one's sanity." Marie patted Jenna's shaking shoulders sympathetically.

"An exercise in the absurd," Gwen agreed sourly, closing the door.

"Really?" Jenna sniffed.

"Obviously, created by some Pilgrim," Jess declared, opening the oven to reveal a pallid-looking turkey. "Some male Pilgrim whose stovepipe hat was too tight—as a vendetta against women."

"Of course!" Marie confirmed, peering into pots on the stove. "Who on earth would plan a menu where the main course takes six to eight hours to cook while its side dishes take only seventeen minutes? A menu where the main dish takes up the entire oven so that everything else that needs to be cooked can't be."

"But don't you take the turkey out half an hour before you carve it?" Jenna asked innocently.

"Yeah, right," Jess chortled. "So you can spend half a day cooking a turkey, then serve it lukewarm. Don't fall for that old myth, Jenna."

"But then how . . . ?" Jenna faltered.

"First, you start by making sure the wine is flowing." Marie put her sack on the counter and pulled out three bottles of Pinot Noir.

"Plenty of it," Gwen concurred, adding her four Chardonnays to the group.

"Start with the expensive stuff and move to the cheap stuff after two rounds." I put my two jugs of miscellaneous white "varietal" in the 'fridge.

"Then," Jess instructed, surreptitiously turning the oven up to 450 degrees, "you hold off serving dinner for at least an hour and a half after the designated time."

"Yep. Make sure they're starving. Desperate for anything." Marie covered the waiting platter of appetizers and hid them in the back of the 'fridge.

"Then, sweetie," I explained, working the dimmer switch, "you turn down all the lights."

"Yes, candlelight only. Gets them in the mood, and they can't see the food. Jenna, where are your . . . ?" Jenna numbly pointed Marie toward a cabinet to find the candles.

"Burned or undercooked—they'll never know," Gwen concluded confidently.

Jenna looked amazed and unconvinced. "But what about the gravy?" she asked doubtfully.

"Ah! The gravy," Jess said gravely.

"Angie, check the door," Gwen directed. I opened the door to verify that no one was standing on the other side, no spies, no eavesdroppers.

"Jenna, that's a team effort," Marie whispered conspiratorially.

"And you must agree to never divulge our secrets outside this kitchen," Gwen warned sternly.

"Uh, okay," Jenna said. Marie, Jess, Gwen, and I whipped bottles, cans, packets and jars out of our purses and slapped them on the counter. "This is what goes into gravy? What about the turkey drippings? And the giblets and the . . ."

"Giblets? Ugh!" Jess shuddered. "Have you ever taken a really good look at those things?"

"Honestly, sweetie"—I put my arm gently around Jenna's shoulders—"this is how it works. From James Beard and Julia Child to the Loaves and Fishes kitchen for the homeless, this is how we all pull off the Thanksgiving feast."

Jenna looked at Gwen, then Jess, then Marie. Finally, she turned her bewildered, trusting eyes to me. "So let's begin," she said, with a deep breath. "Who's got the corkscrew?"

The Thanksgiving meal that year was an unqualified success.

And the conversation at the table became unusually interesting as well, as soon as Tyler asked me about Tim.

"She's not seeing him anymore," Bob broadcast like Barbara Walters with a late-breaking scoop. How the heck did Bob find out?

"Really, Mom? What happened?" Tyler asked with concern. The noisy big happy family fell suddenly silent to hang on my every word.

"Well, um, we had a few disagreements when I quit my job. He seemed to be pretty upset about it."

"Ah," every man at the table murmured, nodding. "Of course."

"What?" Gwen demanded of Wayne sitting at her side.

"What's 'of course' supposed to mean, Jack?" Marie echoed.

The men at the table spent a few moments squirming in their seats, carefully analyzing the ratio of cranberries to turkey slices remaining on their plates. Finally, Jack turned to Tyler. "You brought the subject up, my boy. It's up to you to explain it."

"Well, Mom, Tim may have reacted that way for a couple of reasons," Tyler started hesitantly. "First of all, he was probably feeling guilty that he hadn't protected you."

"'Protected her'?" Lilah repeated quizzically. "From what?"

"From another male," Tom, Lilah's fiancé, explained seriously, patting her hand. "A predator."

"How was Tim supposed to protect her?" Jessica asked, confused. "He wasn't even . . ."

"Tyler's right," Bob pronounced with Sylvester Stallone conviction. "A real man would've protected her."

"And besides that," Tyler continued, "Tim was probably worried about having another mouth to feed." The male contingent around the table nodded in sage agreement as the rest of us shook our heads in disbelief.

"What mouth? *My* mouth?" I asked incredulously.

"But why on earth would he think . . . ?" Gwen sputtered.

"Well, you know, Angie," Bob declared, puffing out his chest (it almost got beyond his belly), "a real man likes to be the provider of the household. Take care of his woman." Clarisse, Bob's prodigious meal ticket, eyed Bob narrowly. The rest of us raced to stuff our mouths with turkey or stuffing or olives or napkins—anything we could find to keep from laughing out loud.

"Mom," Tyler said apologetically a few moments later, "I know these attitudes are archaic. But it's just how guys feel."

"You do?" Angeline asked in amazement.

"Right," Whatsisname, Jessica's fiancé offered. "So, how about those Raiders? Huh?"

After dinner, Tom helped me with my coat. "Angie," he said sincerely, "I'm very sorry that you and Tim are having your difficulties."

"It's not just difficulties, Tom," I said sadly. "I think it's pretty much over."

"Perhaps."

"Tom, I've tried your 'it's good' thing, but I just don't think it's working for me."

"Give it time, Angie. Allow it to unfold."

"But what if it unfolds, and it's still ugly and awful?"

"Ah," he said, nodding wisely, "that's why the gods created firewater. And Prozac." Tom grinned and hugged me. "Remember, Angie. It's not over until the fat lady . . ."

"So, Clarisse is going to . . . ?"

"God, I hope not!"

Bob showed up just then and followed me out to the car. "So, Angie, it's probably obvious by now that Tim just wasn't the guy for you."

"Bob, I don't want to talk about it."

"Sure. Okay, but if you need a man around, I . . ."

"Jack lives right next to me, Bob. And Tyler's always willing to help."

"No, Angie. I mean, if you need a real man . . ."

"Bob! I'm ready to go home!" Clarisse screeched, from the house.

"Sorry, Angie, I've got to . . ."

As I get into my car, I realized that maybe going home all by myself wasn't so bad after all.

Per usual, Christmas raced into town right after Thanksgiving. I felt strange, guilty almost, having plenty of time to shop for Christmas presents. For most of my adult life, I'd crammed my shopping into hectic lunch hours and frantic weekends. My previous Christmas seasons had to be orchestrated with military precision to catch the sales, coordinate schedules around early-opening stores and late-closing stores, and of course, to wrap and find appropriate hiding places for all the gifts. (After the year that Tyler's ant farm invaded Bob's box of chocolate truffles, I took this last task much more seriously.)

Thinking back through all those years reminded me of one of my favorite traditional Christmas errands: Tim's music store. Of course, I didn't know it was Tim's store back then, and I didn't know Tim at all. But for years, I had visited his store right before Christmas to purchase music for the kids, Bob, and my friends. The clerks there were cheerful and helpful, eager to explain to me the difference between Green Day and Cold Play, or Leontyne Price and Loretta Lynn. It was a pleasant stop, never took much time and, by the few returns, everyone seemed genuinely pleased with the CDs and tapes I'd found for them there. But this year? They'd probably all get mittens.

Lilah, in town through New Year's, invited me to go shopping with her one morning. Because it was a weekday, we felt courageous enough to brave the mall. Our shopping lists led us to pretty much the same shops except for . . .

"Frederick's of Hollywood?"

"Yes, dear. I have a little Christmas surprise in mind for Tom, and I need something to wrap it, or rather"—she smiled suggestively—"*me* in."

"Oh. Okay, sure." I had recently expanded my horizons to include Victoria's Secret. But Frederick's of Hollywood was still several light-years beyond my comfort zone. However, I dutifully followed Lilah into the store, careful to keep my eyes well below edible-crotch level. We walked through the store, and I blindly held out my arms so she could fill them with things I was too embarrassed to look at. Finally, we headed into a dressing room.

"So," Lilah began, as she squeezed her small body into a

leather-studded bustier, "have you thought of your name yet?"

"My name?"

"Yes," she said, eyeing herself critically in the mirror. "The name you want your new grandchild to call you."

"Uh, no, I haven't really thought about it."

"Well, I intend to retain 'Gran,'" she continued, exchanging the bustier for a French maid ensemble. "So, I believe that rules out granny, grandma, grandmama. You don't want to confuse the child."

"Lilah . . ."

"Of course, that still leaves nana, noni . . ."

"Lilah, don't you find this grandmother thing strange? I love kids, and I'm excited to be getting grandkids. But when I think of myself as a grandmother, I just feel so . . ."

She flipped her maid's ruffles coquettishly, studying the effect in the mirror. "Old?"

"Yes, old."

"Angie, dear, put it in perspective," Lilah counseled, trading the maid's outfit for Marabou slippers and a fishnet teddy. "I'm about to be a great-grandmother. Do you see me slowing down?" I had to confess that I didn't. "Well, I haven't. In fact, I feel like I'm just getting my second wind. I'm not a senior citizen." She winked at me, "I'm a classic."

"But how do you do it, Lilah? Lately, I'm just feeling ancient and, well, useless."

"It's all in the mind," she replied, testing out a bit of bump and grind in her fishnet. "You know, my dear, they say that being seventy these days is like being fifty."

"Really?"

"Really. So that makes me about, well, I'd say, fifty-four." I'm not precisely certain how old Lilah is. She'd stopped counting her birthdays years ago when, ". . . like my husbands, they just became too numerous to count."

"So, I'm somewhere around thirty-seven?"

"Something like that," she mused, trading the fishnet for an "open tip" bra set. "Personally, I always think of myself as one of the youngest people in the room. Of course, it is a shock at times to pass a mirror and see a wrinkled old woman staring back at me. I choose to ignore her." Lilah practiced flipping the bra open flirtatiously to expose her nipple. "What do you think of this one?"

"Oh, gosh, I couldn't really . . ."

She turned back to the mirror. "And it's wonderful to feel the same sense of curiosity and desire for adventure as I had as teenager, but without the peer pressure."

"Or the acne."

"Or the imposed curfews."

"Or having to make out in the back of '65 Chevys."

"Actually," Lilah admitted with a coy smile, "I still enjoy doing that sometimes." She turned back to the mirror. "You know, Angie," Lilah continued seriously, "you are only a grandmother to your grandchildren. To the rest of the world, you can be whatever you damn well please. Understand?"

"I think so."

"Perk up, Angie! These blues are just temporary; you'll find yourself again. Now, could you get me a smaller size in these panties?"

"Oh, my gosh!" I exclaimed, looking at the bit of lace she handed me. "So *that's* what Brazilian bikini waxes are for!"

When I ventured out of the dressing room, I found myself nose to nose (actually, nose to prominent bosom) with Clarisse. She eyed me narrowly, hands on humongous hips. "So," she declared like Perry Mason cornering the guilty murderess, "you're shopping in Frederick's of Hollywood these days."

"Uh, no. Well, actually, it's Lilah who . . ."

"Ha!" Clarisse huffed and turned to stomp out of the store. "We'll just see about that!"

We will?

The day of our family Christmas party, I went to get my hair cut. Garrauch (the hairstylist who, by his own reckoning, had saved me from "a dowdy destiny") greeted me with a kiss on the hand and a questioning look.

"Angie, *ma petite chou*, you seem less sparkling than your usually effervescent self."

"Really? I guess I'm feeling at loose ends lately. I'm not working right now, so I have a lot of time on my hands these days."

"Ah, but then you have much time these days for"—Garrauch arched an eyebrow suggestively—"a bit of romance, no?"

"No. I may have the time, Garrauch, but there hasn't been any romance in my vicinity lately."

"Ach!" He exhaled despondently. "But that of course is because you live in America. American men know nothing of romance."

"Oh, that's not true, Garrauch."

"It is absolutely true. And you, madam, are to blame."

"Me? I am?"

"Of course, I do not mean you personally. All American women are collectively culpable for this travesty," Garrauch argued passionately. "You allow your men to get away with abhorrent behavior."

"We do?"

"*Vraiment!*" he declared, snipping his shears ferociously. "You American women bestow your favors upon your men despite the fact that they treat you worse than their puppy dogs!"

"Their puppy dogs? Oh, I don't think . . ."

"It's true!" he insisted vehemently. "Frenchwomen never allow their men to be so lazy. They demand poetry and music and flowers and, and, and effort!" Obviously, this was an issue where French national honor was at stake, like the quality of their champagne bubbles or the mold on their Brie.

"Well, Garrauch, I'll keep that in mind if I ever get another shot at it."

"But, of course, you will 'get another shot', *ma cherie*. You are a beautiful woman."

"For my age, right?"

"For any age, my dear." Garrauch winked at me in the mirror. "Especially with the hairstyle I am about to give you. I predict that you will attract a romantic, passionate, debonair man to your side."

I grinned at Garrauch in the mirror. "And are you offering yourself . . . ?"

"Oh, no, madam!" Garrauch gasped in horror. "Not," he paused with hand over his heart, "that I would not be honored and simply delighted to do so. But," he leaned down to whisper in my ear conspiratorially, "my wife would then most definitely use my favorite shears to render me a soprano. And," he concluded thoughtfully, "I doubt she would sharpen them first."

Well, I did seem to attract a man that night, but he was not one I would describe as "romantic, passionate, and debonair"; "rotund, peculiar, and demented" would be more accurate. Bob buzzed around me like a pesky, persistent mosquito all evening.

"Angie, how come I don't see you at the gym anymore?"

"Gosh, Bob, now that you mention it . . ." It's because I'd asked Frank to give me your schedule so I could be sure mine didn't coincide with it.

It had been tricky to figure out the wheres and hows of our family Christmas that year. Jenna was still shell-shocked from Thanksgiving; Tyler's apartment and my studio were too small to hold us all. Lilah's home was still in Macon, Georgia (considered too far a commute), and Clarisse and Bob's house was still considered by some of us (at least one of us) as enemy territory. Lilah solved our dilemma by renting a private room at Viscaya, which offered a buffet.

The gifting that year was also awkward. How are we broken-yet-somewhat reconciled and rapidly expanding families supposed to handle it? Was I supposed to get a gift for Bob now? Eiouw! And if I did, shouldn't I get one for

Clarisse as well? Ugh! I compromised by getting couples' gifts for the official couples (Ryan and Jenna, Tom and Lilah, Bob and Clarisse), individual gifts for my official family (Tyler, Jenna, Ryan, Lilah), and a small gift for Angeline (because I said so).

Midway through the meal, Tyler rose and clinked his glass. "Everybody," he declared, "I have an announcement to make. Well, actually," he amended, grinning at Angeline, "Angeline has an announcement to make."

Angeline beamed her beautiful smile back at him and rose. "We want you all, our cherished family, to know that I have proposed to Tyler, and he has accepted!"

All of us jumped from our seats and surrounded the beaming couple to offer our excited congratulations. All of us except Bob, that is. He sat in his seat sputtering incoherently, "But, but, she can't just . . . it should be . . . a man needs to . . ."

"Angeline," I said, hugging her enthusiastically. "I'm so happy! So I gather you were able to work through Tyler's concerns?"

"Oh, yes, Angie," she said, smiling sweetly. "We talked about his issues at length and in depth. I told him to just get over it." See? A woman after my own heart.

Toward the end of the meal, I left the table to go to the restroom. And Bob was right behind me.

"Angie," he said, trampling on my heels "surely you don't condone this, this unnatural engagement!"

"Unnatural?" I walked faster in an attempt to lose him, but he stuck to me like a bad case of dandruff. "He loves her; she loves him. What's the problem?"

"Well, they can't start a marriage like this! With her taking the lead and wearing the pants . . ."

"Bob, it seems to me that they can both wear pants. I see nothing wrong with it."

"It'll diminish his manhood," Bob protested. I opened the restroom door; Bob followed me in.

"Bob, this is neither the time nor the place to discuss this."

"Why not? It's a family function. We're all together, and . . ."

"Yes, but we're also standing in the ladies' room."

Bob looked around and blanched. I pointed to the exit, and he scrambled through it. I heard a toilet flush and within moments, Clarisse stood angrily before me. "Interesting place for a rendezvous, Angie," she hissed. She stomped through the door Bob had just scurried through. (Doesn't anyone wash their hands anymore?)

What the heck was that all about? Surely, Clarisse didn't think that Bob and I . . . ? No! Too ludicrous!

"Maybe," a little voice whispered, *"not so ludicrous if you put together the fact that . . ."*

"Unh-uh, unh-uh," I warned, running the faucet at full force. The little voice was silenced.

Chapter 16

The holidays came and went. No more shopping, no more parties, no more distractions. I was at a loss. Obviously, I could have started looking for work, or volunteered somewhere, or founded a new nation. But whenever I thought of doing one of those things, I immediately felt the urgent need for a nap. So instead, I became what I had never had the luxury of becoming before: a Domestic Goddess.

I puttered, I erranded, I baked, I sewed. I tidied, I crocheted, I scrubbed, I buffed. I rearranged my closet and my sock drawer. I reorganized my books by topic and my shoes by season. I repaired every loose screw, ripped hem, and squeaky door I could find. And when I had done everything I could possibly do to my little studio, I generously offered my energetic domesticity to my family and friends.

It took just two weeks for them to agree that I had become universally irritating.

Bright and early one morning, when the pups and I were

still lounging in bed, a delegation arrived at my doorstep: four determined women, one of whom I'd birthed.

"Angie," Gwen announced, settling herself at my kitchen table, "we need to talk."

"Hi, everybody!" I climbed out of bed and pulled on my bathrobe. "Isn't it a little early for you all to be out and about? What day is it anyway?"

"It's the fifteenth," Marie responded, without even consulting her Palm Pilot.

"No," I said yawning. "I mean what *day* is it?"

"It's Saturday," Gwen replied impatiently. "See what I mean," she whispered to Jenna.

"You know we love you, Angie," Jessica began, already setting up her flip chart in the corner of my living room/bedroom. "But we think perhaps it's time that you got busy doing something."

"But I am busy doing something!" I protested. "I baked six dozen muffins yesterday and gave you all some."

"Yes, Angie," Gwen acknowledged, with a sigh. "And they are probably very good, but I'm still working on the dozen you brought me the day before. I brought the dozen from the day before that to the office, but they're still working on the dozen you gave each of us four days ago."

"Mom," Jenna said reproachfully, "Tyler says you sent him an e-mail of forty-six different wedding vows."

"Well, I had a little extra time, sweetie, so I looked up marriage vows on the Internet. Weren't they interesting? Like the one where the couple sings a duet and . . ."

"But Tyler doesn't sing, Mom."

"Oh. Maybe he could just whistle along then."

"The real point, Angie," Marie stated calmly, "is that they haven't even set a date yet."

"And do you honestly think he'd want to use a love poem written by his mother?" Gwen asked.

"Well, maybe. It was a simple poem. I used to be pretty good at iambic pentameter. And just in case he needed something spur of the moment . . ."

"Angie," Jessica continued sternly, "tell me you haven't already crocheted eleven baby blankets for Jenna's baby."

"No, I think it's twelve. I'm almost done with October."

" 'October'?"

"Yes. I'm doing one for each month of the year and, if I have time, extra ones for each major holiday."

"Angie, how many months per year are Sacramento temperatures in the nineties or higher?"

"Well, okay, several. But some places use so much air-conditioning that . . ."

"Mom, Auntie Gwen says you trimmed all the plants in her conference room last week."

"Some of them were getting really leggy and I thought . . ."

"But *while* she was using her conference room to make a presentation to the Legal Society?"

"I was really *very* quiet and hardly . . ."

But the delegation had not finished with my supposed infractions. Alphabetizing Marie's pantry ("Isn't it easier to find the pears if you know they'll be right next to the peas?"), making labels for Jack's miniature railroad set ("Well, it may be obvious to *you* that it's a train, but maybe it's not to everyone."), planting peonies and azaleas in Jessica's Zen garden ("But it was so blah! Wouldn't you enjoy a little color when spring comes?"). I tried to defend myself, but my accusers were as relentless and determined as kindling salesmen in eighteenth-century Salem.

"Angie," Marie said gently, gazing at me with compassion, "you're just going through that midlife crisis phase."

"Who says?" I retorted huffily. "Do you see me running out to buy a little red sports car? Wearing gold chains or dating teenagers?"

"Only men do that kind of thing during midlife crises," Gwen interrupted impatiently. "Women are much more likely to go out and start new businesses . . ."

"Or take up exciting, new hobbies, like extreme skydiving . . ." Jess added enthusiastically.

"And often women's midlife crises are preceded by great loss . . ." Marie contributed.

"Like your job," Jess inserted.

"And Tim," Jenna added softly.

"I don't want to talk about it."

"Angie," Marie said, "you don't have to talk about it. What's past is past. But you do have to start thinking about your future."

"Angie, look," Gwen declared, "we're not advocating that you run out and make any big changes or get a job right now if you don't want to."

"But we are advocating that you start getting a life," Jess added.

"Of your own," Jenna clarified quickly. "Mom, you haven't had any real time off in your entire life. Don't you think you could use it to discover yourself?"

"Figure out how you want to spend the next thirty or so years?" Marie suggested.

"It won't come all at once," Jess allowed. "It'll take some time for everything to percolate . . ."

"But the pot has to at least be plugged in for anything to happen," Gwen argued.

"And you're saying I'm unplugged?"

"Unh-huh," they affirmed as one.

"But it all seems so overwhelming!" I wailed. "I'd rather just keep making muffins. If I made the mini ones . . . ?"

"Angie! That is not an option!" Gwen roared. "Bring out the flip chart!"

So, with my reluctant participation, the five of us started planning how *I* might start planning the course of my next thirty years.

The group, with the notable exception of me, enthusiastically titled the project Re-creating Angie. As always, the team started with a project charter stating the purpose and limits of the project:

To develop activities for Angie over the next several months that will help her clarify her goals and open her eyes to new possibilities for her future.

"And keep her from making those damn muffins," Gwen muttered.

"I think we can break down Angie's future life into categories," Jess started.

"Like middle-aged, old, really old, and ancient?" I asked plaintively.

"No, Angie," Marie said firmly. "Like health, career, spiritual, and relationships."

"That's good," Gwen voted. "And since she seems a bit reluctant about the project, perhaps we each need to take responsibility for seeing that she, um . . ."

"Doesn't chicken out?" I offered.

"Yes," they all agreed.

"I'll lead the charge on career possibilities," Gwen volunteered.

"But I don't know what I . . ."

"I could work on relationships with her," Marie offered.

"But I don't want any . . ."

"And I'll make sure she gets some adventure back in her life," Jessica said excitedly.

"But I'm not ready for any . . ."

"And what shall I do?" Jenna asked her aunties. (Why was everyone ignoring me?)

"Why don't you see that her domesticity is channeled appropriately?" Gwen offered.

"Right! She could help paint the baby's room, and I could take her to my Lamaze class . . ."

And so with absolutely no input from me, my next several weeks were planned out in detail.

My midlife makeover started with Gwen, my advisor on Career Possibilities. We met the following Saturday at her beautiful offices in a downtown high-rise. (In Sacramento, any building over four stories qualifies as such.) We walked through her lobby with its panoramic view and African artifacts. We walked down the hallway that was lined with Picasso prints and through her office with its elegant furniture and fresh flowers. Then she ushered me into a small, austere, windowless room that I can only describe as Early Gulag. It was furnished with two wooden chairs flanking a simple square table, and I believe much of the oxygen had been sucked out of it.

"This is where we bring the opposing counsel when we're working on a settlement," Gwen explained. "They tend to settle faster if they aren't too comfortable." She handed me a stack of papers and several well-sharpened pencils.

"Okay, Angie, I've got some work to do. These are various assessment tools, a battery of tests that are mainly multiple choice. Shouldn't take you too long. Knock on my door when you're done. Then we'll look at the results and start brainstorming."

She closed the door, and I looked suspiciously at the stack of forms that were to be the key to my future, the maps to my destiny. And I was pretty sure that I'd prefer baking muffins to struggling with them in my airless cell. But my friends were right (and even if they weren't, I knew they'd never back down); it was time for me to climb back on the world. So I settled myself in and got to work.

An hour and a half later, Gwen reappeared. "Done?"

"Well, I'm nearly done with the first one." It was a personality profile, a laymen's version of the Meyers-Briggs.

"Really? I thought you'd have them all done by now." She glanced at my responses. "Angie," she said, just barely restraining her exasperation, "this was a multiple choice test. Who said you could submit write-in votes?"

"But, Gwen, I wanted to be absolutely candid. And if neither of the answers fit . . ."

"How complicated could this be, Angie?"

"Well, for instance, how about this one: 'Are you more comfortable making a) critical judgments or b) value judgments'?"

"You wrote in 'I try to be nonjudgmental'?"

"Of course. Don't you? And what about this: 'If you must disappoint someone are you usually: a) frank and straightforward or b) warm and considerate?'"

"Your answer was 'I usually avoid the situation until it goes away'?"

"Well, it's true! I do! Really, Gwen, if these tests are going to be accurate, they should give more options."

"Angie, was there a question that said: 'To drive your friends nuts, do you typically a)complicate the simplest issues until those issues are impossibly convoluted or b)wear on your friends' patience until they are ready to scream'?"

"Uh, I don't remember that one, but I think I would have said . . ."

"Angie! Erase all of your write-ins and choose one of the options! Just go with your first impression."

"But what if my first impression is that neither are correct? Like on this one: 'When the phone rings do you: a) hurry to get to it first or b) hope someone else will answer?'"

"And your problem with that is?"

"Shouldn't I check caller ID first? What if it's some solicitor selling . . ."

Gwen responded with a deep guttural sound, similar to the sound of a wounded warthog (I think) and slammed the door as she left the room. Maybe she was just working too hard lately. I wish I'd baked my new strudel recipe for her; that would have cheered her up.

I was wrestling with the "career interests" test when she returned forty-five minutes later.

"Okay, so what's your problem now?"

"Well, I'm supposed to rank these sets of three choices by 'most favorite' and 'least favorite.'"

"And?"

"And they all fall under the least favorite category, so how can I rank them?"

"Angie, they can't all . . ."

"Just listen to this, Gwen: 'a) planning a city sewage system, b) cleaning a patient's teeth or c) deep-sea fishing.'"

Gwen shrugged. "Well, deep-sea fishing doesn't seem too bad."

"But I get seasick."

"Okay, how about the teeth-cleaning thing?"

"What if the patient has awful oral hygiene and disgusting breath?"

"Planning the city . . . ?"

"Gwen, can you imagine a job where all day long you analyze how much poop a city's citizenry might produce?"

"So, just skip that question."

"Okay, but the next one is just as tough. How can I rank 'writing complex mathematical equations'? I don't even know how to write a complex mathematical equation."

"The question isn't whether you know how. It's just whether you would like to do it."

"You mean, if I knew how, would I like it?"

"Yes."

"But how could I know that? I've never done it."

Gwen's fingers gripped the table as if to squeeze the life out of it. "Do the best you can, Angie," she said through gritted teeth, and left the room. Really, she was in dire need of a vacation.

So I did the best I could. I spent the next few hours and wore through several dozen pencil erasers. The choices were rough: removing surgical stitches (Did they mean those nasty infected ones?) versus designing petroleum-plant equipment (Would you trust someone who just learned how to pump her own gas with that responsibility? Would I be somewhere that would require me to wear a burka?), selling dental floss by phone (Could I do that? In all honesty, I rarely floss, so how could I be convincing when . . . ?) versus meeting with people to discuss complaints (I had never allowed my children to whine, and I certainly wasn't going to spend forty hours a week listening to so-called adults . . .).

By four in the afternoon, I was as assessed as I was going to be. I had worked my way through the Personality Profile, the Career Interests Test, and finally the Aptitude Assessment. We sat down to review the results.

"Okay, Angie, according to this first one, your personality type is an ISFJ."

"An insecure, shell-shocked, female job seeker?"

"Cute, Angie," Gwen said with no smile at all. "No, it means that you're a Protector."

"What's that?"

"The explanation says that you like watching out for

people and that you have an extraordinary sense of safety and security."

"Like, um, an air traffic controller?"

"It doesn't mention that. Oh, but it does list school crossing guard as an option," she noted. "And it says that you don't mind long hours and tedious work . . ."

"So, I could work in a sweatshop?"

"Apparently. Okay, let's move on to the Career Interests Assessment. According to this you would be happy working in industrial arts."

"What's that exactly?"

"It means you would enjoy doing mechanical and machine drawings, designing hydraulics and pneumatics."

"Uh, and city sewage systems?"

"I suppose."

"Was there another option?"

"Yes. Food service."

"Baking muffins?" I brightened.

Gwen groaned. "Let's assume that the Career Interests Test was invalid. Okay, now your aptitudes: good in math, verbal, and analytics."

"So I can add, talk, and think?"

"Yes, but you're not so good in perceptual, spatial, and technical areas."

"Which means?"

"That you can't tell the difference between taupe, beige, and raffia, you're not so hot at parallel parking, and you'll never be able to program your VCR."

"I had to take a test to know that?"

"But, Angie, there's good news."

"What?"

"That definitely eliminates city sewage planning as an option. Let's go; I need a drink."

Over glasses of wine at the bar down the street, my friend looked at me intensely. Gwen is fairly (okay, exceedingly) competitive, and I think it was bothering her that Career Possibilities, under her watch, was floundering.

"Look, Angie. Maybe we're being too analytical. Let's try some open-ended questions and just brainstorm."

"Okay. Like what?"

"Like where do you see yourself in five years?"

I saw myself with five more years' worth of wrinkles and cellulite, living in my little studio with Spud and Alli, making muffins and annoying my friends. I didn't have the heart to tell Gwen this. "Um. Let's try another question."

"Okay, what did you dream about as a little girl?"

"Oh, that's easy! I dreamed that there was this witch under my bed who would grab me if I didn't . . ."

"No, Angie!" Gwen said more vociferously than perhaps was absolutely necessary. "What did you dream of becoming?"

"Oh. Okay, then, a mommy."

"Good. And what else?"

"Fashion Queen Barbie."

"Uh, Fashion Queen . . ."

"Yes, with all three wigs and those puffy pink slippers and . . ."

"Okay. Let's try another approach. What did you like to do as a little girl?"

"Besides playing with Barbies?"

"Please, God, yes!"

"Well, I liked to make up stories. And make up what people might say to each other. And I actually could hear their voices and . . ."

"Angie," Gwen said with resignation. "I believe you've just described a career as an institutionalized mental patient."

Chapter 17

Jessica's original assignment in my retooling had been: "Adventure: Make sure Angie gets some fun and excitement back into her life." But after my session with Gwen, the project team (without the project—that would be me—being consulted) gave Jessica a new objective.

"Angie," Marie explained after their summit, "we think maybe your self-esteem has been damaged a bit, rendering you much more hesitant in your approach to life."

"I don't get it. What do you mean?"

"Well, your chi doesn't seem to be flowing with its normal vibrancy," Jess expounded. "You seem to have lost your center and the balance between your yin self and your yang self."

"I still don't see . . ."

"Angie," Gwen interrupted sharply, "you've become a gutless wimp." Oh. "So, Jess is going to help you regain some confidence."

Jessica had decided that the solution to my "gutlessness" was to drag me to a martial-arts workshop. (I'm sure this is how Bruce Lee got started as well.) We met at Kovar's Karate studio bright and early (she was bright, I was only early) on a Saturday morning. In the dressing room, she handed me my uniform for the day.

"But, Jess, these look like pajamas."

"It's a gi, Angie. And here's the belt." My gi consisted of baggy white drawstring pants with a white-cotton jacket on top. The belt was at least six feet long; I tried tying it in a bow.

Our class of beginners and advanced beginners had already gathered when we walked barefoot onto the huge mat. Because I was a "hadn't even begun," an assistant instructor was assigned to watch over me. He was a pleasant young man named Charlie, and his first act was to retie my belt.

"I can tell that you're someone with a sense of humor," Charlie said, smiling. I wonder how he knew that?

The head instructor, Dave, started warming us up. He also wore a gi but his had black pants with a blue jacket; somehow he looked dashing rather than just silly like the rest of us.

"Okay, let's do some warm-ups," he called cheerfully. We ran in place, stretched our hamstrings, even did push-ups (or, in my case, *a* push-up). Next we stood in lines for kicking and punching drills, Charlie constantly at my side, encouraging and correcting. "Firm wrist, Angie, not limp. Great!" "Hit the target with the ball of the foot, not the big toe. That's it!"

Finally, we took a break, sitting in a circle to talk about philosophy. Dave started: "Here at Kovar's, we believe in the value of 'CANI.' Does anyone know what that means?"

To show I wasn't completely gutless, I raised my hand. "Is it asking permission like 'can I go to the bathroom now, sir?'" Jessica groaned beside me, looking mortified.

Dave just grinned. "No, but that's an interesting interpretation. It means constant and never-ending improvement."

"Sounds exhausting," I whispered to Jess.

"And we always have a weekly theme as well," Dave continued. "This week, it's: Wherever you are, be there." I raised my hand again. "Yes, Angie?"

"But how can you be anyplace other than where you are?"

"Angie, hush," Jess hissed.

"Now that is an excellent question," Dave responded. I stuck my tongue out at Jess, who rolled her eyes. "The truth is that we often show up in life with parts of ourselves missing." I quickly checked all my fingers and toes. Nope, all there. "We might show up to make a business decision without our hearts. Or show up to train physically while our minds are wandering elsewhere." I yanked my mind back from its enthralling creation of my grocery list. "To be fully present," Dave continued, "we need to bring everything— our hearts, our bodies, our minds, our spirits—into the present moment. Wherever you are, be there."

Wow.

"Okay," he said rising. "Let's start working with sticky hands."

HEATHER ESTAY

"Couldn't we just wash them, Charlie?" I asked as we positioned ourselves to face each other.

"You are so funny!" He chuckled. (I guess no one takes hand washing seriously anymore.) "Sticky hands is a drill to teach you how to be aware of your opponent and block his moves." Oh, sure. I knew that. "Now just keep your hands and wrists lightly touching mine and follow my moves." He started moving his hands in small circles. "A little more relaxed, Angie. Good. Now soften the eyes."

"Soften them?"

"Yes, soft focus. It's more a matter of feeling and being aware rather than watching." Though very little of what Charlie said to me made any sense, I started to get the hang of it. It was like dancing, following a partner (remember when we used to do that?). Soon, Charlie was turning and step-ping, and I was able to track his movement and his rhythm. "You're doing great, Angie!" he exclaimed. "I think you're ready for sparring. I'll go get you some protective gear."

Sparring? Protective gear? This did not sound like Arthur Murray anymore.

Charlie padded me up in various pieces of thick sponge rubber: a chest pad strapped around my middle, knee and elbow pads, boot-type things on top of my feet, modified boxing gloves, and the pièce de résistance, a mouth guard.

"Mash nosh isht."

"Here, I'll scratch your nose for you," he offered. "Better?"

"Yesh, thash."

"You're welcome. Now just try a few of the combinations we practiced in the drill."

Kick, kick, punch.

Kick, kick, punch.

"Good, Angie, but put a little more intensity into it. You won't hurt me."

Kick, kick, punch.

Kick, kick, punch.

"Uh, look, we usually don't like to approach it this way, but maybe you need to channel a little anger into it. Try thinking of something or someone that ticks you off."

"Tufloon shishlers?"

"Yeah, like telephone solicitors."

Kick! Kick, punch!

"Drubeen wish seel poons?"

"Sure! Drivers with cell phones."

Kick! Kick! Punch!

And those dumb Viagra pop-ups on my computer.

Kick! Kick! PUNCH!

People with thirteen items in the ten-items-only check-out line!

KICK! KICK! KICK! PUNCH! PUNCH!

Those idiots who throw chewing gum on the sidewalk!

KICK! PUNCH! PUNCH! KICK! KICK!

"Uh, Angie . . .

The guy who invented mammograms!

KICK-KICK! PUNCH-PUNCH-PUNCH! KICK-KICK!

"Uh, Angie, maybe we should . . ."

Booger Brain!

KICK-KICK! PUNCH-PUNCH-PUNCH! KICK-KICK! PUNCH! KICK! KICK!

"Whoa, whoa! Angie, okay! Ease up a bit!"

"Shorry. Craree dway. Akin?"

"No, I think we've done enough for today."

Jess and I changed in the dressing room, and as we walked through the lobby to leave, we overheard Dave lecturing to Charlie: "Never underestimate small, skinny women, my man, especially the inexperienced ones. They don't know their own strength. And when they get that crazed look in their eyes, I'm telling you, watch out."

"Jess, who do you suppose they're talking about?"

Jess closed her eyes and muttered to one of her deities for a few moments. "I can't imagine," she finally responded with a sigh. "I really can't imagine."

Jenna, whose mission was to "restrain and/or redirect" my domestic proliferation, kept me busy sewing curtains for the baby's room, laundering the baby's blankets and new outfits, and researching consumer-safety stats on various strollers. (Oh my gosh! Had I known the horrendous accidents that could befall strolling babies, I would have kept Jenna and Tyler safely in their cribs 'til their twenty-first birthdays!) One night when Ryan had to work late, she invited me to be her substitute coach at Lamaze class.

I walked into the gym where the class was held and instantly experienced that déjà vu feeling. My first Lamaze class had been twenty-seven years before and, like Jenna's class, my classmates and I were all in our final trimester, lumbering and huge. The smallest of us looked like the Michelin Man; the largest had to be transported to the grocery store in a semi tractor trailer. Jenna's class was somewhat different: the age range was broader (some of the mommies-to-be looking my age, others seemingly younger than Jenna) and these ladies looked much more physically fit than I remember us being. But the giggling and groaning sounded just the same.

"Now, ladies," the svelte, spandex-clad instructor trilled over the panorama of sixteen tummy mountains lying on exercise mats. "We're going to start with a relaxation exercise. Starting with your toes, relax every little, teensy-weensy muscle. Wiggle them, stretch them, shift them slightly if necessary. But do not move on to the next muscle group until those toes are perfectly relaxed, perfectly comfortable. We'll do the same with every single teensy-weensy muscle until we are completely relaxed. Completely comfortable."

This instruction was directed to a group of women who probably had not been comfortable in any position for months and whose only teensy-weensy anything was their patience. The instructor left the room, saying she would return in a few moments. Jenna and her classmates dutifully practiced relaxing while we coaches massaged those "teensy-weensy" muscles and murmured encouragement.

"So, Mom, how are you feeling these days?"

"Better, I guess. I had a good time at Kovar's with Auntie Jess."

"So I heard," Jenna said, starting to giggle.

"I'm sorry, sweetie. Is that ticklish there?"

"No, Mom." She chortled. "It's okay." The woman next to her looked over, grinned, and started giggling gently.

"Sweetie, are you ready to reveal the baby's sex yet? The name you've chosen?"

"No," Jenna said, not quite suppressing a chuckle, "we're still keeping it a secret. To avoid interference."

I looked at her suspiciously. "Interference? From me?" I asked wide-eyed. "*Moi*?" And I started to laugh, which cracked Jenna up. A woman three bellies over twittered softly, then cackled out loud.

"Oh, no, Mom," Jenna laughed. "You would *never* interfere!"

"Never!" I avowed, tears of mirth running down my cheeks.

"And you know what else is funny," Jenna continued, barely able to speak. "Dad. I think Dad likes you again!" She clutched her big tummy and rolled to her side, gasping with laughter. Six women in our row followed suit.

"No!" The picture of Bob and me together again was bizarre enough to bring me to my knees beside her in full hysterics. "Can you imagine," I gasped, "your dad and me!" Four-fifths of the class had the serious giggles by then; the other fifth had dashed to the restroom on emergency potty runs.

"Oh no, Mom!" Jenna hooted. "Especially not after seeing you with Tim!" A woman on the far wall let out a horse-laugh that made the rest of us guffaw even harder.

"Jenna," I admonished when I could breathe between giggles, "you know that I . . ."

"I know! I know! You don't want to talk about it!" Jenna whooped, collapsing with glee.

When the instructor returned several minutes later, the entire class was laughing out of control, tummies heaving hysterically, the personification of belly laugh. She took one look, turned around, and left again. It was a great class.

Chapter 18

Marie had chosen Valentine's Day to begin our "collaboration to expand Angie's thinking about, and enhance her openness to, new relationships." Marie was very enthusiastic about it; I was not.

"But, Marie," I moaned. "I'm just not interested in any more relationships. I've had it with men."

"Oh, really?"

"Yes, really."

"Well, it is true that many women live out happy, fulfilling lives without any mate or partner . . ."

"See? So, why do I have to . . . ?"

"But," she interrupted firmly, "these are usually women who have made a clear, conscious decision to do so. Not women who are frightened and merely running away from relationships."

"And you think I'm . . . ?"

"Unh-huh." I hate it when my friends can see right

through me. "You know, Marianne Williamson says that relationships are the training ground for the soul."

"I've never met the woman, but you can tell her that my soul is exhausted from all of its training."

"Angie, when you fall off a horse, it's always a good idea to get right back on." I looked at her, totally unconvinced. "Don't worry," she laughed gently. "It'll just be a hobbyhorse for starters."

"As long as it's a hobbyhorse with seat belts," I insisted. "And a safety net."

"We're going to start with visualization. Close your eyes, take a deep breath, and relax your body."

"Okay."

I am somewhat familiar with visualization; you have to be if you live in California. I don't think anyone in this state dares to do much of anything without first getting a "clear positive mental image" of it. Golfers envision their balls soaring in perfect arcs to the flag; dieters picture themselves with slim and svelte thighs. Even our governor probably spends hours imagining an LA with clear skies, a San Francisco with affordable housing, and a state budget that gets approved before the money from the prior year runs out. (Perhaps someone should tell Arnold that it's simply not working.) I was never sure that positive imagery really helped me much personally. Those perfect parking spaces at the mall remain elusive, and my teeth are still slightly crooked. But then again, maybe life in California would be even worse (and LA even smoggier) without all of this rampant visualization.

"Now I want you to just imagine your perfect male companion," Marie began. "Keep breathing deeply and stay relaxed. Just let the image unfold slowly," Marie crooned, like a hypnotist on a Las Vegas stage. "You might start with his personality; what is he like?"

"Okay. Well, he's friendly and warm."

"All right. Good qualities. And . . . ?"

"And, um, he listens to me when I have something to say. He may not always understand me, but he's still attentive."

"Good, Angie. Very good. What else?"

"He's very affectionate physically, a great snuggler. And he's always glad to see me."

"That's it. Keep going."

"He doesn't take offense easily. And even though he's not a macho kind of guy, I know he would always defend me."

"Very good. And . . . ?"

"And he's not overly concerned about appearances but he does groom himself."

"He grooms . . . ?"

"And he doesn't have many bad habits except when he licks himself in public and . . ."

"Angie, stop!" I opened my eyes and saw Marie eyeing me suspiciously. "You're describing Spud, aren't you?"

"Well, Spud is a perfect male companion. Except for that licking thing and the fact that he sheds."

Marie groaned, shaking her head. "Angie, do you honestly see yourself living the rest of your life with just Spud and Alli?"

"Well, I . . ."

"Don't answer that!" Marie stared at me thoughtfully for

several moments. "Okay, we need another approach. And I know just the thing. Angie, get dressed."

"But where are we going?"

"Don't look so worried, Angie. We'll still take it slowly."

"So, no singles bars?"

"Absolutely not."

"No Internet matchmaking?"

"No Internet matchmaking."

"No speed dating?"

"Nope."

"Okay. So, then where are we going?"

"To a cardio belly-dancing class."

Right.

Marie's rationale behind our excursion into the world of belly dancing is that I needed to reopen the sensual, womanly side of myself and "break down the stone walls of resistance" I had erected.

"Open my chakras again?" I asked warily, putting on the leggings she instructed me to wear.

"I suppose that's what Jess would call it. Look," she said, handing me my coat, "if nothing else, at least you'll be getting some exercise." I was still skeptical, but fearing that Marie would revert to the singles-bar option, I followed her to her car.

Delilah's Bazaar and Oriental Dance Studio was offering a two-hour seminar that afternoon in honor of Valentine's Day. The studio was located in a strip mall, wedged between a chiropractic office and a medical-supply store that offered a "50% Off!" special on back braces and ice packs.

"Marie, do you think Delilah's is located here because . . . ?"

"No."

The class was just gathering as we arrived. A beautiful, large woman of North African descent stopped us at the door. "No, no, no, no!" Delilah exclaimed in an intriguing accent. "I must see your bell-lee!" She rolled the waistband of my leggings so it was below my navel, then tied my T-shirt below my bust. Next, she wrapped a flowing scarf around my hips. She did the same to Marie and sent us in to line up.

Twenty or so women of various sizes and ages were packed in the large bright room lined with floor-to-ceiling mirrors. And at this point, I realized that the downside of belly dancing would be staring at my bell-lee in the mirror for two whole hours. (I dare you to try this at home.) I don't mind my tummy under clothes, but my exposed bell-lee looked scrawny, pale, and wrinkly, like an undercooked biscuit. The ladies with luscious, rounded bellies, like Marie and Delilah, were definitely sexier (I swear that this is not just my stone wall of resistance talking).

"Now, lad-dees," Delilah began, turning on the rhythmic music. "We will first learn to walk. It is called the Camel Walk."

My classmates and I shuffled forward to the music. Apparently, out of twenty women, I was the only one whose shuffle was so spastic that it required special attention (maybe I was walking with two humps, and she wanted one?).

"No, no, no, no!" Delilah admonished me. "Small steps only! And to the beat: Da da dum! Da da dum!"

Da da dum. Da da dum.

"Now, we will shimmy the shoulders!" Delilah called out, demonstrating the move. "Shim shimmy. Shim shimmy. Da da dum!" I tried it. "No, Angeeee!" she protested (she had learned my name pretty quickly). "These, these are your shoulders!" Delilah tapped my shoulders. "These are your arms," she said, tapping the aforementioned body part. "The arms stay still like so. The hands stay out like so. Only the shoulders move: Shim shimmy! Shim shimmy! Da da dum!"

Da da dum. Da da dum. Shim shimmy. Da da dum. Shim shimmy.

"Now we will add the hips," Delilah instructed the class, demonstrating a rhythmic undulation. "No, Angeeee! You don't move the hips by moving the hips!" Of course not. How silly of me! "You move the hips by squeezing the buttock. First, the right buttock *squeeze*, then the left buttock *squeeze*. Da da dum! Da da dum! Shim shimmy, right *squeeze*. Da da dum! Shim shimmy, left *squeeze*!"

Da da dum. Da da dum. Shimmy shim—no, shim shimmy. Right squeeze. Da da dum. Right—no, *left* squeeze. Da da dum. Chim chimney, chim chimney, chim chim cheree! Da da dum.

We spent the next hour moving specific body parts (that I'd not known I had) in certain ways (that I didn't know they could move). My navel was instructed to smash against my spine, then relax shamelessly, like a walrus sunbathing. My rib cage was supposed to detach from my waist, and my pelvic region was ordered to "find its own voice" (I am not *even* going to explain that one.)

At our break, panting and sweating, Marie asked how I

was doing. "So, is your inner sensual self releasing, Angie?" she asked optimistically.

"Marie, I am maintaining the tightest possible control over all of myself," I replied. "I think if I release anything, my whole skeleton will fall apart. The thighbone's no longer connected to the . . ."

"Okay, lad-dees!" Delilah clapped her hands to bring us to attention. "We will now add the zagat! The finger cymbals!"

All righty then.

So we lined up to have Delilah strap tiny cymbals to our middle fingers and thumbs. The fact that these cymbals cut off all circulation to our fingertips was not the issue. The issue was that we had to clang them in a rhythm that matched no hip, shoulder, or foot rhythm we had learned thus far.

"So," Delilah began. "The cymbals, alternating right hand and left hand, touch and touch and: 'one two three four five six seven.' With me now, lad-dees: 'one two three four five six seven.' Very good," she said, turning to play the music. "And begin: Da da dum. Da da dum. One two three four five six seven. Shim shimmy. Left squeeze. One two three four five six seven. Right squeeze. Da da . . ."

All I can say is that what happened next must have been a Zen moment. My mind and body parts were at a total loss to keep up. Every bling of the cymbals stumbled into a da of my feet and tripped over the shim of my shoulders. The total impossibility of what I was trying to do must have thrown me into a previously unknown state of consciousness. So I had an epiphany:

"I love him." I stood stock-still in the astonishment of the moment.

Unfortunately, the line of budding belly dancers to my left did not stand stock-still. They crashed into me like a bad pileup on I-5. But, because I was epiphanizing, I remained as still as Stonehenge while my classmates fell like dominoes at my feet.

"I love him," I repeated in ecstatic revelation.

"Him who?" Marie asked from under the tangle of arms, scarves, cymbals, and legs of our classmates.

"Tim," I said with the certainty of the Oracle at Delphi. "I'm in love with Tim."

"Angie, are you sure you . . . ?"

"Marie, I know this like I know my own name." I yanked Marie out of the pile. "I love his five o'clock shadow and his morning breath." I stood Marie up, untied her hip scarf, and whipped off my own. "I love when he drones on about his work, and I love that sometimes he doesn't understand me." I dragged Marie toward the exit. "I love what's perfect about Tim and what's imperfect. If he never changes a thing, that's great. Or if he reinvents himself, I'll still love him." I hauled Marie through the parking lot to the car. "Marie, I don't know what kind of work I want or what my cosmic destiny is. I'll figure those things out later." I shoved her into the driver's seat and ran around to the passenger side. "But right now, I do know that I love Tim. And I know that I need to go tell him right now! So, let's go!"

"Well, that's great, Angie. But there's just one problem."

"What?"

"This is not my car. Mine is in the next aisle."

Oh.

Chapter 19

After getting into the right car, we drove home, arriving at about five o'clock. This was perfect! I would be letting Tim know how I felt on Valentine's Day! How romantic is that? I jumped into the shower. As I put on my makeup, my hands were shaking. But it didn't matter! Tim would be so happy to see me that he wouldn't notice the uneven blusher or my overdrawn eyebrows. (Okay, so maybe he would notice that blob of mascara on the bridge of my nose. I grabbed a tissue and wiped it off.) As I looked for something to wear, I scripted what I would say to him:

"Tim, I'm back. And for good this time." No, that sounded too much like a threat.

How about: "Tim, I've been thinking about us a lot. And . . ." And what?

"Angie," a little voice whispered. *"Don't you think you should call first in case . . ."*

"I can't hear you!" I screamed, hands over my ears.

I pictured Tim at his door, grinning one of his bashful

213

grins, surprised and thrilled to see me. Oh, heck, maybe I should just throw my arms around him and do whatever comes next! That should get the message across (especially if the something next was what I hoped it would be).

"*But, Angie, what if . . .*"

"Leave me alone!"

Should I stop and get a Valentine's gift? No, I didn't want to take the time, and my mind was buzzing so wildly that I couldn't think of what to get him anyway. Besides, it wouldn't be fair. He didn't know I was coming back to him, so he wouldn't have one for me. We can't start our new life together on an uneven footing.

"*Angie, maybe you should . . .*"

"Hush!"

But I had to bring something, so I cut out a heart from a scrap of wrapping paper and wrote "Angie *heart symbol* Tim." Sweet, but not too mushy, right? Maybe he would fold it up and carry it in his wallet for years to come. Maybe I'd find it someday, when we were both in our eighties, rocking away on some cozy porch somewhere together. It might rekindle our flame and . . .

"*But, Angie, you might want to . . .*"

"No!" I hollered. "And when I walk out that door, I don't want you following me!" I slammed the door and ran to the car.

I was so excited that I took three wrong turns in as many blocks. My stomach was doing flip-flops, and I felt myself grinning inanely. This was going to be great!

The lights in Tim's front room were dimly lit. Poor guy! He was probably spending this Valentine's sitting morosely in front of the TV watching a replay of some old sports event. He'd be in his old sweats, unshaven, probably drinking a beer to dim the pain of being alone on Valentine's Day. Was he in for the surprise of his life!

I practically flew up his front walk and rang his bell. My heart was pounding and I held the little paper heart behind my back. Open up! Open up! Open up!

Tim opened the door. "Angie?" He didn't flash his thousand-watt smile but merely looked startled. Poor guy! Perhaps the surprise had been too much. "Angie? I, uh, wasn't expecting you."

"I know! I thought I'd surprise you." I gave him my most heartfelt smile.

"Oh. I, uh, didn't realize," he stammered. This was not going exactly according to plan. He was so stunned at seeing me that he hadn't even opened the screen door yet. How could I throw myself into his arms through the wire mesh? Of course, we hadn't left on the best of terms. He couldn't know about my epiphany and that he was about to get all that he desired.

"See, I was in this cardio belly-dancing class when I realized that . . ."

"Who's that, Tim?" a female voice called from the kitchen. Maybe it was his mother? Oh, God, please let it be his mother! As Tim turned, Liza rounded the corner, wiping her hands on a pretty apron.

That's when I noticed that the dimness of the room was not due to the TV but to the candles on the table set for two.

That's when I noticed that the room wasn't filled with the noise of a football announcer but soft music.

That's when I noticed that Tim wasn't in his old UC Berkeley sweats with a five o'clock shadow but was dressed nicely, clean-shaven, and smelling of aftershave.

That's when I noticed that his house didn't smell like nachos and beer but some kind of aromatic concoction.

That's when I noticed that my complete humiliation would not dissipate my cells into the atmosphere and leave only a puff of smoke behind no matter how sincere I was about wishing it was so.

Tim and I stood frozen in place; Liza spoke first. "Angie, it's so nice to see you again," she said warmly, smiling. "Would you like to join us for dinner?"

"Thank you, no," I said, wondering why my voice sounded so far away and who was controlling it. "I just came by on my way to, uh, somewhere else. Just to say 'hi.'" I felt my knees start to give way—the traitors!—and I knew I'd better move before I collapsed in a pathetic heap on Tim's doorstep. "So, well, hi. Gotta go. See ya' around. Another time." Fortunately, whoever was controlling my voice took over my shaky limbs and got them moving back toward the car.

"Angie!" Tim called, and I heard the screen door open. The mystic force operating my body shifted me into high gear. My body flew to the car. I dove in, slammed it into drive, and peeled away from the curb.

Three blocks later, I stopped and put on my seat belt. (My mystic puppeteer obviously did not adhere to California driving code.) My thoughts were racing around and, like high-speed channel surfing, I couldn't quite catch them as they roared through. But I was pretty sure I wouldn't like them if I could. I concentrated all of my energy and brainpower on getting home and not ramming the nearest light pole. It's only when I drove safely into my driveway that I realized I was still clutching my little paper heart. And that's when I started to cry.

Fifteen minutes later, Marie and Jack walked out of their front door and found me there. They were obviously dressed up for a romantic evening on the town. Jack moved diplomatically to the background as Marie came up to the driver's side window.

"Angie, what's wrong?" she mouthed through the closed window. I shook my head, unable to speak. "Is it Tim?" I nodded slowly. "It didn't go well?"

I shook an adamant "no" and started crying again. "He had a date!" I wailed.

"Oh, Angie! I'm so sorry," Marie said, full of concern. "Look, Jack and I were just going to dinner. Do you want to join us? Or do you want me to stay with you here?"

I took a deep breath and shook my head again. "No, I'm okay," I mouthed back at her. "Go have fun. I'll see you tomorrow."

"Are you sure?" Poor Marie sounded so concerned. I nodded once more. "Okay, if you're sure. But I'll come by tomorrow, okay?" I tried to get my mouth into something like an encouraging smile. She finally turned and left.

A few minutes later, I entered my little studio to the enthusiastic greeting of Spud and Alli. The phone was ringing but I couldn't think of anyone I wanted to talk to, even if I could find my voice. I didn't want to talk about it. I didn't even want to think about it.

I flopped onto the bed and waited for the tears to come. "So, I suppose," I said tearfully to myselves, "you want to tell me that you told me so."

But there were no little voices coaching, analyzing, fantasizing. The silence was even more depressing; even myselves had deserted me. Spud and Alli curled up next to me on the bed. "At least, you'll always love me, huh, guys? And things will definitely look brighter in the morning, right?"

Things did not look brighter in the morning. They looked bleaker, and I felt even stupider (which perhaps is not a real word, unless you are feeling stupider, in which case, it absolutely is). My message light was blinking furiously at me. Nine messages. Two were from Marie, three from Jessica, and three from Gwen (the other was from a company that would be thrilled to come out and assess the condition of my chimney—this despite the fact that I had no fireplace). The jungle grapevine was definitely in action; all of the messages were full of sympathy and concern (except for that clueless chimney sweep).

"Angie, look," Gwen's last message stated firmly. "I know you and I know you'll be beating yourself up and making yourself even more miserable. You can't stay alone without a rational mind to steer you straight. Meet me at Arareity Jewelers at eleven forty-five. We'll go from there, and I'll buy you some lunch and pound some sense into you. And Angie," Gwen continued, "this isn't necessarily the end of the world. You told him to give you breathing room, and he did. It doesn't necessarily mean that it's over."

I can't say that last thought cheered me up (I was too far

gone for that), but it did dislodge me from complete and utter hopelessness, elevating me to mere hopelessness. And though one of the last things I felt like doing was listening to Gwen's sharp and piercing logic on the situation, I knew she'd come after me if I didn't show up. So I pulled on my scruffy sweats and headed out the door.

Chapter 20

Arareity Jewelers is a beautiful little shop located in a redeveloped warehouse in downtown Sacramento. I'd been there a few times with Gwen, who likes to design her own jewelry in collaboration with Carole, Arareity's owner. I'm not a big jewelry person. But even I can start salivating when I see the exquisite pieces and unusual artwork Arareity displays. The pieces in their showcases weren't the trite, common offerings of mall stores. They were handcrafted by local artisans or created by Carole herself, individual artistic expressions rather than mere ornaments.

But on that particular day, I was too numb and unhappy to enjoy the designs and the sparkles and colors. I stood in the tiny shop, staring forlornly at the clock, waiting for Gwen to show up or my life to end, whichever came first.

"May I help you?" Carole, the owner, asked politely.

"No," I replied with a pathetic sigh. "It's unlikely I'll ever need jewelry ever again in my life," I sniffed.

"Well, but you are in a jewelry store," Carole said cautiously. "You know that, don't you?"

Obviously, my scruffy appearance and puffy red eyes were making her leery. "Don't worry about me." I sighed again. "I'm just waiting for someone." She eyed me dubiously but returned to her work behind the counter. I turned to stare out her storefront. And that's when I realized that my life just might end before Gwen arrived. Because that's when I saw them.

Liza and Tim.

Arm in arm.

Headed straight for Arareity.

Oh, shit.

And though I normally avoid that kind of language, circumstances warranted my saying this out loud and with feeling. "Oh, shit!"

"What?" Carole asked, startled.

"Oh, shit!" I repeated, bounding around the counter. "Quick! You've got to hide me!"

Carole first looked panicked, but then a look of determination came over her face. I prayed she would only incapacitate me with pepper spray and not blow me away with a Colt .45.

"Look, I'm not a burglar, and I'm not a lunatic." Carole did not look convinced. "Okay, so maybe I am a little nuts. But this is an emergency!" Tim and Liza were almost at the door, too absorbed in each other to see me yet. "Please!" I begged as pathetically as I could.

Carole still looked wary but pointed to a corner behind the counter. "There," she commanded. "Crouch down."

"But won't they see . . . ?" My words were muffled as Carole threw a huge pile of winter coats over me.

I heard the faint jingling of the door opening and Carole's pleasant voice. "Good afternoon," she said kicking my purse under the coat mountain that engulfed me. "May I help you?"

The coats muffled Tim's reply but I could distinctly make out: "We're looking for a ring." Oh, God! Could this nightmare get much worse? Carole directed them to a showcase on the other side of the shop, so I thankfully couldn't hear their exchange. But I had the distinct impression that their voices were happy and excited. Finally, Liza's exclamation penetrated my protective covering: "This one! It's perfect. Don't you think, Tim?"

Why me? What had I ever done to deserve this? Can't I be like normal people and just get dumped cleanly? Do I have to show up at the celebration of the dumping? Do you know what a moan feels like if you don't get to moan it? It kind of sits in your chest and knifes through your heart. It chokes all the breath from you and makes your face crumple up like a cheap bumper hitting a stone wall. It makes your limbs go all wobbly while your brain tries to eat itself, making the ugly, screechy noises of an amateur violinist. Trust me; I know this for a fact.

Apparently, Tim agreed that this was the perfect ring because many painful eons later, their transaction was completed. "Thanks so much," Carole said. "Enjoy." I heard the door jingle once more as Tim and Liza exited. Carole lifted a corner of my coat mountain. "Would you like to come out now?"

"No, thanks. I'll just stay here for a while, if you don't mind."

"Suit yourself." Minutes later, the door jingled again and I heard Gwen's brisk assertive voice. "Hi, Carole. Nice to see you. I'm meeting a friend here. Has she shown up yet?"

"About five-four? Brown hair? Crazy as a loon?"

"Yes," Gwen replied with absolutely no hesitation. "That would be her."

Gwen led me down the street to Fox and Goose and sat me down in a booth. She stared at me fixedly, barely acknowledging the waiter who came by.

"Just bring us two of the specials," she said, still eyeing me intently. "And iced tea or something." Gwen waved a hand in front of my face. "Angie, are you in there? Can you say something?"

"I don't want to talk about it," I whispered. My body had gone numb, and I wondered if I would ever feel anything again. I kind of hoped not.

Gwen shook her head sadly; her cell phone rang, and she answered it. "Yes, I've got her . . . No, it doesn't look good . . . Well, from what Carole told me . . ." Gwen turned her face away from me and started psst-pssting into the phone. "Okay, wait, and I'll find out." Gwen turned back to me. "Angie, Jessica has some herbal tea she wants you to take. She said it will help you rest and, uh, something about realigning your fifth house."

"No," I said numbly. "No tea." I wondered if I would ever want anything again. I kind of hoped not.

Gwen mumbled into the phone again and ended the call.

The waiter brought our food, two Philly Cheese Steak Specials. The two of us stared at our plates. "Oh, my God," Gwen muttered, "what on earth is this?" Neither of us ate. Gwen's phone rang again. "Yes, Marie . . . she won't talk about it . . . no, she won't eat either . . . well, I can try. Hold on a minute." Gwen turned to me again. "Marie wants to know if she should pick up some Chinese food for you for dinner tonight. Or would you rather have a pizza?"

"No. No Chinese," I mumbled. "No pizza. No food." I wondered if I would ever be hungry again. I kind of hoped not.

"She says . . . No, I don't think so. Angie, you're not going on a hunger strike, are you?"

"No," I said, getting up from the table.

"Angie, where are you going?"

"Home."

"Well, call me when you get there."

"I'll call you."

Chapter 21

But I didn't call her. I quickly packed up my bags and put them, along with Spud and Alli, into the minivan. Then I went to find Jack. He was in the basement working on his miniature railroad. The smile that started when he saw me quickly faded as he looked into my face.

"I'm leaving, Jack. I'm going to Phil's cabin in Tahoe for a few days. Or maybe a few weeks, I don't know." I bit hard on my lip to keep from crying. But Jack's gentle, concerned eyes were making it difficult. "I want to keep it a secret, but I thought someone should know in case I got eaten by a bear or something."

"Angie, is everything okay?"

"No, Jack. Everything is not okay," I blurted out. "Everything is absolutely and positively not, not, not okay." I started to cry again, and Jack handed me a tissue silently. "Why is it that life seems to work out okay for everyone else? But somehow I always muck it up. How can I be so utterly clueless? What good is an epiphany if it comes too late?"

Jack looked helpless and a little scared now. "Angie, shall I call Marie? She's better at these things than I am."

"No, Jack. No Marie. I need to figure this one out by myself. I'll be okay," I said, with very little conviction as I turned to go.

"Wait, Angie! Let me get you some things to take with you." Jack hurried up the stairs and into the house. I waited on his back step. In a few moments, he reappeared with a small grocery sack. "Okay," he said, pulling out a well-worn copy of *Walden*. "I'm not sure if this will help." He reached back in the sack and pulled out a full bottle of cognac. "But I'm sure this will." He smiled hopefully.

I tried to return his smile but was not too successful. Instead, I rifled through the sack to find a flashlight, a corkscrew, some doggy treats, and a map. I pulled something that looked like a kazoo. "What's this?"

"It's a duck caller." He shrugged. "Or maybe a moose caller, I forget which. I haven't tried it out myself. It just seems like anyone heading out to the wilderness should have one."

I started to laugh, hiccoughed, then found myself crying again. "Jack, you truly are one in a million. Are you sure you don't have a brother for me somewhere?"

"I do have a brother. He's a mortician in Idaho with several teeth missing and questionable personal hygiene." Jack grinned, then looked at me with compassion. "I know you can do better than that, Angie, if being with someone is what you truly want."

"Thanks," I croaked and headed to the minivan before I really broke down.

The trip to Tahoe was relatively uneventful (the only events being the minor upchucking Spud and Alli each did to let me know their dislike of long car trips). I stopped crying long enough to get us on the right road; Spud and Alli, after generously smearing the windows with nose prints, settled on their blankets and snoozed.

We made the two-hour trip into a four-hour trip, stopping to clean up the doggy vomit (me), pee (Spud and Alli), cry (me), and, of course, stopping to shop at Ikeda's farmers' market (even in the midst of a mental breakdown, you've absolutely got to stop at Ikeda's for a fresh-fruit milk shake). The sky, bright blue as we left Sacramento, looked faintly ominous as we drove through the foothills. As we reached higher elevations, sprinkles of a late-winter snow dusted the windshield.

Phil's cabin was on a dirt road off a dirt road that came off another dirt road. Fortunately, Phil's map was great because my sense of direction is not. (Phil, obviously aware of this, included instructions such as "if you see the red barn on the left, you've gone too far." I saw those red barns more than once.)

By the time I drove into the dirt driveway that led to Phil's cabin, it was nearly dusk, and the snow had started in earnest (not that it had been insincere previously, just that it really let loose). Getting out of the car, Spud and Alli let me know that, as much as they disliked regular water, this frozen version was worse. It took half a box of doggy cookies to convince them that death was not imminent if they walked twenty yards to get to the cabin door.

The cabin itself was seemingly rustic but secretly full of creature comforts. The main room had a large stone fireplace flanked by two overstuffed couches and ottomans. Off to the side was a large wooden table with benches and a small railway kitchen with a Franklin stove (and a microwave, double oven, and stovetop hidden behind cabinetry). The walls of the main room were lined, floor to ceiling, with fully loaded bookshelves (the surround-sound speakers were disguised as encyclopedias). Behind a door I found the bedroom, with its own small fireplace and a queen-size bed with an eiderdown comforter (and a dual-control electric blanket underneath). There was an enclosed loft area above that held another bed. The master bathroom featured a deep, claw-footed tub (with Jacuzzi jets).

"This is my kind of Walden," I told the pups with a sigh. "Peace. Quiet. No one around for miles. Just a roomful of books, you two, and me and my thoughts."

"Angie! Are you in there?" Jessica's voice ripped through the silence and set off a beagle barking frenzy.

I opened the door to see her stamping snow off her boots. "Jess, what on earth are you doing here?"

"Me? I came to find you, of course, and make sure you're okay. But you certainly made it difficult to find you."

"That was kind of the idea. How did you know where I was?"

"Well, Marie called and . . ." We were interrupted by the aforementioned Marie driving her ancient Land Rover up the now snow-covered dirt driveway. As she got out of the car, Gwen's Jaguar pulled up beside her.

"Well, if I'd known you two were coming," Gwen exclaimed in exasperation as she exited the car, "we could have carpooled. Who put this cabin so far out in the wilderness?"

"Marie? Gwen? How on earth did you find me?"

"Well, Jack told me what happened and . . ."

"Jack wasn't supposed to tell anyone!"

"He didn't tell just *any*one. He told me," Marie declared earnestly. "So of course I called Jess . . ."

"Who called me. And *voilà!* Here we are," Gwen added. "Though next time you run away to the outback, at least you could run away closer to town," she grumbled. Gwen was not what anyone would describe as the outdoors type.

"Angie, we were just afraid you'd do something rash," Marie said sincerely.

"I wasn't contemplating suicide if that's what you were thinking."

"Suicide? Over a man? Of course not! What a ridiculous idea!" Jess exclaimed.

"We were thinking more along the lines of dyeing your hair purple or eating seven quarts of Häagen-Dazs." Gwen declared with all seriousness.

"You three drove all the way up here so I wouldn't dye my hair purple?"

"Actually, we were more worried about missing out on that Häagen-Dazs," Jess admitted.

"Look, you are my very best friends. But the point of coming up here was to get some alone time, to do some thinking, to figure things out."

"Well, that's why we're here. To help you figure things out," Marie said. "Besides, I brought a pot roast and some Häagen-Dazs in case we couldn't talk you out of eating yourself to death."

"I brought the flip chart and seven colors of Magic Markers," Jess said hopefully. "They only used six colors when they planned the Hubble spacecraft launch; seven will certainly handle your life."

"And I brought the wine," Gwen added.

"But how can you stand to deal with me anymore!" I wailed. "I can't even stand to be around myself!"

"It's true that you have been extraordinarily irritating these past few months," Marie agreed.

"Difficult, depressed, self-absorbed . . ."

"Grouchy, uncooperative, pessimistic . . ." Jess contributed.

"Okay, okay, I get the picture."

"But we're your friends, Angie," Gwen asserted. "We're not going to desert you just because you've become a royal pain in the . . ."

"And we want to help," Marie added.

"Besides, Angie, it's getting dark, and that snow is really coming down. You wouldn't want your best friends to drive home under those conditions, would you?" Jessica entreated dramatically. All three of my buddies (obviously trained by Spud and Alli) turned innocent, beseeching eyes toward me. Good grief!

Thirty minutes later, we had wood stacked in the fireplace, ready to light; the pot roast was reheating and the wine opened.

"I propose a toast," Gwen began brightly. "To the second

half of Angie's life. And to future possibilities and surprises and . . ."

BAM BAM BAM BAM! We froze at hearing the pounding on the door.

"Oh, my God! Don't open it! It might be a bear!" Gwen exclaimed.

"Gwen, bears don't knock," Marie said. She crossed to the door and flung it open.

"Angie, I came to . . . Marie?"

"Tim?" Tim stood in the doorway with a large backpack on his shoulder and a bewildered look on his face. I tried to rise up from the cushy couch, but found that my knee joints had gone wobbly and numb.

"Well, come on in, Tim." Marie beamed hospitably.

"Let me get you a glass of wine," Gwen offered graciously.

"Uh, actually, I came to talk to Angie," Tim stammered.

"Oh, okay," Jess said, settling herself comfortably between Gwen and Marie who had settled themselves comfortably on the second couch. "So, go ahead."

"Uh . . ."

"All right, you three," I commanded from my still-frozen position. "Out." I didn't know what Tim wanted to talk about, but I was pretty sure whatever new pain or humiliation I was about to experience should be done one-on-one. My three friends filed into the adjoining bedroom reluctantly. I heard the door close, then the whisper of it being opened a crack.

"Oh, hell! This isn't the way I planned it. I brought all these candles and some wine . . ." Tim said, distressed. He took a deep breath. "Angie, the way we left it months ago I thought we'd never . . . but then you showed up at my place and Liza was . . . well, I came up to . . . but all your friends are here, and . . ."

"It's okay, Tim. They're gone." I felt like the air had been punched out of my stomach. Tim really is a nice man, and he obviously felt bad about our last encounter, the humiliating scene the day before. But why couldn't he just get on with it? Apologize and leave so I could continue with my nervous breakdown?

Tim took another deep breath and sat down beside me. "Angie, I stayed up all night last night just thinking about you and me. And about Liza," Tim squirmed uncomfortably. "See, to tell the truth, I had started to like her. A lot, actually."

Well, isn't this great? Couldn't he just say he's sorry? He drives all the way up here to explain that he's in love with another woman. Where's that Häagen-Dazs? Next time, Tim, just send me an e-mail!

"But I knew all along that what I liked about Liza was that she's kinda like you." Oh, great! Well, this is even better. "Kinda like you, but not you. And it's you, the original, not a copy that I'm in love with. Liza and I talked about it, and we're still friends. She even helped me pick out . . . no, I'm getting ahead of myself."

Wait. Did he say "in love with"?

I'm not particularly eloquent at dramatic moments. If you catch me in the shower hours later, I'm brilliant and witty. But at that exact moment? My mind, anticipating another blow to my ego, had traveled out of the county on its own recognizance. My mouth opened, but no sound was emitted.

"Look," Tim continued earnestly, "I'm really sorry about the way I acted. But when you quit and then you said you were going off to have adventures . . ." He raked his hand through his already disheveled hair. "Well, you were doing all those things without me. Without me! And I love you, so I just thought . . . "

"Why?" Uh-oh. Had my mouth just spoken? Without my mind in attendance?

"What?"

"Why? Why do you love me?" Yep, that was my mouth. I heard a chorus of groans from behind the bedroom door.

Tim stared at me for one of the longest moments of my life. Then his face broke into a grin. "I knew it!" he slapped his hand on his knee triumphantly. He reached into his shirt pocket, brought out his glasses, and a folded piece of paper.

"Uh, you knew what?"

"I knew that you wouldn't let me just say 'I love you' and leave it at that." He grinned and adjusted his reading glasses, unfolding the list from his pocket. "That you would insist on proof or the details or something. So, I prepared." He smiled, pleased with himself. "I've got a list. May I read it?"

"Oh, well, gosh, sure."

"Number one: your sheets."

"You're in love with my sheets?"

"No," Tim said gently, touching my hand. "I'm in love with the way you always wash and iron them before I come over. Like I'm someone really special to you."

"Oh. Okay," I said shyly. Did I put on waterproof mascara that morning? I hoped so, because I was pretty sure that I was already crying.

"Number two: You put ice in your Chardonnay." Gwen's groan was audible. Tim looked at me lovingly. "Which says to me that you'll always be your own person." Or maybe that I'll always be clueless? I liked Tim's interpretation better.

"Number three: I love that you think your children are perfect. Which," Tim hastened to add, "of course, they are." He put both of his hands around mine, and said, "And I love the way that you know that I'm not perfect and yet you seem to, um, seem to . . ."

"Love you?"

"Aw!" The Greek chorus sighed behind the bedroom door.

"Yeah. Look, Angie, I've got this whole list and we can . . ."

"Look at it some other time?"

"Right. Angie, I've wanted to ask you to marry me for the longest time. I even dreamed about it once. But I was afraid that you might say no. And if you said 'no,' I wouldn't even have the possibility that someday you might . . ." Tim stopped uncertainly. "But if I never ask, I'll never know, so . . ." He took a deep breath and looked deeply, meltingly into my eyes. "Angie, I love you. Would you . . ."

Now, of course, in most people's lives, this moment would have ended in a romantic embrace. Tim would have finished his sentence with ". . . marry me?" I would have said breathlessly, "Oh, yes!" and we would have fallen into each others' arms and shared a blissful, romantic evening (once we had thrown Gwen, Marie, and Jessica out into the snowstorm, that is). Unfortunately, I do not seem to live most people's lives.

"You hussy!" A huge snow-covered behemoth burst through the door. "Where is he? I know he's here!" Clarisse, a crazed look in her eyes, stormed into the cabin, flinging open doors and hunting under furniture. She threw open the bedroom door, at which point my eavesdropping friends stumbled into a heap on the living-room floor.

"What are you talking about? Who are you looking for?" Gwen demanded, picking herself up.

"Bob, of course!"

"Bob's here, too?" Tim asked, puzzled.

"He's here somewhere! I know he is! You two thought you were so clever setting up this little tryst. But I've been following you, Angie, and . . ."

"You're having a tryst with Bob?" Jessica asked, appalled.

"Don't be daft, Jess. Of course she isn't!" Marie declared. "You aren't, are you, Angie?" she asked, less certainly.

"Of course I'm not! I haven't seen Bob since . . ."

"Yoo-hoo! Angie, darling!" Bob's voice came from outside. The six of us froze like a tableau in Madame Tussaud's Wax Museum. This one would have been titled *Walden* meets *The Jerry Springer Show*. "Are you in there, darling?"

None of us moved, carefully avoiding eye contact. But you can only wait so long for that other shoe to drop. I yielded to the inevitable: "Come on in, Bob, and join the party."

Bob entered the room, confusion all over his face as he took in the crowd. "What are all these people doing here?"

"You sneaky son of a . . ." Clarisse hissed, fingernails positioned in attack mode.

"I'll handle this, Clarisse," I said, with militant authority. I was seething with the fury of a woman who has just had the most romantic moment of her life interrupted. "Everyone just sit down." No one moved. "Sit down!" I bellowed. And they sat. (It's not for nothing that I was the mom elected to drive the "behavior issue" kids on field trips. Tyler and Jenna were never defined as such, of course, but the ones who *were* learned to fear my wrath. But that's another story.)

I stood in front of the assembled menagerie like Hercule Poirot ready to deliver his denouement. "So here's the story. Marie"—I pointed to her—"is here to save me from dyeing my hair purple. Tim is here to ask me to marry him. At least I think that's what he's here for; we keep being interrupted. Jessica wants some of the Häagen-Dazs she's afraid I'll gorge myself on. And Gwen is here to make sure that we have decent wine for the occasion. Oh, and Clarisse showed up in a fit of jealous rage with the intention of killing me and apparently mutilating you, Bob, in some unspeakable way." I took a dramatic breath, and continued, "As for me, I'm here to get some peace and quiet, some private alone time to contemplate my life and do my nails. So now it's your turn, Bob." I whirled around to face him. "What the heck are you doing here?"

But Bob wasn't looking at me anymore. He was gazing

amorously at Clarisse. "You came all the way up here just because of me?"

"Yes, Pooky," Clarisse sniffed. "I was going out of my mind thinking that you might be interested in another woman."

"'Pooky'?" Gwen muttered under her breath. "She calls him 'Pooky'? I think I'm going to be sick."

"Just wait," I whispered back. "It gets better."

"Dumpling," Bob declared ardently (the audience groaned), "I've been a fool. To think that you care so much for me that you were ready to kill Angie and maim me for life! You are all the woman I will ever need." He walked over to Clarisse with adoration in his eyes. And what happened next is truly too icky for me to relate.

"Eiouw!" Marie muttered with a grimace. "This is like watching manatees mate on the Nature Channel."

"Okay, so now that *that* is out of the way," Jess said brightly. "Tim? You were saying to Angie?"

"Uh, well, I . . ."

"Hi, Mom!" We all turned to see Jenna waddling through the open doorway. She was covered with snow from head to foot, an animated pregnant snowman (snowwoman?). "Wow, is this a party or something? It is snowing like crazy out there! They were closing the roads right after I passed through. In fact, your driveway is completely blocked, so I had to hike up here. Not easy when you're hauling Baby Bubba around!" She grinned, her face flushed and sweating, then grimaced as she clutched her bulging tummy. "Ow!"

We all stared at Jenna in astonishment. And then at

the growing puddle forming between her feet. "Ooops!" she said, with an embarrassed grin. "Guess I'm dripping, huh?"

"No, Sweetie," I said with a calm that I did not feel. "I'm pretty sure your water just broke."

And, of course, that's when all the lights went out.

Chapter 22

"Shit!"

"Don't swear in front of my daughter!"

"Dad, that was me who said 'shit.'"

"Oh."

"My God, I can't see a thing!"

"Can someone light the fireplace? Get us some light in here?"

"Wait! I've got all those candles in my backpack. But I can't remember where I put it," Tim said.

"Damn! I just found your fricking backpack. I think I broke my leg on it," Gwen groused.

"But, a lighter. I didn't bring a lighter," Tim fretted.

"I've got one," Clarisse offered. "I was planning to torch the house."

"Aw, Dumpling, that's so sweet!"

Amid general confusion and bumbling, we finally got a few candles lit, then lit the fire. We stood around looking like ghouls at a séance. For some reason, all eyes were on me, Hercule the Unflappable, for the next move.

"All righty then. Sweetie, have you felt any contrac . . ."

"Arrrgh!" Jenna screamed, clutching her tummy.

"I'm going to take that as a 'yes.' Okay then, let's get her into the bed." No one moved. "Gwen! Jessica! Marie! Move it! Now!"

The platoon came back to earth with a start, and as one woman we bundled Jenna into the next room. Marie and I pulled off her boots and parka as Gwen and Jess lit the bedroom fireplace and placed candles strategically around the bedroom. I kissed Jenna's slightly feverish brow.

"Are you okay, sweetie? You shouldn't have come up here."

"I was worried about you, Mom. I wanted to help and . . . Arrrgh! Ryan! Mommy, I want Ryan," Jenna moaned.

"Yes, sweetie. We'll try to get him on our cell phones."

"Angie!" Tim whispered through the crack in the door. "We can't get cell phone reception up here. I just tried."

"Terrific." Clearly, the life of Henry David Thoreau had some drawbacks.

"Sweetie, excuse us for just a moment. The aunties and I have a little strategizing to do." I grabbed all three of my very best friends by their respective necks and hauled them into the far corner of the room. "Okay," I said menacingly. "Let's plan!"

"Calm down, Angie," Gwen commanded. "We need to think this through."

"Maybe the snow will stop and the power will come back

on and we can call for help or get her to a doctor," Marie offered hopefully.

"Sure, and maybe Santa and his reindeer will pop by and offer us a ride back to Sutter Memorial Hospital," I retorted.

"Hush up, Angie. Good, Marie. Yes. Let's consider that Plan A," Jess declared. I could see she was itching to bring out her trusty Magic Markers and flip chart.

"Besides, this is her first baby. Doesn't labor last longer for first babies? We've probably got plenty of time," Marie said optimistically.

"Tyler came out within three hours of my first contraction."

"Uh-oh," Gwen said. "Then we'd better have Plan B in place."

"Which is?" I asked.

"Which is we deliver Jenna's baby ourselves," Marie declared.

The four of us looked at each other and took a collective deep breath.

"How hard could this be?" Gwen, the mother of none, remarked nonchalantly. "Women have babies all the time." When she caught our glare, the three of us who'd had nine childbirths among us, Gwen looked much less cocky. "Okay, so how about if I just follow instructions?" she offered meekly.

"I think we start with a project charter," Jessica stated with professional assurance.

"The purpose of the project is to deliver my grandchild safely before I strangle all three of you!"

"Angie, quit being so testy. We need to work together on this. Okay, let's break down the various tasks. Someone needs to help Jenna with her breathing through the contractions," Marie said.

"I'll do that. I went through Lamaze for all five of my pregnancies," Jess volunteered. "I've got a Ph.D. in panting and pushing."

"Good. Then someone needs to catch the baby as it comes out," I said.

"Twelve years of coed softball," Marie said, flexing her fingers. "I'm your guy. I just wish I'd brought my mitt." I growled at her. "Just kidding, Angie. Will you lighten up?"

"And we need to boil water," I continued.

"Why?" Gwen asked. We all looked at one another, totally stumped.

"I don't know," I admitted. "They always boil water in the movies."

"Maybe it's for a soothing cup of tea?" Jess postulated.

"Let's just boil it. We'll figure it out as we go along."

"Okay, I'll do that part. I can keep the water at a slow simmer until we're ready for it," Gwen volunteered. "And I'll find some towels and warm them up to put the baby in."

"Good. Then, someone needs to cut the umbilical cord," I remembered. My enthusiastic volunteers looked squeamish.

"Angie, as the grandmother, I think that privilege should be yours."

"Gosh, thanks," I said. "What do I cut it with?"

"I brought toenail clippers," Gwen offered.

"I think I saw a cleaver in the kitchen," Marie said.

"Wait, I might have brought scissors in my crochet bag,"

I remembered, wondering how an umbilical cord compares to three-ply worsted.

"Okay, team, are we feeling confident?" Jess said enthusiastically. "Are we ready to get into action?" We looked at each other uncertainly . . .

"Arrrgh!" Jenna shrieked.

. . . then took a collective deep breath. "It's showtime."

Over the next hour, the team got organized. Gwen pulled out every pot in the house, filled them with water, and set them on the Franklin stove to simmer. Marie flexed her catching muscles and massaged Jenna's feet as Jess worked with our soon-to-be-mama on breathing. I mainly paced the floor, trying to remember all I'd ever known about childbirth. But my last delivery was twenty-four years before, and I could barely remember last Thursday, so not much came to me.

Meanwhile, Tim hauled in all the firewood he could find and stacked it up by the fireplaces. He trudged down the road to see if it was being cleared (it wasn't). Then he climbed up on the roof to try again for cell reception, an adventure that resulted in torn pants and scraped knees and elbows, but had no luck reception-wise.

"Why didn't you just open the skylight in the loft?" I asked as I bandaged him up.

"Uh, well, Bob and Clarisse have been up there and the sounds they're making . . ." He smiled bashfully.

"Ah. I get the picture." And it wasn't a pretty one.

"I'm sorry I'm not much help, Angie."

"Tim, you're wonderful. Just having you here is . . ."

"Arrgh!"

"Sorry. Gotta go."

"Angie," Jess said, when I entered the room. "We need to help Jenna find a focal point so she can concentrate on it during contractions. It should be something familiar to her."

"Like what?"

"A favorite picture. A stuffed animal, something that . . ."

"I know, I know!" Jenna cried. "Mom's nose, I could use Mom's nose."

"My, uh, nose?"

"Yes, Mom. I've stared at it for years. Whenever you were lecturing me, I stared at it to pretend I was listening."

"You stared at my . . . ?"

"That's perfect," Jess ruled. "Angie, bring your nose into position and be ready for the next contraction."

So, I did. Jenna's contractions got more consistent and a little stronger. After a while, Jess increased Jenna's breathing to medium speed, humming a familiar tune.

"What's she humming?" Gwen asked.

"'Yellow Submarine,'" Marie replied. "It's the perfect tempo. In the town where something something," Marie sang softly.

"Yada yada," Gwen warbled along. "Doh dee doh. We all live . . ."

So, over the next couple of hours, Jenna stared at my nose as we sang along to her contractions. We were perhaps not quite accurate with the lyrics (and never did figure out the words after 'sea of green'). But our harmony wasn't bad, and it gave us something to do.

But after about twenty choruses, the miraculous happened! The type of thing that only happens in sappy movies desperate for resolution: Ryan, my competent veterinarian son-in-law, walked through the door!

"Jenna!" he croaked, heroically staggering into the cabin with frozen limbs and snow-drenched hair. "Where are you?"

"She's in there. Her water broke, and her contractions are getting closer," Tim said, directing Ryan to the bedroom.

Ryan visibly paled as he stumbled to her side. "I'm here, sweetheart. Everything will be all right now."

"Arrrgh!" she screamed with her latest contraction.

"Oooo," Ryan moaned, as he slid to the floor in a dead faint.

"I'm thinking that we're back to Plan B," Gwen noted.

"Tim, could you help me drag the father-to-be by the fireplace to warm up?" Marie asked, grabbing an ankle of my prone son-in-law.

"Breathe, Jenna. Stare at your mom's nose; that's it. Breathe through the pain, sweetie. In through the nose and out through the mouth. In the land . . ." Coach Jessica crooned.

Half an hour later, the contractions were coming faster and harder. Jessica increased the tempo of Jenna's breathing again—"Pant, pant, pant, blow!"—and the four of us joined her, like a pack of winded greyhounds. Between contractions, the delivery team was getting a little tense. Gwen, having run out of pots to boil, was particularly testy. "I'm just not used to having no control over the outcome," she fumed.

"Well, then, go out there and see if you can talk some sense into Ryan."

Several minutes later, Gwen and Tim came to the bedroom door.

"Angie," they whispered. "We've got a plan."

"What?"

"Ryan is conscious again. We talked about it. He thinks he can talk you through the birth if he stays in the living room and pretends that it's just some farm animal."

"Worth a try. Let's give it a test."

So we positioned ourselves. Ryan sat on the couch in the living room; Tim stood on the outside of the bedroom door to transmit Ryan's instructions to Gwen on the other side of the door who relayed the information to the three of us by the bed.

"Okay," Tim started. "Ryan is pretending that Jenna is a cow."

"Not too flattering," Marie observed. "Couldn't she be a gazelle?"

"He says he's more familiar with cows. Now he wants to know what kind of cow she is," Tim continued.

"Obviously, a pregnant cow," Gwen said impatiently.

"No, what breed?"

"Jenna, sweetie," Marie asked softly, "if you were a cow, what breed would you be?"

"Arrgh!"

"I think she said Holstein," Marie called to Gwen.

"Okay, Jen," Jessica chanted. "Remember pant, pant, pant, blow. Look at Mom's nose."

"Now he wants to know the cow's name," Tim reported.

"Clara Belle!" Gwen screamed through the door. "Just tell us what the f—k we're supposed to do next."

"Okay, okay. He says that since she's a heifer . . ."

"A heifer?"

". . . she'll probably be particularly agitated."

"Well, she's not laid-back and chewing her cud, if that's what you mean," Marie offered.

"I'll kill him! I swear I'll kill him!" Jenna screeched, rising from her bed.

"Gwen, tell him that she's definitely agitated," I said, then turned to comfort my young heifer. "Don't worry, sweetie, the aunties and I will kill Ryan for you when this is all over. Just let us know how painful you want it to be."

"Okay, Ryan says we need to figure out how close she is to delivering. He wants to know if her tail is arched up."

"Uh, not that I can see," Jess answered doubtfully.

"He's asking if she's bagged up."

"Is that like 'are her suitcases packed'?" I wondered.

"No. How full are her udders?"

"Which part is the udder?" Gwen whispered.

"Are they dripping milk? Are the teats poking out?"

"Mom!" Jenna screamed in panic. "The baby's coming! I can feel it coming!"

"Keep breathing, Jenna. Don't stop breathing."

"Dammit, Ryan. Her teats are out, her bags are packed, and she's ready! So tell us what to do next!" Gwen hollered.

"He says to stay calm."

"That little son of a . . ." Gwen fumed.

"He's right," I said, holding on to Jenna's hand and my

composure as firmly as I could. "We just need to stay calm. It's okay, sweetie. Keep her breathing, Jess."

"Ryan wants to know if you have all of the supplies ready."

"Like what?" Gwen asked.

"Like a bucket of hot water . . ."

"Got it," I confirmed.

"With some disinfectant to wash your hands."

"I brought some Listerine," Jess offered. "Will that work?"

"He says yes, and he says you need, um, chains and rope."

"Chains?"

"The rope is to tie Clara Belle up so she doesn't kick you or maim you with her hooves. He says we need chains to pull out the calf if that becomes necessary."

"I'm going to kill him, Mom! I'll rip off his . . . Aaargh!"

"Look at her nose, Jen. Pant, pant, pant, blow."

"Angie, don't we have to make sure she's fully dilated?" Marie asked anxiously. "I'm pretty sure the cervix is supposed to be dilated to ten centimeters before she does any pushing."

"Fine, okay, I'll check. But how big is ten centimeters?"

"Precisely 3.973 inches," Gwen declared. "So, that's a little wider than the mouth of a wineglass. Red wine."

"About the length of your cell phone," Marie added.

"Closer to your Palm Pilot," Jess corrected.

"About the size of a softball," Tim contributed. "Not a regulation baseball but a . . ."

"Enough! I get the idea!" I washed my hands with soap

and water, splashed them with Listerine, then rinsed them again. Thank goodness, I had bitten my nails to the quick over the past few weeks. I tried to remember everything I'd tried to forget about my four decades of pelvic exams. Of course, for those occasions, I played the feet-in-the-stirrups role. This would be an entirely new perspective. "Okay," I said feeling gently. "The opening seems as wide as a tennis ball and . . ." My fingers brushed against a different texture. "Oh my gosh! I think I can feel the baby's head!"

"Okay, Jenna, we're close now," Jess instructed. "With the next contraction, be ready to push."

Over the next thirty minutes, Jenna screamed and pushed and denounced Ryan, then rested and screamed and pushed and denounced again. The audience in the living room was eerily silent, but the team in the bedroom kept up a lively chorus of encouragement.

"That's it, Jenna! You're doing great!" Marie hollered.

"Yes, that last push was exceptionally well-done!" Gwen exclaimed, flushed with excitement.

"You're doing great, Jenna. Deep breath. Relax for a moment."

"Mommy, I don't think I can do this . . . Aaargh!"

"Sure you can, sweetie. That's good, very good."

"Oh, my gosh! Angie, I can see the top of the baby's head!" Marie exclaimed from her strategic position.

"We can see the baby calf," Gwen whispered through the door.

"Easy, Jenna. Now, get ready to push with the next contraction. Big breath in; half breath out. Ready?"

"Aaargh!"

"Ryan wants to know what part of the calf you see. If it's a tail, that's bad."

"No, don't worry. Tell him it's good. It's all good."

"Okay, Jenna. Deep breath, let some out and . . ."

"Aaargh!"

"Okay," Marie reported excitedly. "The head's staying in position. It's crowning."

"Crowning? What's crowning?" Gwen mumbled anxiously. "I've heard of silver spoons but not . . ."

"Okay, Jenna, now we're just going to breathe with this next contraction. Easy on the pushing," Jessica coached.

"Mommy, Mommy," Jenna whimpered.

"We're almost there, sweetie," I whispered. "You can do this."

"Aaargh!"

"Okay, I've got the head! The head's out!" Marie announced.

"We're almost there, sweetie. Grab my hand and . . ."

"Aargh!"

"It's coming out! I've got it! I've got *her*!" Marie yelled like an enthusiastic outfielder. She held the baby carefully and gently put her in my arms. Her! My granddaughter! I held the tiny precious baby and brought her to Jenna's breast.

"Oh, my God. She's beautiful! She's my beautiful baby girl."

None of us had heard the door open, but I felt his presence at my elbow. "Yes, sweetheart," Ryan said with a husky voice, a turkey baster in his hand. "She's our beautiful baby girl."

"Oh, my God!" Gwen gasped. "He's going to baste the baby!"

Ryan gently suctioned the baby's mouth and nose as Jenna looked on adoringly. I wish I could freeze that tableau and preserve it forever. Jenna lying in bed flushed and exuberant with the baby at her breast; Ryan, proud and loving, kneeling beside them; Gwen teary-eyed and sniveling into one of her warm sheets; Marie grinning from ear to ear and flexing her fingers; Jessica looking stunned, still mumbling "breathe, Jenna, breathe" to herself.

But, of course, we couldn't freeze there. We still had work to do. Ryan, now fully recovered, clamped and cut the umbilical cord (with the scalpel he happened to carry with him, not the toenail clippers Gwen once again offered). He tied the cord off carefully, then helped Marie tenderly clean and wrap our baby girl in the sheets Gwen had warmed. Jess massaged Jenna's tummy to help release the afterbirth as I held Jenna's hand and smoothed her brow.

"Mommy," she whispered. "She's beautiful, isn't she?"

"She's beautiful, Jenna. So, now, will you tell us her name?"

"Savannah."

"I like it. Savannah. Much better choice than Agurtzane."

"Huh?"

"Hey, that's funny," Ryan said from across the room. "I've got a cousin named Agurtzane."

"Hmmm . . . So your father was right for once, Jenna."

"About what?" She yawned sleepily.

"Never mind. Get some rest."

"So, I'm really a mother now, huh?" Jenna murmured, as her eyes closed.

"Yes."

"And you're really a grandmother now, huh?"

"Mmmm. I'm a grandmother. And it's good, Jenna. It's all good."

The four of us left the room to give Ryan and Jenna some privacy, but Ryan followed us to the living room.

"I just, um, really want to thank you all for taking care of Jenna and our baby," he said with tears in his eyes. "You must think that I'm a total . . ."

"Gosh, Ryan," Jessica broke in quickly. "It was so fortunate that we had you here. I mean, who else would have thought to use the turkey baster?"

"Absolutely," Marie chimed in. "And the Listerine? Who would have thought to use it?"

Even Gwen rose to the occasion. "And your instructions? Invaluable," she declared heartily. "Especially that one about keep calm."

Ryan shook his head and grinned at us all. He may be a little conservative, shy, and squeamish at the sight of his wife in pain, but the father of my granddaughter is not stupid. I put my arms around him and whispered in his ear, "You're a great husband, Ryan, and you're going to be a great dad. I mean that sincerely."

"Thanks, Angie," my son-in-law said clearly, gratitude in his eyes. He went back to join his little family.

"Looks like Jenna's forgotten about killing him." Gwen smiled.

"Just wait 'til her next labor." Jessica grinned.

"Hey, where did Tim go?" Marie asked.

He was nowhere in the cabin. His jacket and backpack were gone. We looked but found no note, no trace.

"That's so odd," Marie mused. "I wonder if it means . . ."

"Stop!" I interrupted forcefully. "We don't know what it means. And we won't know until I get the chance to ask him. Directly. In person. So, no more speculation, okay?"

"Okay," they agreed sheepishly.

"There's probably a very reasonable explanation for his disappearance," I continued with conviction. "I mean, not all men are irrational, irresponsible, inconsiderate, and . . ."

"Hey, Angie," Bob called as he stumbled down the stairs, scratching at his tummy poking out from his undershirt. "How's a guy to get some breakfast around here?"

My friends looked at me pointedly. "Okay, so then again, some of them, well, are."

Chapter 23

Three hours later, the snow had stopped, and the light of the new day was just peaking over the pine trees. Jenna, Ryan, and Savannah were still snoozing in the bedroom. Bob and Clarisse (after decimating the pot roast and finishing off the Häagen-Dazs) had retreated to the loft above. The four of us were camped out all over the living room, trying to get some sleep.

I couldn't sleep at all; just too much life in my life the past twenty-four hours, I guess. I listened to the quiet morning, the familiar sound of Bob's snoring coming from above, Gwen humming "Yellow Submarine" fitfully in her sleep. My mind was too exhausted to stay organized and it allowed a mishmash of voices to spin through it: "It's all good, Angie." "You can be whoever you damn well want to be." "Wherever you are, be there." "But what if they name her Gurutz?" "I love you, Angie." I heard that last one several times: "I love you, Angie." I even had witnesses this time. But where was he? Did Tim decide that the craziness of my life was too much after all? That he'd prefer the copy and someone not quite so "original"? And what am I supposed to do with my life? Or just, what am I supposed to do next?

A rumble like heavy machinery broke through the quiet of the morning and the racket in my head.

"It's a parade," Jess mumbled, sleepily rubbing her eyes.

Gwen stretched and squinted out the front window. "Of baby snowplows?"

The parade consisted of three small all-terrain vehicles with snow shovels in front. As they roared up to the cabin, we could see that each carried two men bundled in parkas and hats.

"That's Jack!" Marie exclaimed. "And it looks like Tyler!"

"Who's that with them?"

"It looks like Stanley." Marie said, now jumping up and down. "It is! It's Stanley! He's our next-door neighbor and an obstetrician!"

The parade stopped at the porch steps, and Tyler hopped off the lead plow. "Hi, everybody," he said cheerfully, giving me a hug. "I hear we missed all the fun."

"But we brought Stanley, just in case," Jack added.

"Jack, you told me it was a home delivery. You didn't say the home was in Tahoe," Stanley grumbled. "Okay, where are they?" Marie greeted Stanley with a big hug, which seemed to cheer him up, and directed him to the new little family in the bedroom.

"But, how did you know where to find us?" Gwen asked.

"Tim." Tyler looked at me significantly. "Tim hiked about seven miles from here until he found a cabin with a working phone. He called Jack and arranged for these ATVs."

"He hiked through the snow? That is so romantic!" Jess gushed.

"That is incredibly romantic!" Gwen agreed.

"That is absolutely the most romantic thing I've ever heard of." Marie sighed. "No offense, Jack."

"No offense taken."

That's where he went? But . . . "So, where is he?" I said, still somewhat shell-shocked.

"There was only room for three of us on the snowplows. He thought it was more important for the rest of us to get here." Tyler smiled. "But he's waiting at the gas station down the road until we get back. I'll bet one of the guys can take you there."

"Angie! You have to go to him!" Marie insisted.

"You stay right here," Gwen commanded the ATV drivers. And my three friends bustled me into the cabin. Jessica hunted for my coat while Marie grabbed a brush and started untangling my hair. "Angie, this is it," Marie said seriously. "There are many important moments in a woman's life . . ."

"Turning points," Jess inserted.

"Yes, turning points. And this, Angie, is one of them."

"So, don't blow it," Gwen warned sternly, spritzing me with perfume she'd found in her purse.

"Right." Jess echoed. "Don't blow it."

"And what we mean by that, Angie," Marie said sincerely, "is that you just need to be yourself."

"Just yourself," Gwen concurred.

"And," Jess added excitedly, "keep your chakras open and your third eye alert and let the wisdom of your Essential Feminine flow and . . ."

"Jess!"

"Right. Okay," she said wrapping me in my coat. "Just do what Marie and Gwen said. Get moving!"

We ran out the cabin door and over to the first snowplow. Tyler made the introductions. "Mom, this is Buck. Buck, you know the guy who paid you? My mom is the woman he said he wants to marry."

"He said that?" I said weakly.

"Yes, ma'am." Buck took off his hunting cap and wiped a tattooed arm across his eyes. "The guy said it's true love. That's the only thing that woulda gotten Boots and Buster and me out this morning so early."

"Well, and that baby," Boots (or perhaps Buster) added.

"Turning point, Angie," Marie murmured in my ear.

And at that moment, it all came together. Suddenly my chakras were galvanized, and all of me, from my big toe to my heart, was present. And I knew exactly what to do next. "Okay, Buck, then let's roll!" I climbed into the passenger seat of Buck's tiny plow and fastened my seat belt. "And don't spare the gas pedal!"

"Yes, ma'am," Buck said enthusiastically. He flipped the switch, and the little machine roared to life.

I was perhaps a bit too zealous in my instructions to Buck. It turns out that he is the Mario Andretti of the snowplow set. Perhaps if I'd been armed with Dramamine, this would have been okay, except for the fact that ATV snowplows are apparently not equipped with shock absorbers. So all of the shock (and at eighty miles per hour over hill and dale, there's a heck of a lot of shock) was absorbed by my personal backside. By the time we got there (which I'm sure was some kind of land record for miniplows), I could barely walk.

"Thanks so much for the ride, Buck," I said shakily, pleasantly surprised that I was still alive.

"No problem, ma'am. Will you be needing a ride back?"

"Oh gosh, no. I mean I couldn't possibly impose . . ."

I found Tim sitting on a bench, looking bedraggled and weary. His face was bruised, his jacket was torn, and his pants were covered with mud. "Tim?"

"Angie!" He leaped up, spilling coffee all over himself. "Oh, heck!" I started to laugh, and he grinned sheepishly, lighting up the entire horizon. "Angie, I . . ."

"No, Tim," I said firmly. "It's my turn to talk. First of all, you can't just go running off like that, even if it's to be heroic."

"Uh, okay."

"And you have to remember that I'm a little bit crazy."

"Unh-huh."

"And I don't always know exactly what I'm going to do next."

"Me neither."

"But, no matter what I say or how I act, you're not to forget how much I love you."

"I won't."

"And my family will always come first."

"All right."

"And when you become family, you'll come first, too."
Tim started to laugh. "No, I didn't mean it like . . ."

"I know exactly what you mean, Angie," he said, smiling.

"And I'll always be happy to wash the sheets for you."

"Check."

"But you have to do your own laundry."

"Absolutely."

"Unless I have extra room in a load I'm doing."

"Agreed. But Angie, have I told you yet how much I love you?"

"No. But could you just save that for later?" I took a hesitant step toward him. "I'm so tired of talking and thinking and . . ."

"Yeah, me too."

"So," I whispered, "I thought maybe we could just . . ."

"Works for me."

And it was good. It was all very good.

Epilogue

The wedding was so much more beautiful than I ever imagined it could be. Spring had blossomed early that year, so we were able to hold the ceremony under a candlelit tent in William Land Park. I stood behind the bower of flowers, waiting for my entrance. I peaked at the large crowd of wedding guests; I spotted The Guys from the Twenty-ninth Street Gym, my three best friends and their significant others, Bob and Clarisse (Heck, what party would be complete without them?). Ryan, sitting up front, raised Savannah's chubby little arm to wave at me.

Standing at the altar, Tyler looked absolutely dashing as the best man. He stood by the clearly nervous groom and beamed happily at me. Angeline and Jenna, radiant bridesmaids, smiled encouragement to me from their positions across from their handsome fiancé/brother.

I heard my cue in the music: First whistles, then the chanting voices, flutes, drums, and rattles. It was exotic and hypnotic, and I felt my heart beating to its beat. I swayed gently to the rhythm. All eyes were on me as I moved slowly down the aisle with tears running down my cheeks. I couldn't remember when I had last been this totally happy.

The groom looked at me with love in his eyes. And then he grinned as his beautiful bride, dressed in traditional Hopi bridal robes, white with red stripes at top and bottom, made her entrance behind me. Lilah, looking absolutely luminous, grinned back at Tom, obviously having the time of her life. (She had confessed to me earlier that her only disappointment was that, in Tom's tribal traditions, the bride was not topless. "And I had to grind corn for three days straight to present as a gift to his family. Thank God for Cuisinarts!") Tom and Lilah joined hands to become husband and wife.

After the ceremony, Tim pulled me behind a flowered pillar to give me one of his Truly Extraordinary Kisses. We'd shared thousands of those in the past couple of months but they still made me giddy.

"Us too?" he murmured. "Sometime soon?"

"Sometime soon," I promised. He hurried off to begin the music for the reception.

I found my three best friends sitting with Jenna and Angeline. Tyler soon showed up to claim Angeline for the next dance, and Ryan followed carrying Savannah. "I'd like to dance with my wife," he said smiling. "Angie, would you mind holding Bubba for a bit?"

"Ryan!" Jenna protested. "Don't call her Bubba!"

"Well, Bubbles, then?" he teased, leading Jenna to the dance floor. "Bubbalina? Bubblicious?"

"So, Ryan does have a sense of humor after all," Gwen observed, taking Savannah from my arms. "My turn," she said firmly. It wasn't really, but you can't argue with Gwen at all when she's around that baby.

"Okay, Angie," Marie said, pouring us all more champagne. "When are you and Tim going to tie the knot?"

"Oh, I don't know," I sighed contentedly. "We're still practicing our loops and bows and . . ."

"And position number thirty-two of the Kama Sutra?" Jess giggled.

"Hush!" Gwen hissed, covering Savannah's ears. "Not in front of the baby!"

"You know, the only thing that hasn't worked out yet is my career," I mused. "I still don't know what I want to do with my life."

"Why don't you try your hand at writing?" Marie suggested.

"About what?"

"Well, how about your adventures of the last two years?" Jess offered. "Not that anyone would believe it."

"That's a great idea," Gwen enthused. "So when would you say it all began? When we gave birth to Savannah?"

"Technically, Gwen, we assisted at the birth. I think Jenna was the one who . . ."

"No, it should be back to Jenna's wedding," Marie insisted. "The one we put together in three weeks."

"I think it was before that," Jess claimed. "When we had to steal back Angie's black-lace thong from that smarmy guy's . . ."

"Nope," I said definitely. "I know exactly when it all

started. It was my forty-ninth birthday. And if I ever did write a book about it all, which of course," I stated confidently, sipping my champagne, "I never, ever will, I know just how I'll start it: 'Obviously, I never should have gotten out of bed that day.'"

Want More?

Turn the page to enter
Avon's Little Black Book —

the dish, the scoop and the
cherry on top from
HEATHER ESTAY

Q & A with Heather Estay

Heather Estay, author of *It's Never Too Late to Look Hot*, grew up (though never matured) in Denver, Colorado, then moved to California in 1969 to attend Stanford University. She graduated four years later (much to the surprise and chagrin of the Alumni Association) and has remained in northern California ever since due to loopholes in California's extradition policies. Heather graduated with a degree in psychology (along with half of all Californians at that time) and eventually got her real estate license (to join the other half of the population). She spent many years in a variety of jobs, looking for an occupation that would pay her to be a goofball. Her seventeen years in commercial real estate were pretty goofy, but they wouldn't let her wear her jammies to the office. So she became a writer. Heather is unintentionally single and resides in Sacramento, California, with Spud, her Wonder Beagle. *Little Black Book* caught up with her there for this interview:

Disclaimer: The opinions and outrageous attitudes expressed herein are not those of HarperCollins, Ms. Estay's agent, editors, or beagle (or even, actually, of Ms. Estay herself).

So let's talk midlife crisis.

Yes, let's. Besides going through my own midlife crisis a couple of years back, I did some extensive research on it (which consisted of twenty-two minutes surfing the Internet and a few Web sites, one of which was devoted to Elvis trivia). I discovered that "midlife" starts at forty—did you know that? So apparently if you are an overachiever, you can legitimately start your crisis then. (I'm a bit of a sluggard so I didn't have mine until I was fifty-one or fifty-two.)

The other interesting thing I learned (other than that Kurt Russell, at age ten, kicked Elvis in the shins) is that men and women relate to this midlife thing differently. Women tend to reinvent themselves positively: begin new careers, find cures for infectious diseases, become US senators, etc. Many men, on the other hand, concentrate on turning back the clock to act out fantasies of a younger, more virile self than they probably had ever been. Hence, those little red sports cars, ventures into extreme sports, and invasions of foreign countries. (Okay, for those of you who are yelling: "Foul! That's a gross generalization!," I just want to point out that this is a *statistically supported* gross generalization.)

I don't think anybody knows what causes this particular gender difference, but I'm guessing that our friends have a lot to do with it. Think of this: a fifty-five-year-old guy takes up with a sexy, tattooed eighteen-year-old, starts wearing a bad toupee, and buys a car he can't afford. What will his buddies say? "Yo, dude! Nice wheels!" A woman who exhibits similar behavior will be subjected to an annoying number of friends who take her out for lunch to find out "what's really going on." As a woman, it's just easier to form a major corporation than to act outrageously and have all of your friends on your case.

The other factor is probably the "crisis" part of a midlife crisis itself, the part that feels depressing and hopeless and rotten. Many men aren't used to feeling this way, so they're not sure what it means or what to do about it: "Gosh, maybe a new

chain saw/wife/big-screen TV would make me feel better."
Women, who've grown up feeling these things at least once a
month, know that talking it through with their friends or a good
psychotherapist might be a better starting place—not that this
can't be combined with a really good shopping spree.

**Angie seems to have a little trouble getting into the
sexual swing of things. Is that realistic in this day and
age?**

Gasp! Choke! Swallow! How old are you anyway? Oh,
never mind . . .

Look, I gave an interview recently on "Sex and Women
over Fifty." When I heard about the interview, my first response was "What sex?" My second response was to verify
that the interviewer knew that I write strictly fiction.

I know scads of single, attractive, sexy women over fifty.
But for many of us, the most sex we've experienced in the past
several years was *Sex and the City*—and I hear that's been
canceled. WE'RE NOT GETTING ANY!

"Why?" the pleasant, safely married interviewer asked me.

I had to think about this issue (as opposed to just complain
about it, which is, frankly, a lot more fun). Of course, when
you're being interviewed, you have to think in "sound bites,"
not full, coherent thoughts. So here's what I came up with:
Sex Plus.

"What's that?" she asked. "Like sex for larger women?"

"No," I responded as if I had a clue about what I was about
to say next. "Sex Plus. Meaning sex plus something else:
friendship, relationship, romance . . . something."

"Oh."

Then, of course, being a writer who is paid to expand a
two-sentence thought into a three-hundred-page novel, I
expounded. As I recall, I told her that I think most of us are
not looking for just the physical experience of sex—nothing
wrong with it, we just like our sex to come with something
more. Like, um, a gin and tonic with *extra* lime. We don't re-

ally need to order a Tom Collins. But we would like that extra lime anyway. And without that extra lime, it just isn't as good. Have I lost you completely? Suffice it to say, we tend to like our sex with at least a little extra something on the side to make it a truly satisfying experience.

Also, if we are really, really, *really* honest with ourselves, we women tend to get more emotionally involved with our sexual partners than is considered strictly cool. (Right? Oh, come on now, be honest. *Cosmo* is not going to find out and expose you as a "Don't" if you confess to it . . .) I don't think this is just a generational issue. There has got to be some brilliant anthropomorphic rationale behind this, but all I remember from my psych studies was how rodents learn to thump on levers to get food. But based on B.F. Skinner's work, here is a simple mathematical equation we can use to predict how frequently a woman might get involved: Take number of years lived times annual frequency of relationships times 95 percent (this total equals postrelationship hurt experienced). Divide this number by her IQ added to her singledom satisfaction quotient and—voila!—you will have the number of times she is likely to get involved over the next twelve months. (Hint: The answer is often zero.)

So, though many of us over forty or fifty are still hot to trot, we're a bit clearer on what makes us truly happy and what doesn't (even without using the calculations above). When I was twenty, I could cheerfully snarf down an entire box of Dolly Madison powdered sugar doughnuts and feel just fine. At this age, I'm clear that I'll just feel icky afterward. So I tend to avoid them. (Okay, okay! So every once in a blue moon, I forget, do the doughnuts, and feel icky. But the incidence of such rampant doughnut bingeing is way less than in my younger years.)

As a friend put it, we still know how to ride bikes and would enjoy doing so. We just can't find bikes worth riding.

Gin and tonic, powered sugar doughnuts, bicycles . . . What was the question again?

Uh, let's move on. Where did you get the idea for Angie's internal voices?

Now *that* part could definitely be considered autobiographical. Don't you have a variety of voices who run your life? No? How dull for you.

A few years ago, I was involved in a nonrelationship with a guy. You know the kind of relationship I'm talking about: He rarely calls (but you know he really wants to!), he's never romantic (but he's just shy about showing his true feelings!), he doesn't introduce you to his family (but when he does someday, you just know that they'll love you!) blah dee blah blah blah.

It occurred to me one day (after an embarrassing amount of wasted time thinking about this guy) that the only relationship we had was the one in my head. I counted up the number of times we'd actually been together (without using all of my digits), then the number of hours I spent thinking about him (enough to have earned me early retirement). Our "real" relationship was nonexistent, but the one in my imagination was phenomenal! (Ladies, if you want to turn all that wasted romantic fantasy time into a profit center, just write it all down, make sure it's double-spaced, and submit it to your local publisher.)

When I write, I often think: Hey! If I am dumb enough to think/do/feel a certain thing, then probably a lot of us think/do/feel the same way. I don't believe that this Walter Mitty life I carry around with me is all that unusual. (If it is, well, maybe my books should be displayed in the Beyond Self-Help section.)

Not all of us are alike, of course, in this or anything else. For instance, I once told a friend that I always use a Stairmaster in the back of the gym so I can watch the guys with great butts and calves. "Oh my God, I would *never* do that!" she cried. "After all the work I've done on my buns, I work out in front to give everyone else a treat! In fact, I should charge admission . . ." (See what I mean? She's from New York, practically a different planet. But I wonder if we are of the same species . . .)

Your books are pretty "innocent" and wholesome. Not much swearing, not much graphic sex. How come?

(Okay, I nominate this as one of the dumbest interview questions ever asked.)

Cuss words: Being a relatively conscious being (until that third glass of Merlot kicks in), I know that swearing is offensive to a lot of people. Since it's not an integral part of me or how I express myself, I don't bother with it unless it is really critical to some scene or character. (Being an uppity woman is offensive to some as well. However, since that *is* an integral part of who I am, I just let it rip.)

Sex scenes: Okay, so maybe I need to go to one of those seminars on Writing Erotica. My personal erotica is, um, pre-verbal, so whenever I read "hot, steamy sex scenes," I become choreographically challenged: *His left hand moved slowly up her right thigh while he clutched the back of her neck, pressing her to his manhood as his lips brushed the lace covering her ample bosom . . .*

Wait! Okay: You put your left hand out and your right hand in, your tongue on the breast and you shake it all about, you do the hootchy cootchy and you . . .

Personally, I've read very few explicit sex scenes that are truly sexy. I have a very good imagination; I'm betting you do as well. So until I attend that Erotica Seminar, make it up for gosh sakes!

Angie has apparently fallen in love, and to a really nice guy this time, but she still hasn't gotten married. Why not?

I don't know. It just hasn't turned out that way. As I'm writing along, a story takes on a life of its own. I may try to get a character to do or say something, but sometimes they just resist my initial ideas. I had other versions of the ending of this book where Angie gets married—but she just wasn't ready. (We argued about it at length. She locked herself in the bathroom and wouldn't come out until I'd rewritten the scene.)

And let me ask you something: Does "happily ever after" *always* have to include marriage? It's one of the options for us (and Angie), but is it the only one? The best one?

Nora Ephron claims that the major achievement of the Women's Lib movement in the seventies was the Dutch treat. But along with that questionable gain, it also gave us greater freedom to determine how exactly our own "happily ever after" will look. And it might look different in one stage than another. So now that Angie has had a taste of all of this new-found freedom, I don't think we should rush her into anything. (But when she comes out of the bathroom, I'll ask her if she knows what she plans to do yet.)

So what's next for you?

I'm working on a series of mysteries; the main characters are a foursome of female golfers. I'm having a little trouble though: the murder victim is locked in the bathroom with Angie and won't come out until . . .

HEATHER ESTAY

HEATHER ESTAY lives in Sacramento, California, with Spud, the Wonder Beagle (who snores but swears he doesn't). *It's Never Too Late to Look Hot* is her third humorous novel (What? You didn't think it was funny?). She spends most of her days writing goofy stuff to avoid getting a real job, which is a constant embarrassment to her mother. Oh, and Heather plays golf—poorly.